SEXY PUCKING
POLAR BEAR

PARANORMAL HOCKEY LEAGUE

JENNY FENSHAW

Book Cover Designed by Dark Water Covers Premades and Formatting

Editing by Empowered Writing Author Services, HEA Author Services, and Patricia Raine Lam

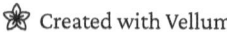 Created with Vellum

CONTENTS

1

BURKE

I PEEK THROUGH THE CRACK OF THE CURTAIN TO CHECK OUT THE CROWD gathered in the scorching August sun on the world-famous Atlantic City Boardwalk. There's a good-sized crowd waiting for the introduction of the folks entering training camp for the Atlantic City Devil Birds, a team in the newly-formed Paranormal Hockey League.

I'm amazed at how many people are here to meet us and see the introduction of the team's mascot. I'm sure a lot of the crowd is random people watching from the beach or who have wandered out from the casinos lining Atlantic City's Boardwalk, but many are wearing t-shirts bearing the team logo of an angry seagull with bulging muscles holding a hockey stick. I guess there are some hockey fans in the crowd.

Sean Waller, another defenseman trying out, nudges me with his elbow.

"I bet you never dreamed you'd be trading test tubes and safety goggles for a hockey stick and skates when you were in your classroom up in Canada."

I shake my head. "No, never in a million years."

When I heard a professional hockey league was forming for

shifters and other types of paranormals, I took the chance to see if I have what it takes to play hockey professionally. It's a dream not possible for generations of shifters.

It's been over ten years since a grizzly bear bridezilla got in a snit and shifted on camera while being filmed for the trashy "Brides Behaving Badly," a cable television show. That outed shifters to the non-shifting public, and we've been in the public eye ever since, but restricted from participating in professional sports.

Shuffling my feet, I can't wait for this shindig to start. I'm a polar bear shifter, and my bear longs to take a quick dip in the Atlantic Ocean a few hundred yards away and cool off. Or go back inside the air-conditioned comfort of The Nest, the nickname for the pier that's home to the team.

I'm not built for this kind of heat and humidity. Neither is my bear, and his comfort is important to me too. We're in the same body. My bear is part of me, and I'm part of him. We need to work together and consider each other when we make decisions. If he had his way, we'd be eating raw seal, and that's a giant no in my book. Out of consideration for him, I didn't sign up for the Las Vegas team and plop his polar bear butt in the desert.

I miss Canada. For the thousandth time, I'm questioning the wisdom of giving up my job and my home. Heck, I'm giving up my country to chase this dream. What if I'm not good enough?

I'm twenty-seven years old. I'm not a kid. How am I going to compete with a bunch of guys younger than me who didn't spend all their time in a classroom? Other than skating with the high school teams I coach, I haven't played anything other than a couple of beer league games since I graduated college.

My heart is racing, and my palms are sweaty. If I was home, I could go swimming in the lake. It wouldn't feel like Satan's armpit back home. Back home, I wouldn't be on the verge of what I think is my first panic attack either. But I'm not home. I'm here.

Sean takes his own peek through the curtain and lets out a low whistle.

"I think this crowd is bigger than the population of the whole county I'm from." Sean is a moose shifter from rural Maine.

"Yeah." I wipe my forehead on my sleeve and add, "I wish we could have done this in the rink where it's cooler. This heat is a bitch."

"Get the flock out of here," Jake Whitman, our team's general manager and a team owner, mutters when he sees a bunch of seagulls settle along the railings and on light posts around the area where they set up the stage for today's event. He somehow looks polished in dress slacks and a gray button-down dress shirt. His top button is undone and he doesn't wear a tie—his only concessions to the heat and humidity that are making me wilt.

"It's nice your extended family wants to be here with you," Teagan Penhall, majority owner of the team, says, looking cool in her sheath dress in Devil Birds-blue. She's stunning with her honey-blonde hair and big blue eyes, the same shade as her dress. She could be a model, but instead operates one of her family's casinos and now co-owns a professional hockey team with her two best friends.

"Yeah, I appreciate it, but they couldn't have come in their human form? You know they flew here as their gulls to avoid paying for parking. And Uncle Enzo keeps posing next to the Devil Birds' banner because he's hoping people notice the resemblance, realize he was the model, and want to take selfies." Jake sighs. "I swear, if he sticks a Sharpie in his beak to sign autographs, I'm going to put myself up for adoption."

"You're almost thirty years old, Jake," Teagan says.

"I don't care."

I hide my grin as the team's social media person, Daphne, approaches with her clipboard. She's the Mistress of Ceremonies for today's event. She shoos me and Sean away from the curtain with a smile and a wave of her hand.

"Ready to go?" she asks the team owners. "Kennie is here with the kids. Hey, Rowena, you all set?" Daphne asks the little red-haired girl with pigtails holding the hand of a petite blonde.

Wow! She's gorgeous—the blonde. The little girl is cute, but the woman with her is a knockout. They're both wearing gray Devil Bird shirts with denim shorts. For being tiny, the blonde has legs that appear to go on forever. I assume she's the little girl's mother, and I feel like a creeper scoping out a probably-married woman, but I have eyes. I can't help but see her.

The little girl nods and takes Daphne's hand, the blonde slipping away. I guess she's going to stand in front of the stage.

Daphne grins and looks us over. "Okay, Teagan is going to give the opening remarks, Rowena is going to introduce the mascot who will do his thing, then Coach Morgan is going to introduce the training camp candidates—goalies, forwards, and then defense. We have assigned you a number that tells your place in the order, and it's on your shirt. Make sure you follow along. Give your name, your hometown, your animal if you're comfortable sharing, and your position." Daphne giggles. "Pretend you're in the Miss America pageant!" She waves the hand holding the clipboard to show our surroundings. "This is the place for it!"

"They used to hold the Miss America pageant in Atlantic City," Sean whispers to me like that was something I needed to know. I nod.

After making sure all is as it should be, Daphne nods, signaling the curtains can open. The crowd roars, the seagulls squawk, and when we step out of the shadows and onto the stage, their cheers are deafening, exhilarating.

Taking the microphone and welcoming the crowd, Teagan talks about how excited the team owners are to bring professional hockey to Atlantic City and support the shifter community. I'm ashamed to admit I tune her out as I look out to the crowd in search of the blonde. She's in front of the stage with a bunch of kids. Most are younger, probably around the little redhead's age, but some are early teens. She's obviously older than them. At least I don't have to worry I've been checking out a teenager. I shudder at the thought. She's holding her phone up to film the event.

"Now, to introduce the Devil Bird's mascot is Rowena, a first grader at Pine Grove Academy." Teagan steps aside and hands the little girl the microphone as the crowd applauds. Like a pro, she waits for the audience to quiet.

With a regal tilt to her chin I wouldn't expect to see in a six-year-old, Rowena confidently announces, "Ladies and Gentleman, meet Shifty!"

That's what she said. I heard her. It's what everyone on the stage heard her say. Unfortunately, right as she said "Shifty," the speaker crackled, and what the crowd heard was "Meet Shitty!" During the crowd's stunned silence, I clearly hear the guy in the Shifty the Seagull costume say, "Are you fucking kidding me?!"

Then the crowd chants, "Shitty! Shitty!" as Daphne shoves the mascot to the front of the stage.

Rowena stamps her foot in her tiny pink Converse sneaker. "I said Shifty!" she yells and bursts into tears.

Everyone stands there frozen, at a loss for what to do. I can't stand to see little kids cry, so I scoot up to Rowena. She's relinquished her microphone to Coach Morgan, who is introducing the players. I lead her to the side of the stage behind my potential teammates. She doesn't need to be on display while she's distressed.

"Hey, don't cry, Rowena. You did a great job!" I squat on my haunches, to be closer to eye to eye. In this position I still tower over her, but it's less than if I was standing at my full six foot six height.

"I said it right! Shifty! I didn't say a bad word!" Tears flow from her big brown eyes down her freckled cheeks, and my heart tugs. Poor little mite.

"I know, sweetheart. You did nothing wrong. The speaker crackled and messed it up. Let's get you to your mom, okay?"

Rowena lifts her arm to wipe her face on her sleeve. "Mommy isn't here. She's at work."

"Okay, well, the lady you were with before. Let's get you to her."

"She's my teacher."

Then there she is—the cute blonde, kneeling down to hug the

little girl. "Rowena! Don't cry! You did *such* a good job! I got it on my phone to show your mom and dad. They will be very proud of you!!" She looks over at me and smiles. "Thank you for taking care of her and getting her back here."

I smile back and am about to reply when a forward calls out to me. "Bedard, it's almost your turn. Get up front!" I rise to my full height, ready to take my place in line.

"No problem, happy to have helped. Great job, Rowena. Be proud of yourself." I hold my ham-sized fist out for her to bump with her tiny one.

I make it to the front of the stage in the nick of time. Walking up to the microphone, I introduce myself.

"Hello, I'm Burke Bedard from Ontario, Canada. I'm a polar bear shifter, and I play defense."

The rest of the introduction program goes well. Rowena and her teacher join the rest of the kids in front of the stage. She's stopped crying. That's a relief. It broke my heart. I'm such a marshmallow, which is funny considering I could tear a person limb from limb when I'm in my bear form. But when confronted with little kid tears, all I want to do is make it better.

"How did you get good with kids? You have some?" Trevor Carter, one of the centers, asks me as we go into The Nest. It's a remodeled shopping center built on a pier extending into the Atlantic Ocean. Besides our arena, there are sporting goods and athletic wear stores, a bookstore, some restaurants and other sporty things like batting cages, an indoor driving range, basketball and tennis courts on the roof. It's a neat space.

"No kids of my own," I say. "Only my students. I teach high school chemistry now, but when I was getting my degree, I subbed for all grades. I covered the younger grades a lot because I like little kids."

The next event for the day is a meet and greet with ticket holders and a tour of the locker rooms with the school kids.

They break us into groups of three and send us to our assigned tables throughout the lobby of the rink. Each table has a stack of photos showing a group shot of the training camp attendees with spaces for us to sign our names underneath. For some of us, this will be our only brush with fame. I hope everyone soaks in the experience and appreciates it. I know I will. I wish Bobby had this chance too. It's not fair he never got his shot.

"Who's the blonde? She's cute," Sean says as we settle at our table. I take the center seat. Trevor is our third and sits on my other side.

"What blonde?" he asks, looking around.

"The one with the school kids. Is she a mom or a teacher?" Sean jerks his chin toward the group of school kids entering the lobby with their chaperones.

"The tiny one?"

Sean nods.

Trevor groans. "Dude, forget about it. She's off limits."

"Why?" I ask. "Is she your girlfriend?" It doesn't matter. I'm here to play hockey, not to get involved with anyone. I'm curious. That's all.

"Nah, nothing like that. We're friends."

I didn't realize I was tense until I felt my muscles relax.

"She's Coach's little sister."

Well, damn.

There's a code understood by hockey players everywhere that you don't mess with a teammate's sister. You never mess with the coach's daughters. I assume the code extends to the coach's sisters. This is the first time I've had a coach young enough to have a sister I'd want to date. Not that I want to date her.

Focus, Bedard, you are here to play hockey, save up as much money as possible, and go back to Canada. That's where your life is. Where your future is. Find a good woman to marry, have some kids, go back to teach-

ing, and have a comfortable life with the nest egg that pro hockey gives you.

When I look into the most beautiful crystal-blue eyes I've ever seen, my pep talk flies right out the window.

"Hey, Kennie!" Trevor says as he rises from his seat and goes around the table to hug the woman we were just speaking of. He bends down to embrace her because her head doesn't even reach his shoulders. She pulls away first.

"Hi Trev. Nice turnout," she says, looking around the lobby. People are entering, and the chatter of the crowd is getting louder. She smiles at me and Sean.

"Rowena wanted to come over and thank you for helping her on stage, Mr...."

"Bedard. Burke Bedard." I rise and reach across the table, holding out my hand. Kennie places her small palm in mine. It's delicate, but her grip is firm as she gives me a quick shake and pulls back.

"Sean Waller. Call me Stone." The third member of our group holds out his hand as he stands.

"I'm Kendall Morgan. Nice to meet you all. And you've already met Rowena."

"We did," Trevor says. "You did a great job announcing Shifty. I'm sorry the speaker malfunctioned." He gives her a fist bump and a warm smile.

Rowena sighs as only a little girl can, her shoulders rising clear up to her ears before dropping dramatically. "Those things happen. It's a small part of the program and someday it will be a funny story to tell my children."

She says it so matter-of-factly, I'm taken aback. She's about six years old and speaking with the wisdom of someone ten times her age. I glance at Kendall—I can't call a woman that beautiful Kennie —and she's trying to hold back her laughter. Somehow, I do the same.

"I'm Rowena Emerson. Thank you for helping me before. It was very kind of you," the pint-sized philosopher says, holding her hand out to shake mine.

"Burke Bedard," I tell her, "I'm glad I could assist you." I give a bow over our clasped hands. I'm not sure why I'm being this formal, but even in a t-shirt and pigtails, she has such a regal bearing. She's a spitfire. I hope I have a little girl like her someday.

"Can I hug you?" she asks. With her head tilting to the side, she looks like a little bird. "It's important to ask permission first before hugging people. It's the polite thing to do. You can say no if you don't want to."

I smile, glad to know she's being taught these lessons. Everyone should learn them.

"Absolutely. I'd like that very much." I come around the table and kneel to make it easier for her to reach me.

"Okay to get a picture to send to her parents?" Kendall asks.

"Of course," I say as Rowena's slender arms hug my neck. I give her a gentle hug and then pull away.

"You give wonderful hugs, but your beard tickles," Rowena says with a giggle.

"Oops, sorry."

"Ro, do you want to get a picture with Mr. Waller and Mr. Carter too?" Kendall asks.

"Mr. Carter? Really? It sounds like you're talking to my dad, Kennie," Trevor complains. "Call us Carter"—he points to himself—"and Stone." He points to Waller.

As she takes the picture of the three of them, I see Coach Morgan approach. Kendall startles when he rests his hand on her shoulder.

"It's me, Ken," he says.

"Hey Liam, sorry. You startled me." Kendall looks around the lobby. "Great crowd. You guys must be thrilled."

"We are. Here, give me your phone. I'll get your picture with this motley crew."

"No, that's okay," she protests, but he plucks her phone from her hand and gestures for her to join us. We crowd together, and I notice the tense set to Kendall's shoulders. Carter gives one a quick squeeze as he guides her and Rowena to stand in front of us.

"Try smiling this time, Ken," her brother says as he gets ready to take another picture. I guess the second time was the charm because he hands her back her phone.

Coach leans down and holds out his hand for a high five from Rowena.

"Thanks for doing such a great job today, Ro. Sorry the speaker messed up. You're a rock star."

The little girl giggles and says, "No, I'm a FLOCK star. Flock of seagulls. Get it?"

"Oh, my Go...sh, you're brilliant. You gotta tell Teagan." With that, Coach leads Rowena away to where Teagan and Jake are standing with some important-looking people.

Before she leaves to follow them, Kendall smiles at us. "Thanks for the pictures. I'll bring her back around for your autographs since Liam dragged her off. Mr—Burke," she corrects herself, "thank you for your kindness."

"Nice meeting you," I say as she walks off to join her brother and student. I'm not checking out her pert ass hugged by denim shorts. Nope. Not gonna do it. There will be plenty of time to look at cute, perfectly-shaped asses after I've had a successful and lucrative professional hockey career. For now my focus needs to be on pucks, not butts.

2

KENDALL

It takes all my willpower not to look back over my shoulder at Burke. I feel a tingle between my shoulder blades signaling someone is watching me walk away. I hope it's him. Wait — no, I don't. There's no point in him noticing me. I don't want him to notice me. I don't want anyone to notice me. Let me teach my kids and live my life. No guys. Especially not big, hot shifter guys.

If I'm ever ready to date again, I'll see if my brother's girlfriend, Mallory, knows any nice, quiet lawyers. She's a paralegal in the legal department of my family's property development company. This pier is their latest project. Usually, they do retail-focused projects like outlet malls and shopping centers. This time they did something different, including the rink and other sports things. Anyway, next time I'm looking for someone different. Not an athlete. Especially not one who plays a violent sport like hockey.

"Teagan, Rowena had a great idea of what to call our fans. Tell her, Ro," Liam encourages as we join his co-owners.

"Flock stars. Because they are like a flock of seagulls." Rowena speaks with the absolute confidence of a six-year-old. When I grow up, I want to be like her. I *used* to be like her. Hopefully, life and men don't knock her down like they did me. Hopefully, she's stronger than I am.

A gorgeous smile spreads across Teagan's face. She already looks like a supermodel with her long blonde hair and perfect figure. Add in that she's a brilliant businessperson, generous, and kind, and I have a bit of a girl crush on her. Maybe that should be my plan. Date girls. Nah, I'm a fan of peen. Damn it.

"What a great idea, Ro! I wish we could hire you for our marketing department. Are you sure you want to go to first grade?" Teagan asks.

"It's not that I *want* to go, but the playground has all kinds of cool things, and I have to be a student there to play on it. And they have pizza Fridays."

"Those are important things you're smart to consider, Rowena," Jake agrees. "When you graduate high school, come see us."

"Thanks, but when I graduate high school, I'm going to go to college to become a doctor and join the Army like my daddy."

"Splendid plan," I say. "How about we walk around and get everyone's autograph? Okay?" When Rowena nods, I take her hand, say bye to Liam and his crew, and start going from table to table, meeting the players.

At one table, there's a woman about my age seated with two guys. Rowena's eyes widen, and she asks breathlessly, "Do you play hockey?"

"I do," the woman answers, flashing Rowena a smile as she signs her name on the picture and passes it down the table. "I'm a goalie, and my job is to make sure the other team doesn't score a goal."

"Do you play with the boys?"

"I do. I grew up playing with my brother Sean. He's at the table over there." She points to the table where Burke and Trevor are sitting with Stone Waller.

"Oh! I met him! He's nice. What's your name?" Rowena has never met a stranger, and if she does, they don't remain a stranger long.

"My name is Bridget Waller, and this is Declan Mackenzie." She gestures to the man in the center who is now signing his name. He nods and smiles. "And he is Nathan Crosby."

The man on the other side of Declan grins as he takes the picture to sign. "What's your name?"

"I'm Rowena Emerson. This is my teacher, Miss Morgan."

"Any relation to Coach Morgan?" Declan asks. I hear an accent in his voice. Scottish, maybe?

"Yes, he's my older brother," I answer.

"You serious?" Nathan hands Rowena back her photo.

"As a heart attack," I say.

Rowena is vibrating with excitement. "Did you know girls can play hockey, Miss Morgan?!"

"I did. Girls can do anything," I answer.

"I want to play hockey!"

"That's something you'll have to discuss with your parents, Ro." I know the Devil Birds are going to have youth hockey teams, but I remember how expensive and time-consuming hockey is from the years Liam spent playing. Any activity, especially if it's a team sport, is an enormous commitment of time and money. My gymnastics and cheerleading were just as demanding as Liam's hockey. I don't know Rowena's family situation well enough to know if they have money and time for hockey.

The meet-and-greet is ending as we approach Burke's table for their autographs. The rest of the crowd is funneling out of the rink lobby, leaving the players and my school group as the last inhabitants.

Rowena skips up to the table and exclaims to Sean, "Your sister plays hockey! That's cool! I wanna play hockey too! Is she better than you?" She hands him her photo. "Can you sign this, please?"

With a laugh, Sean takes the picture and signs it, passing it to Burke and then answering her questions.

"It *is* cool that Bridget plays hockey. Her nickname is Brick because our last name is Waller, like Brick Wall. She's such a good goalie, it's like trying to get pucks past a brick wall. She's better at being a goalie than I am. I play defense, and my nickname is Stone like Stone Wall. My job is to keep the pucks from getting to the goalie. We are each good at what we do."

"What's your nickname, Burke?" Rowena asks.

Studmuffin McHottypants is my guess.

"I don't have one yet, Rowena. We'll see what happens once training camp starts."

Trev hands Ro her picture as my brother stands in the center of the lobby and whistles to get everyone's attention. He's such a coach.

"Okay, Pine Grovers, who's ready to take a tour of the rink and the locker rooms?" he asks.

Everyone cheers. Teagan, Jake, and Daphne walk through the crowd handing out Devil Birds knapsacks to the kids, as well as their chaperones. I peek inside my bag. There's a puck, a water bottle, and other branded trinkets. At my suggestion, there's also a folder for them to put their photos in so they don't get dropped or ruined.

There is no need for a whistle because I have a teacher's voice. But since I have the height of a twelve-year-old, I climb up on a chair to get everyone's attention. "Take your folders out of the bag and put your photos in them. Once you're done, hold your folder up." I wait until I see everyone's folder in the air. "Now put your folder in your bag and put your bags on your backs. A strap over each shoulder. We will not replace lost bags. Help your buddies."

I have some of the older kids matched with the younger kids. The older kids think we matched them because the little kids need help, but really, it's helping keep the older kids from getting in trouble. I've found if people think they have someone who needs them, they'll often behave better than they would have without the responsibility.

"Can I go with Calvin and Miss Reimer?" Rowena asks me after I jump down from the chair.

"Sure. Have fun." I watch to make sure she connects with my co-teacher, Abby, who nods to acknowledge she's taking Ro. Most of the players are going on the tour, but a few are hanging back. I've seen the locker rooms and other areas of the pier through its renovation.

My family did a wonderful job rehabbing the property. But right now, I want to sit for a moment in the relative silence. I sink into the chair I had used as my stage and close my eyes with a sigh.

"Would you like a bottle of water?" a deep voice asks from alongside me. I gasp and pop my eyes open. I'm a cougar shifter. Normally, I can sense when someone is approaching.

"Yeah, thanks," I say, taking the bottle from Burke. I open it and take a deep sip. The cool liquid feels good going down my throat. I smile as I look into his deep brown eyes.

He sits next to me.

"So, how many kids do you have?" I ask with a laugh.

"One hundred and twenty."

Even though I'm choking on my water—because *one hundred and twenty*—I can appreciate the way his eyes crinkle at the corners when he joins me laughing.

"I'm a high school chemistry teacher and my school's hockey coach. My students and athletes are all my kids, but I don't have children of my own. No wife or girlfriend either," he says.

I ignore his not-very-subtle statement. "How long have you been teaching?"

He sips his water, and I force myself to tear my gaze away from the sight of his tanned throat flexing as he swallows. Oh, lordy. I cannot allow myself to find this man attractive. He is all wrong for me.

"Five years teaching, seven years coaching. I started coaching while I was in college. How about you?"

"This will be my first full year teaching. I took over for a teacher on maternity leave in January, and when she decided not to return, they hired me to fill her spot. Pine Grove Academy is a private K-12 school catering to the growing shifter population in the area. Many go through the public schools. My brother and I did. But with a shifter-focused program, it's easier for some kids. You know how it was before shifters were out. People in power claimed shifter kids had behavioral issues or labeled them as hyperactive when, in truth, they were dealing with some extra critter hormones."

"It's cool there's a school like that. I teach in the public school system at home, but it's Canada. We're a bit more chill up there. No pun intended."

I chuckle because regardless of whether he intended it, his pun was funny.

"My mom teaches at the local public high school. My grandmother taught there too. History, both of them. I prefer working with the little kids. I'm still taller than they are."

His rich laugh washes over me, and it almost feels like a cozy blanket settling around my shoulders. Oh, this is not good, Kendall.

"Well, I don't have that problem. I'm bigger than almost everyone I teach."

"I bet you are." That came out way throatier and more flirtatious than I intended. Even if I was thinking about it, I didn't intend to express it. With my luck, I'm flushing a deep red. Awesome.

I jump up. "I should catch up with the tour."

Burke rises as well. "Let me show you the way."

"No, it's okay. I know where it is, thanks." Rushing away, I feel the tingle between my shoulder blades again. Not good.

I am in no position to date again. Especially not an athlete. The last time I dated, I ended up married to a minor-league-baseball-playing squirrel shifter who wanted me for my trust fund. I'll gain access to it when I turn twenty-five, but he wanted me to get an early disbursement. Since I was twenty-two, the decision fell to my father as trustee, and Dad didn't think we needed it as two healthy, college-educated adults.

Kregg took out his disappointment on our dishes, lamps, and walls. Not on me, physically, because I got out of there just in time, but words and betrayal hurt too.

I should have known he was bad news as soon as I heard how he spelled his name. K-R-E-G-G, pronounced *Craig*. He insists his parents were going with the "traditional spelling," but I met his parents, and the truth is they are a pair of squirrel shifters from Nowhere, Ohio who don't know how to spell. It would be okay if they weren't nasty, greedy people who justified their son lying to me and trying to cheat me out of my trust fund.

I hurry down the hallway to the locker rooms like I will outrun my memories. Thinking about what I went through with Kregg causes bile to rise in my throat. I duck into the ladies' room and lose the water I drank. Most of my family doesn't know about how Kregg treated me. It would break their hearts, especially my father's. I can't stand the pity. They think I must have come to my senses and left. They don't know he cheated on me. Or about how I lived in fear he would start hitting me when he ran out of things to throw and break.

The shame I feel is enough of a burden. I'm a cougar shifter. I could have shifted and protected myself, but I didn't. My cougar cowered like a frightened kitten from a fucking squirrel. Calling him a fucking squirrel is an exaggeration because he wasn't good in bed. Forget nuts. He barely had acorns, and saying he had a twig was being generous. How he found women to cheat on me with, I don't know. I guess there are women who want to say they slept with a professional athlete even if he is a minor league baseball player with subpar equipment.

With shaky breaths, I look in the mirror. I know I have nothing to be ashamed of. The verbal abuse and cheating were not my fault. I've been to therapy at the insistence of my cousin Andy. He is the only one in my family who knows what I went through, and I've sworn him and his boyfriend Harrison to secrecy. They were college team-mates of Kregg's. I met him when Andy brought him home for Thanksgiving. Once Kregg realized how wealthy my family was, he pursued me like crazy, and I was naïve enough to think he loved me.

Never again. If I ever have another relationship, it will not be with someone prone to violence, and it won't be with a professional athlete. I'm not taking a risk on someone who can hurt me or cheat on me again. I'd rather be alone. My career needs to be my focus. The kids are enough for me. They have to be.

Every few weeks, we get together as an extended family for dinner. I love that we are close, but I skip them as much as I can. There are four of us kids—me, Liam, and our cousins Logan and Andy. By my calculations, that means I need to show up a quarter of the time.

I'm the only single one and it's awkward. I get questions about if I'm seeing anyone. Why aren't I seeing anyone? Do I want to die alone? The nights I get ambushed by the handsome teacher from Mom's school or the earnest associate attorney from Aunt Holly's law firm are the worst. No skipping tonight though. It's Mom's birthday, and they would hunt me down if I did my usual "Sorry! Can't come tonight! Busy! Love you!" text. Doesn't matter we were all together at the Devil Birds thing today. This is a command performance.

I'm not lying; on Friday nights, I often schedule extra practices for the cheer team I coach or give private lessons to those who want to improve their skills for tryouts for their school squads. I love my family, and I know they love me. Everyone wants me to be happy, but they don't understand I'm not ready to date again.

I know they think I'm flaky and that I've decided to throw in the towel because being married wasn't as fun as I thought it would be. I should be ready to jump into the dating pool and try again. Shifters almost never get divorced. I grew up hearing the fairy tales about fated mates and happily ever after. I thought that's what I had, but I was wrong. My Prince Charming was anything but.

Tonight, Logan and Daphne share they are trying to have a baby. I walk outside and sit on one of the lounge chairs beside the pool. I need a moment.

"You okay?" Andy asks. He knows the baby talk isn't easy for me.

"Yeah, I'm fine. I'm excited for them."

I *am* excited for them. They will be great parents. Mom and Aunt Holly have been dying for us to have babies. I thought I'd be the first. I had such high hopes when Kregg and I ran off and got married. It was romantic. I had daydreamed about our future and our family. We were both young, but I've always wanted to be a mother.

Kregg said he wanted the same things, but all that was a lie. He was telling me what I wanted to hear to get me to marry him so he could get my money. We had a pregnancy scare, and that was why we eloped. Turns out I wasn't pregnant, but I didn't know until after we had stood before the Justice of the Peace and spoken our vows. If he had gotten me pregnant, a baby would have tied me to him forever. Still, I'd love to have a baby. Someday. Somehow.

"You know," I say, "if you and Harrison ever want kids, I'll carry it. Harrison's sperm, obviously."

Harrison looks like a cross between Denzel Washington and Shemar Moore. If ever there were genetics to be carried on, those are the ones. He's a wolf shifter from Atlanta and even his wolf is gorgeous, with solid black fur, lustrous and dark, and striking gray eyes. Whether in human or wolf form, he turns heads. However, Harrison only has eyes for Andy. They are the cutest couple. I'm grateful they are my best friends.

Andy bumps my shoulder with his. "We'll see. But you are going to find someone to love and have a family with. I know you're scared, and I don't blame you. But there are good men out there."

I open my mouth to comment, but he cuts me off.

"Straight men. Men who want you for you, not for your money, not for your connections. They want you because you're wonderful and not too ugly."

Count on Andy to make me laugh. I'm not conceited, but I know I'm not ugly. Okay, I'm shorter than average, at a smidge over five feet tall, but I have long blond hair, blue eyes people say are pretty, and a body guys seem to like to see in a bikini. I'm attractive enough.

"Yeah, okay. But Harrison and I would make pretty babies together."

"Harrison would have pretty babies with a lamppost."

"I don't think I want to know," Liam says as he walks up behind us. "Food is ready."

Andy and I rise. Before I can follow Andy to the house, Liam lays a gentle hand on my arm. He is one of the good ones Andy was talking about. Mallory is lucky. But so is Liam because Mallory is awesome.

"Are you okay, Kennie?" he asks.

I smile my cheer smile, the one I perfected during my years as a competitive cheerleader. It's my shield to hide behind and it's always been effective.

"Yeah, why?"

"I know the past year has been hard. I worry about you."

"Don't, I'm fine."

"You haven't been dating."

"I'm focused on my career. And I'm only twenty-four. I'm in no rush."

Let him think I'm uninvolved because of work, not because I don't trust my judgment in men.

I shrug. "And I'm not in a target-rich environment in an elementary school. My best friends are two gay men. When I'm ready, I'll find someone."

Liam sighs and waves to his girlfriend, Mallory, as we start up the path to the patio.

"Okay. But don't shut yourself off. One failed relationship shouldn't dictate your life."

"It's not. I'm fine." Mostly.

3
BURKE

I can't believe it. My first official team event. Coach is having a cookout for the team, staff, and families at the house he shares with Carter's sister, Mallory. I'm ecstatic. I've conquered the first challenge—making the team. Making the team with people like Carter, Mackenzie, and the Wallers, who are quickly becoming true friends, makes this all the sweeter.

Walking through the house where the party is being held, I admire how roomy and comfortable it is. I don't need a house as big as this, but something with this vibe is what I dream of having for my future family. Carter grew up in this house, and he said it was great with his older siblings plus the cousins who live on the farms down the road. I can see Kendall through the screen on the sliding glass door. I'm glad she's here, but I wasn't expecting it.

The conversation she's having with a woman who must be her mother drifts through the screen.

"Why do I have to be here at the team barbecue? I'm not on the team, Mom. I don't even like hockey!" Kendall says. She stomps her foot in her flip-flop, and I grin. It's an adorable display of temper, and reminds me of something the first graders I've had in the classes I subbed for would do when they didn't get their way.

"We are going to support your brother, and it's a party. It will be fun. Have a burger, take a dip in the pool, enjoy the view…" Her mother wiggles her brows suggestively.

Kendall's shoulders rise and fall with a sigh. "I'm not dating again, Mom."

"Who said anything about dating? You're young and single. Have some fun!"

Kendall gasps. "Mother!"

Her mom's laugh tinkles like bells as she walks away.

Sliding the screen door open because I don't want to look like a creep if Kendall turns around and sees me standing there, I step out onto the patio running the length of the back of the house. It's shaded by a second-floor deck and has lots of seating and tables set up for the party.

She gives me a guarded smile.

"Hi," I say.

"Hello."

We stand there looking at each other. I don't know what to say.

Carter approaches the patio from across the lawn and throws an arm around Kendall. She jumps.

"Just me, Ken. Why are you always jumpy?" he asks.

She smiles up at him, but it looks forced. "I was daydreaming. You surprised me, that's all."

"Thinking about how you'd rather be at the beach?"

"Guilty."

"Hey, Bedard. Oh, good, there's Mac, Brick, and Stone." He holds up his hand in greeting as they join us on the patio. "Glad you're here. Follow me to the barn. I have something to show you." He grabs Kendall's hand. "You too."

Carter leads us through the woods to the big red barn barely visible from the house. Punching in a code on the keypad next to the largest door, Trevor opens the big door and flips on the lights.

Stone whistles. "Dude, you have your own rink? Is it crazy expensive to keep the ice going? Is there ice? It's not cold."

Brick and Mac look around, and I approach the boards. Opening the gate, I squat to touch the surface.

"It's synthetic?" I look over my shoulder to where Carter still holds Kendall's hand.

Until she pulls it out of his grasp.

"Yeah," he says. "My mom is a chemical engineer, and when we were kids, she invented this improved polymer that created a synthetic ice surface with less friction and longer wear time than what was available then. We were the guinea pigs. This is the original surface still, hasn't had to be replaced in over fifteen years."

"Wow," Brick says. "How cool to have your own rink. Stone and I waited for the pond to freeze."

"This used to be stables?" Mac asks.

"Yeah, but none of us ride. It made sense to convert it to something we can all use."

He leads us through the ground floor of the barn, showing us the locker rooms and gym.

"This is the part Kennie will like." Carter opens a door and turns on the lights.

Kendall lets out a gasp of what I assume is delight. Before us stretches an expanse of blue mats, and at the back is a dance floor with mirrors. Kendall skips out onto the floor and spins around, with her arms outstretched.

"I wish I knew you when we were kids, and your parents could have adopted me. A cheer gym to use whenever I wanted would have been great."

Carter nods. "My cousins did cheer and dance. Since we had this space, my parents made it a spot where they could come over and practice. Their farm is right next door. I did it with them when I had no one to play hockey with. Wanna tumble?"

"Hell yeah!" Kendall says, putting her hair up in a ponytail with the elastic she had around her wrist and kicking off her flip-flops.

They stand at the edge of the mat and grin at each other before taking off in a flurry of cartwheels, flips, handsprings, and twists. They're laughing when they reach the far end of the mat and bow at our appreciative whoops and hollers.

Carter holds his hand up for a high five, and since he's a foot and a half taller than she is, Kendall needs to jump to reach it.

"That's insane," Brick says as they walk back to the group. "You make it look easy."

"Well, I had years of training and experience. I'm sure you make skating and playing goalie look easy, and I know it's not. I can't skate," Kendall says.

"You can't? How did that happen?" I ask.

"While Liam was in the rink, I was in the gym. I enjoy tumbling and dancing. And the rinks are too cold. I like to be warm. I'm a summer girl. Bring on the heat."

I grin. "So, no moving to Canada, then?"

She shakes her head vehemently. "No moving anywhere. I'm a Jersey Girl born and bred. I'm here to stay."

Carter gives her a hug from behind and kisses the crown of her head.

"We weren't letting you go anywhere, anyway. I missed you."

He releases her and she steps away to slip into her flip-flops.

"Come on, I wanted to show you upstairs." Carter turns and leads us up a staircase next to the gym. At the top, he opens a door to a large living area with couches, a pool table, a huge tv with gaming systems and a kitchen area.

"Nice setup. I could live here," says Mac.

Carter smiles. "Funny you should say that, Mac. There are two apartments, three bedrooms each. I was wondering if you guys wanted to move in here with me. This is more space than I need for myself, and I like you. I think we'd have fun."

He opens a door in the wall alongside the foosball table. "This is my apartment. I have the bedroom with the attached bath. The other two rooms share a bath. There's a powder room there." He points to a door. "Kitchen, living room, here are the other two bedrooms. This one is for one of you, and the other is staying empty. The other apartment has the same layout."

"How much are you charging for rent?" Stone asks.

Carter names a figure so low he must be joking. Way below market value, based on the ads I've been checking out.

"Seriously?" Mac asks. "You're crazy."

"I want to cover utilities. I don't want to be out here in the woods alone, but it's stupid to pay rent somewhere else to not be alone. Everyone cleans up after themselves and buys their own food. If you want different furniture, bring it in. What's in there now is stuff Mal and Liam moved out when they remodeled. New mattresses."

"Can we see the other apartment?" Brick asks.

"Sure." Carter says, leading the others to the second apartment. "You'll have full use of the rink and gym equipment. It's about thirty minutes to The Nest, which isn't ideal, but there's room to run, which you won't have if you stay in Atlantic City or rent an apartment here on the mainland."

I glance at Kendall. "Will you live here too?"

"What? No. I have a condo," she says.

"I thought the empty bedroom was for you."

She shakes her head. "Nope, not for me. I guess he's keeping it as a guest room."

Stone pokes his head out of the other apartment. "Burke, you want to see this?"

"Yeah, on my way."

Brick is in the doorway of what I assume is a bedroom when we walk into the second apartment.

"Dibs on this one," she says. "I'm not sharing a bathroom with any guys."

"I'll take the room over there." Mac says, gesturing to Trevor's apartment.

Brick blows a raspberry at him. "You're tired of living with me, aren't you, Mac?"

He gives an emphatic nod. "Yes, Brick, I am. You're a lovely lass, but you're a lot to deal with. I can put my younger siblings in a head-lock or throw them in the loch, but you'd hurt me."

"Well, I'll take the bedroom here. Did you want the other, Burke?" Stone asks.

I walk around and look out the windows. It's a great space, and the price can't be beat.

"Are you sure about this, Carter?" I ask. "You're going to be with us at the rink and traveling with us. You want to be stuck with us at home too?"

Carter shrugs. "I'm the youngest of four. Being here by myself would be lonely. If you bug me, I'll shift and go for a run. If you want to be here, you're welcome."

"Then count me in! Thanks, man. I appreciate this." I shake his hand.

Kendall checks her phone. "We better get back to the house. My brother gets annoyed if people are late for things."

They're holding hands as we walk back through the woods. Again. For people who are supposed to be "just friends" they sure hold hands a lot. I don't hold hands with any of my friends like that. Is he somehow excused from the "no being involved with your coach's family" rule?

I like Carter and understand he has connections because Coach is dating his sister. But it doesn't mean he gets to be all up on Coach's sister. I wonder if Coach knows how cozy they are? Why do I care? *Here to play hockey, Bedard, not crush on your Coach's little sister.*

We arrive back at the main house as the rest of the team shows up. Coach introduces us to his girlfriend, Mallory, and his parents, Will and Faith. Mallory is Carter's older sister. She's pretty with red hair and green eyes, but she's not a knockout like Kendall.

"Oh, Burke Bedard! We've talked about you at our dinner table quite a few times these past few weeks." Mrs. Morgan...Faith, as she insists we call her, says.

They have? I feel a flush creep up under my beard. "Um...okay. Thank you?"

"Mom!" Coach comes over. "You can't say that to our players. Sorry, Bedard."

"All good." I'm trying my best to lower my eyebrows because I know they are almost to my hairline.

A pretty pink flush sweeps up Kendall's face. Coach sighs, again. I'm getting the impression he does that a lot around his mother.

"Mom!" Kendall reaches out and grabs Bridget. "Have you met Bridget Waller? She's a goalie. Bridget, this is our mother, Faith."

"Run," Coach says under his breath. Don't need to tell me twice. I always listen to my boss. I smile in the general direction of the group and slip away.

"Beer?" Carter asks as he opens a cooler.

"Nah, is there pop?" I don't indulge often but a Coke sounds delicious. The can is cool in my hand, and I relish it. I miss being cold. It doesn't get this hot and sticky in the part of Ontario I'm from. It's at least thirty-five degrees. Wait, I'm in the US now. Ninety-five degrees. I'm going to have to get used to thinking about miles, gallons, and Fahrenheit. My science teacher's heart experiences a pang. I miss the metric system.

"Can we have sodas, Uncle Trev?" Two boys walk up to us. My guess is they are around eight and ten years old.

"What's your dad say?" Carter asks.

"He says yes!" the younger one says.

"EJ?" Carter asks the older one.

"We're allowed to have one each, and then we have to drink water the rest of the day."

Carter hands each boy a can. "Burke, these are my nephews, EJ and Matt."

"Hi. I'm Burke." I hold out my hand to shake.

EJ shakes my hand. "Defense. Polar bear shifter. Canadian."

"Yep."

"I play defense too," he says.

"I play center, like Uncle Trev!" Matt says as he pumps my hand. You can tell the boys are brothers from their looks. Both have dark hair and bright blue eyes, but EJ seems far more reserved and serious than his younger brother.

"Nice to meet you both," I say.

"This is their dad and my older brother, Ethan," Carter inclines his head toward the man approaching us. He's a few years older than I am, in his early thirties. Leaner than Carter, but still tall and muscular. Not as tall or muscular as I am, but most men aren't.

We shake hands.

"Hey, heard a lot about you," Ethan says.

It seems I'm quite the conversation topic. "Good, I hope?"

"Absolutely." Ethan smirks. "Not that I'd tell you if it wasn't."

We all laugh.

"Bedard is taking a room in the barn," Carter says. I'm surrounded by Carters. I guess I should call him Trevor today.

"Oh, well, you'll see these two all the time then." Ethan rests a hand on the shoulder of each boy. "We have a cottage over toward the farm."

Trevor points to the woods opposite the band of trees shielding the barn. "Our uncle's Christmas tree farm is over there."

I nod. "Are the woods okay to run in?"

"Yeah, absolutely," Ethan says. "There's a river back there too. You can take a dip in there. No icebergs, but we get some snow."

A little bundle of happiness runs into me and attaches itself to my leg.

"Burke!"

"Hey, Rowena. How are you doing?" I step out of her grasp and squat down.

She bounces on her toes, and her red ponytails swing back and forth. She's adorable. "I'm good. Auntie Teagan brought me here today. Mommy was supposed to, but she got called into work. I lost a tooth! See?" She smiles and sticks her tongue through the space on the top row where her tooth used to be.

"Wow!" I say. "Did the Tooth Fairy visit?"

"She did! She brought me a dollar and guess what else," she says breathlessly.

"What?"

Rowena roots in her little pink backpack and pulls out a book. "A hockey book! And it has polar bears like you!"

Teagan joins us. "Hey Burke. Apparently, all Ro has been talking about is ice hockey and polar bears for weeks."

"Oh!" Rowena says. "I'm a bitch!"

I swear half the team chokes on their drinks. Anger surges in me. Who would call this adorable little girl something so ugly? Doing my best to keep a rein on my temper so I don't scare her, I put a gentle hand on her tiny shoulder.

Kendall rushes over and kneels down next to me. "Rowena, who called you that?" Kendall's tone is gentle.

I'm trying not to growl.

"No one. Daddy is a bear and Mommy's a witch. I smushed the words together like you taught us and got bitch." Her proud smile makes my heart twinge.

"Okay. Good job. But we can't smush all words together to make contractions. It's only certain words like *I'm* and *don't*," Kendall says kindly.

My heart twinges again. It's gotta be the caffeine in the pop. I should stick with water.

Rowena tilts her head. "Well, what am I then?"

I remove my hand from her shoulder after giving her the gentlest of squeezes. "You're a very smart, very special little girl."

Kendall turns to look at me with a sweet smile, and I want to swim in her ocean blue eyes. I also want to swim in the pool. Or take a cold shower. A cold shower would be the best choice right now. Cool me off from the heat of the day and help other parts of me from getting too hot. Think about ice water, Burke. Sliding down snow-banks. Cold things.

Teagan holds out her hand to Rowena. "Come on, Ro. Let's go in the shade and put more sunscreen on you. If I don't, you'll be more bacon than little bear." She looks back over her shoulder as she leads the little girl away. And winks.

When I rise to my full height, I'm struck by how small Kendall is next to me. I dwarf most people and think little of it, but with Kendall it stirs an instinct in me to protect her. I know Coach is a cougar shifter. I assume Kendall shifts as well, since she teaches at a shifter charter school and talked about being a shifter kid in the public school system. She's not weak, especially if she's a cougar too. She doesn't need protection, but my instinctive need to protect her remains. It's not something I've felt before.

"Do we need to get you in the shade too?" she asks. "I can't imagine you're loving this kind of heat and humidity."

"I'm not. I was longing for a nice iceberg to lounge on. A dip in the pool would work in a pinch. Want to join me?"

She looks out at the pool where some of my teammates are hanging out. A few brought their wives or girlfriends. She wouldn't be the only girl.

"Yeah, okay. Give me a minute to change."

"Sure," I say. "I'll meet you at the pool."

Since I'm already wearing my swim trunks, I only need to take off my shirt to be ready to swim. I'm spraying on sunscreen when Kendall walks over to drop her towel on a chair. The bikini she's wearing is modest as far as bikinis go, but I swear it's the sexiest thing I've ever seen. The turquoise of her top makes her eyes shine with a vibrant blue. The bottoms are like shorts with how they cover everything. But damn, they do incredible things for her ass.

After seeing the way she tumbled across the mat in the barn, I knew she was athletic, but the combination of curves and toned abs is hot. I didn't know my type was sexy sporty, but it is. At least it is now. Wait. No, it's not. I don't have a type.

Hockey is my focus. Play my best, save my money, and go back home to my real life. I can't get distracted by a woman. Especially not my coach's sister. That's the surest way to get my ass benched or kicked off the team. Hockey code is clear—you don't mess with the sister or daughter of a teammate or coach. You don't violate the hockey code without facing the consequences.

"Will you spray my back if I spray yours?" Kendall asks.

"Um...yeah. Sure. You gotta rub it in though."

"No problem. Can you do me first?" She turns her back to me.

"Sure." My voice cracks worse than it did when I was twelve. Clearing my throat, I try again. "Sure." I swallow hard as she sweeps her ponytail over her shoulder, exposing her back. Have backs always been sexy? After I spray the lotion, I hand her the bottle. I rub in the lotion at her shoulders and work my way down the supple muscles along her spine.

Icebergs. Think of icebergs. But not even that works as I sweep down her back and approach the waistband of her swim shorts. She shivers when I run my thumbs along the elasticized band. I don't think it's the temperature that caused that reaction.

I clear my throat and step back. "All good."

Kendall glances over her shoulder, and her blue eyes look hazy. Did my touch affect her like it did me?

She gives me a slow smile. "Your turn."

4

KENDALL

I WISH I WAS WEARING A SWEATER, JEANS, AND A PARKA TO HIDE MY BODY'S reaction to Burke's touch. My nipples are stiff peaks, and I am grateful for the light padding in my bikini top to hide them. I haven't reacted to a man's touch like that in forever. If ever. I know he-who-shall-not-be-named never affected me like that.

Burke does the sexy one-handed pull the shirt off over the head thing that hot guys know how to do. Is it something taught in middle school when they separate the boys and girls to go over the birds and the bees? Do they still do that? I feel like I should know, but with first graders we focus more on not sticking crayons up our noses and zipping up coats than taking off shirts.

I watch the red cotton drop on the lounge chair and look up, up, up to his face. It's a long way up. Past tight abs, firm pecs with a light dusting of dark hair, the strong column of his throat. He quirks his sexy lips to the side and his deep brown eyes sparkle. The jerk knows he affected me. Well, two can play that game.

"You're very big," I purr. I'm a cougar shifter. We purr, not roar. I watch his Adam's apple bob with his swallow. "You should sit down so I can handle—" I lower my chin, drop my gaze down toward his board shorts, and then look back up at him through my lashes."—everything."

It's my turn to smirk as a blush spreads from under his thick, dark beard. I hold out my hand for the sunscreen. "Sit."

Burke hands me the bottle and settles on the lounge chair. Even with him seated, we are almost the same height, but he's still taller. I spray the sunscreen across his wide shoulders and then down his spine. I drop the bottle on the chair next to Burke's thigh. His muscular thigh. It's my turn to swallow hard.

His skin is warm as I rub in the lotion. His muscles are firm beneath my touch. I've dated athletes before. They're my catnip. Toned, muscular bodies aren't unfamiliar to me. But this is the best one I've ever encountered.

I scratch my nails along his back. Goosebumps break out on his skin and he gives a slight shiver. I smile and move down his lats, diligently rubbing in the lotion. He has a light tan. I catch a tiny glimpse of how white the skin is under the waistband of his trunks. No naked sunbathing for this guy. He picks up his discarded t-shirt and holds it in his lap. I'm grateful my pebbled nipples are easier to hide than whatever he's packing.

"Icebergs."

"Hmm?" I ask, leaning against his back to speak near his ear. My nipples brush his back, and the pressure feels fantastic. I swear, I could make myself come from rubbing my breasts against him.

He leans back slightly, increasing the amount of contact between us. I gasp. But don't move away.

If he turned his head, our lips would almost touch. I wonder if his beard is soft or scratchy.

"Are you going in the pool too? I have my floaties!" Rowena, the most adorable mood killer I know, is next to me. I'm reminded we are at a team barbecue. At my brother's house. With my parents here.

Oh no. Teagan is looking at us with raised eyebrows and a knowing smirk. She's been like an older sister to me since she's always been one of Liam's best friends. I could talk to her about things I didn't want to discuss with Mom or Aunt Holly. With a brother and male cousins, there were things I needed a feminine peer's perspective on, and she provided one.

I straighten quickly and step back. "Sure are! I like your bathing suit."

"Thank you! I look like Ariel because my hair is red, and my suit is...blue? Green? I forget the color." Ro sticks her little tongue out in thought.

"Teal. I think that's the color name you're thinking of, Rowena," Burke says as he rises from the chaise. "I'm going into the pool." He turns to Teagan. "I can watch her if you aren't getting in."

Teagan shakes her head. "Thanks, Burke. I'm going in. If she's in the water, so am I. That's the rule." She holds out her hand. "Come on Ro, we're going in at the stairs."

Burke looks down at me. "Ready?"

To swim? Yes. To deal with the emotions he riles up? Nope?

I jump in.

"I guess you are," Burke says as he eases into the pool. Good thing he didn't jump in, he's huge. The splash would have been like a tsunami.

Ro paddles over to us with her hot pink glitter floaties on her arms. Teagan is with her. We are at the point it drops off to the deep end. I'm still able to stand in the shallow water, and Burke is in the deeper area but also able to stand with the water above his waist. I think that was his primary concern.

Ro scowls at Burke. "I thought you were a polar bear?"

He tilts his head. "I am."

"Your fur isn't white!"

"What?" I ask her.

"Daddy's a grizzly bear. The fur on his chest is brown. His—" she points at Burke. "—should be white."

Teagan chuckles. "Honey, that's not how it works. People's hair color has nothing to do with the color of their fur or feathers in shifter form."

"But Daddy said it's because his bear is brown!"

Oh, no. The lip is trembling. I glance at Burke.

"Actually," Burke says, "polar bears have clear fur. It's not white."

Ooh, distraction. Good tactic.

Rowena eyes him suspiciously. "They do?"

"They do. It's clear. There's a protein in it called keratin. We all have it in our hair. But in polar bears, the keratin makes it look white even though the strands of fur are clear. And my skin is black. It absorbs the sun like a solar panel."

"Prove it," she says with a glinty-eyed stare.

"Note to self," Teagan says. "Don't play poker with Ro."

"Rowena, it's not polite to ask people to prove things to you," I say.

Burke shrugs. "Discovering and showing proof is the basis of science. I can prove it by shifting, but I don't want to make things weird at a team barbecue."

"It's nothing folks haven't seen before," Teagan says.

Trevor swims closer, his leg brushing against mine. "I've never seen a polar bear in person."

On the deck of the pool, Matt jumps up and down, waving his arms. "I wanna see a polar bear!"

Teagan leans toward Burke. "It's whatever you are comfortable with. We will never ask you or expect you to shift, but if you want to show the kids, I bet they'd get a kick out of it. Carter too."

Burke nods. "Okay, let me get out of the pool and I'll shift into my bear. You can see how my fur is."

"Can we touch it?" Ro asks.

"Sure," Burke says. "Can I shift behind the pool house? I don't want to do it in front of a crowd."

I nod.

"Will you come with me?" he asks me.

I nod again, and we get out of the pool. We towel off and Burke hands me his t-shirt to throw on as a coverup. It's like a dress on me. I resist burying my head along the shoulder to breathe in his manly scent of cedar and mint. It's like running through the forest in winter.

"Are you going to be okay as your bear in this heat?" I ask. I love the heat but it's so humid today, even I find it oppressive.

"I need to stay in the shade and can't stay as my bear too long since I can't sweat to cool down."

"Okay, what do you want me to tell them? And can they touch you?"

We walk behind the pool house and out of view of everyone. Would be a great make out spot. If we had a reason to make out. Which Burke and I do not.

"I'm good with you touching me."

What? Oh. As his bear.

He shrugs. "They are shifter kids. They should know the basics of etiquette. Don't pull on my fur. Don't climb on me without my permission. I'll nod if it's okay, but they will need help because I'm big. They can pet me."

"What am I telling them about your fur? It's clear?"

"We don't need to make this a big science lesson. Let them look, and then I can answer questions after I shift back."

We stand there, looking at each other. It should be awkward, but it's not. Then it is.

Burke shuffles his feet. "I guess I'll shift now?"

"Oh! Yeah! Sorry." I turn around to give him privacy.

I can feel the air vibrate the way it does when a shift happens. It's magical. I hear a thud behind me and feel the ground shake. Startled, I turn around.

"Holy shit!" I try not to curse because I don't want to slip up in front of the kids, but I can't help it.

"You're huge." I approach Burke in awe. Everyone is big compared to me. But he's beyond huge. He's massive. He's standing on four paws and he's still taller than I am. I can't see over his back. "Can I touch you?"

He nods his majestic head, and I reach out a hand to lie on his shoulder. His fur is coarse, but I flex my fingers and feel softer fur underneath.

"Oh! You have a double coat. Kinda like tigers do. Makes sense." I run my hand over his ear like I'd do with a puppy or a kitten. He leans his heavy head against my hand. I haven't been comfortable around a man bigger than me since my breakup. Even with my family or Trevor, when I know I'm completely safe, it takes a moment for me to relax. But I instinctively know I'm safe with Burke. I snatch my hand back. I can't be comfortable. Nothing can happen.

"Ready?" I ask. I give my biggest top of the pyramid cheerleader smile. It's fake, but it's my force field. I have to remember to keep my distance.

I lead the way back to the party. I can feel Burke behind me. The shiver running down my spine is one hundred percent because of his presence. It is way too hot to be because of the air temperature.

Murmurs of "wow" and "holy crap, he's huge" come from the crowd assembled in the yard as we emerge from behind the pool house. I lead Burke to a spot under the oak trees where he isn't in the direct sun. It's still hot but a bit more bearable. I chuckle. Bearable. I'm too young and too female to be starting with the dad jokes.

The kids rush over, eager to check him out. I can't help it. I go into teacher mode and give the teacher clap we all do to get our class's attention.

"Okay," I say, "We are going to treat Burke with care and respect. You can touch his fur. No pulling on fur or ears. You all know how to behave, and I know you'll be great." I lay a hand on his side and feel him huff out a breath. "It's too hot and not polar bear weather. Burke is going to shift back in a few minutes."

The kids—and adults—are respectful and curious. About fifteen minutes later, I'm leading Burke back behind the pool house to shift. I wait a few minutes to allow him privacy then follow. He's adjusting the waistband of his shorts. Through some kind of ancient magic, or something along those lines, we can shift with our clothes. Scientists are trying to figure it out. It has something to do with some sort of scientific mumbo jumbo Burke understands. I don't care how it works, only that it helps us avoid a lot of awkward nakedness.

"Hey," I say, "Liam said you're welcome to use the shower in the pool house to cool off."

Burke sighs. "That would be awesome."

"Follow me." I turn and enter a side door then look back over my shoulder. Oh, no. "Hey, are you okay?"

Burke's shoulders are drooped, and his eyes are half-closed. He's swaying like one of the big pine trees this part of the state is famous for, but during a nor'easter, and the tree is about to come crashing to the ground. I think they'd make the same thud.

"Oh, no," I rush to his side. "Don't faint, Burke." I slip my arm around his waist and guide him to the sofa where he relaxes back on the cushions.

Shit. He faints. I rush to the bathroom and wet a couple of wash-cloths in cold water. I grunt as I lift his legs onto the couch. I'm tiny but strong. I apply a cool cloth to his forehead, and his big brown eyes blink a few times before they fully open. Burke tries to sit up, but I lay my hand on his firm, muscled, gorgeous chest. Ack, need to stop focusing on those things.

He covers my hand with his. It's massive. His hand completely hides mine. I should feel trapped. I should be straining to pull away. But I'm not. It feels right. It belongs there. This is bad. But good.

"Hey, big guy. Welcome back." He gives my hand a gentle squeeze, but my heart feels it too.

"How long was I out?" he asks. I can feel his heart pounding underneath my palm, and I swear the vibration travels up my arm to my own heart where it matches the rhythm.

"Maybe a minute? Not long."

He squeezes his eyes closed and groans. I think more from embarrassment than discomfort. "I feel stupid."

"You made it to the couch and laid back on your own. I was getting cold cloths to help you cool down. I'm not sure if you were all the way unconscious or were resting. Does this happen when you overheat?"

He blushes. "Yeah. I avoid shifting outside in the summer. I know better than to let myself get overheated. I haven't fainted since I was a boy. But I wanted to teach interested kids about my bear."

"You couldn't resist teaching." I grin in understanding.

The sliding door opens, startling us both. "Hey Ken, you in here?"

I pull my hand out from under Burke's and jump to my feet. Mallory is looking at us with raised eyebrows.

I paste on my cheer smile. "Hi Mallory. We're good. Burke overheated, he was resting for a moment to cool down." I push a strand of loose hair behind my ear to give my hands something to do.

Burke takes the cloth off his forehead and pushes himself to a seated position. I watch him, but I think he's going to be okay. Maybe a little fuzzy for a couple minutes but should be okay as long as he doesn't overdo it.

Mallory's eyes go wide. "Oh, no! Do you need a doctor? Let me get you some water." She rushes to the fridge in the small kitchen and pulls out a couple of bottles.

She pushes one into his hand. "Drink."

"Thanks." He opens it and gulps some down. When he finishes the bottle, Mallory puts the second bottle in his other hand as she takes the empty.

Burke takes a couple of sips from the second and sighs. "I'm okay. I don't need a doctor. I know better than to shift when it's this hot, but I underestimated how fast it would hit me. I am going to respect the humidity from now on."

"Okay. Well, you're welcome to stay in here. Or sit on the patio. There are fans there. Whatever you need."

"Thank you, Mallory. I appreciate it. I'll take a couple minutes and then park myself on the patio for a while. Now you know why I play ice hockey and not soccer."

Mallory and I laugh.

"Hon, are you in here?" Liam walks in. He takes in the scene and puts his arm around Mallory's shoulder. "What's going on?"

"Nothing," I say. "We were talking."

"You okay, Bedard?" he asks.

Burke nods. "Yeah. I got overheated when I shifted. Rookie mistake."

I can see he's nervous this is going to jeopardize his spot on the team.

"Is it a problem because you shifted or do you overheat normally?" Liam asks. "I haven't dealt with polar bear shifters much. If we need to monitor your playing time in a game, we can adapt, but we need to know." He is giving off a concerned vibe, but not like he's freaked out. That's good.

Burke grins. "It's too hot, and I'm too furry. Guess it's a good thing I didn't go to a team in Vegas or Florida."

"Ugh, you'd die in Florida," Mallory says. "No matter how oppressive the weather is here in New Jersey, it's worse down there. My parents live in Orlando. They do the Shifter Sprint in the theme park each Thanksgiving. US Thanksgiving, in November. Anyway, there are usually a few polar bears running, but they look kinda miserable around mile twenty-nine. They are the first in the Lazy River when the race is done."

Burke rises from the couch, and I rush to his side on instinct like I'm somehow going to hold him up. Uh-oh. Judging by Liam's raised eyebrows, I bet he's getting ideas. Liam's ideas always screw up my life somehow. Like I need his help.

"Well, I'm going to go back to the pool for a bit if you're okay, Burke?" I look up at him. I have to tilt my head all the way back to see him. How such a large man can give off such a gentle air, I don't know. And he's an apex predator shifter! I could understand if he was something like a giraffe shifter or maybe a cow, something mellow that eats grass all day. But he's not. His animal is on top of the food chain where he's from. He's not a teddy bear. He's a freaking polar bear!

"I'm good. I'll sit on the patio and relax. Thank you for your help. I appreciate it." His deep voice wraps around me like his t-shirt does, and I want to cuddle in it.

"Oh!" I say. "Your shirt! Here, take it back."

I grab the hem and pull it over my head and hand it back to him. I worry he is going to faint again by how unfocused his eyes went for a moment as he looked down at me.

"Um, thanks." He swallows with a gulp and looks at Liam before his gaze flickers around the room. Everywhere but at me. A faint tinge of pink I'm pretty sure isn't sunburn touches his cheeks. A bloom of satisfaction blossoms in my chest. I still got it. Who cares if my scumbag ex didn't appreciate it? His loss.

***

I make my way back to the patio with Mallory after spending some time laying out and chatting. I'm glad she's with Liam. They make a good match.

I stop short when I get into the shaded part and look around. Ouch. My ovaries might have exploded at the sight of Ro napping on Burke's chest, and he's chill with it. Like little girls fall asleep in his lap every day. Not in a creepy way, in a sweet way. I wonder if he has nieces and nephews or if he's naturally wonderful? I'm not used to being envious of a six-year-old. Well, they make some adorable kid sneakers I'd wear if I could, but being able to drive, vote, and drink is a fair compromise.

Liam pulls Mallory onto his lap, and she giggles as he kisses down her neck to her shoulder. They are adorable together. I miss having someone to cuddle with. My gaze strays back to Burke, and it's all I can do to hold back my gasp when I see the intensity in the deep brown eyes looking at me. Then he blinks, and it's gone. Maybe I imagined it? The remaining open seat is next to Burke. If I don't take it, I'll look rude.

I wave my finger at Ro sleeping on his lap. "How did this happen?"

Burke gives a one shoulder shrug. "She wanted to read her polar bear book with me. She was asleep by page three."

"Does this happen to you often?" I ask with a smirk.

"Putting women to sleep? Not like this." He winks.

I can't believe we're flirting above the head of a sleeping child. This is inappropriate on countless levels. And in front of my brother! I glance at Liam. Everyone at the table is watching us with varying expressions of amusement—Teagan and Mallory, or consternation —Trevor and Liam.

Ro, bless her heart, chooses that moment to wake with a start and sit up.

"I have to go potty, Auntie Teagan. Where's the bathroom?"

Teagan gets up and walks around the table as Burke lifts Ro off his lap.

Ro places her hand in the one Teagan holds out to her. "Come on, I'll show you. Then we'll get you something to eat."

I feel like everyone is waiting for them to be out of earshot before speaking.

Liam looks between me and Burke. I want to crawl under the table.

"You're a professional," Liam says to Burke, looking him in the eye. He sweeps his gaze to include me in his next statement. "I trust you both to handle your business. Don't screw up the team."

"Th...there's nothing going on." I trip over my tongue.

Burke looks pale.

Liam shrugs. "Okay. I'm not doing the patriarchal bullshit of telling my team you're off limits, Ken. You're a grown woman, and God knows you'll do whatever the hell you want. But don't mess up the team."

My brother is lucky my cougar is hiding because if I ever wanted to shift to beat him up, it would be now. My face is flushing from both embarrassment and pure fury. How *dare* he? He has no say in my life and for him to say something like that in front of Burke, in front of anyone, is insane. My chair screeches on the flagstone of the patio as I shove it back to stand. I know people are glancing over, our parents included, but I don't care. Let them see.

I lean over the table and point my finger right in Liam's face. His expression shows both shock and the beginning of his own rising temper.

"What I choose to do with my life is no concern of yours, Liam. Who do you think you are? I don't want to date anyone. No offense, Burke."

Burke holds up his hands in a *no offense taken* gesture.

"But the last thing I want is to date one of your players or anyone affiliated with your team. You don't have to worry about me screwing up your precious team."

I turn and stomp the best I can in flip-flops through the French doors and into the kitchen. Teagan and Ro enter from the hallway where the downstairs powder room is as I grab my bag off the back of a stool at the breakfast barn.

"You okay, Kennie?" Teagan asks.

"Talk to your best friend." I take a deep breath because I don't want to cuss in front of Ro.

"Liam? What did he do now?"

I look in my bag to make sure my wallet and phone are in there and take out my keys then put the strap over my shoulder. "Butted in on something that's none of his business."

Teagan rolls her eyes. She knows what Liam is like.

I force a smile as I look down at Ro. "I'll see you at school, honey. Have fun today."

I see Mom approaching the French door. I just can't right now.

Turning, I call my goodbye over my shoulder with a wave and hurry to the front door. I've gotta get out of here before I do something I'll regret. I have too many regrets already. I don't want to add to the list. Thank goodness no one blocked in my Mustang. That would be the straw that broke this cougar's back.

As I drive the winding road through the woods, I hit the button on my steering wheel and say, "Call Andy's iPhone."

He answers on the second ring.

"Do you have food?" I ask before he finishes saying hello.

"Hello to you too, Kennie. I thought you were at your brother's party? They didn't feed you?"

"I left early. Do you and Harrison have plans tonight? If not, I can pick up subs or pizza, and you can listen to me bitch about my brother."

I can hear Harrison chuckle in the background. Andy must have me on speaker.

"How can we resist an offer like that?" Harrison calls out. "Get pizzas. Do you want margaritas, wine, or something else?"

"Margaritas! I'm driving. Can you order the pizzas?"

"Yeah," Andy says. "The usuals?"

"Yes, please. Oh! Add in some garlic knots too. Do you have any cake? Cookies?"

I hear the clang of a pan hit the counter.

"Starting the brownies! Do you have ice cream in your freezer? If not, snag some," Harrison calls out.

"We're good. I have a few containers. Go snag what you want." That's an advantage of being next-door neighbors. It's easy to pop into each other's condos for whatever we need.

I pick up our pizzas and head home. Andy meets me on our shared front porch to grab the pizzas. I thank him and go into my condo to change into comfier clothes.

After changing, I walk through their front door and almost swoon at the rich scent of chocolate wafting from the kitchen. If I ever get married again, I think the ability to bake brownies will be a requirement for any candidate. Andy has much better taste in men than I do.

"Sit! Relax! We are serving you. You look like you need to decompress." Andy hands me a plate loaded with two slices of pepperoni and sausage pizza—my favorite. Harrison follows with a watermelon margarita. Another favorite.

"Why can't we be a throuple?" I whine. "Well, no, Andy and I are first cousins. That won't fly. Are you sure you really love Andy, Har? What does he have that I don't?"

I see the smirking glances pass between them. "Okay, other than *that*." Hard to compete with a peen.

I flop back on the couch and huff. "Fine."

"You're still our best friend, Ken." Harrison sits next to me with his own plate full of mushroom and pepper pizza. He places his strawberry margarita on a coaster on the coffee table in his typical precise manner.

"You know if Harrison was going to turn straight for anyone, it would be you, Kennie," Andy says from my other side. His bite of ham and pineapple pizza is half the slice. Since he isn't a margarita drinker, he has a bottle of his favorite IPA on the end table next to him.

Harrison bumps me with his shoulder. "So, what's going on, Kennie Kitty? Did something happen at the party?"

I chew my bite of pizza and then take another one. The point of being here is to vent to them and know they will be on my side. They are always on my side. For once I have cheerleaders instead of being the one cheering.

Swallowing, I lean forward and put the plate with my second slice on the coffee table and grab my margarita. I take a sip and let the watermelon and tequila work its magic.

Sighing, I rest my head on Harrison's shoulder and close my eyes. Normally, all my stress would flow out of me, but not tonight. I sit back up and tell them what happened.

When I stop to take a breath, Andy snorts. "How do you flirt accidentally?"

I elbow him again, and he shoves a throw pillow into the space between us to act as a barrier from future attack. If he didn't act like a goober, I wouldn't elbow him.

"Do you want to hear the story or not?"

Harrison pats my leg soothingly. "We want to hear. Spill."

"So, we're flirting. *Accidentally*. Liam and Mallory are at the table. Trevor and Teagan too. Ro wakes up and Teagan takes her to the bathroom." I take a fortifying sip of my drink and end up draining the glass. Oh well.

"You're not going to believe this part. Liam actually gave me permission, *permission*, to date his team as long as I don't screw it up. He straight up gave Burke and I permission to date! I don't want to date him! I don't want to date anyone! No more athletes, especially."

The timer for the brownies beeps, and Harrison rises from the couch. "Hold the thought, Kennie."

"Ken…" Andy says.

"The brownies smell incredible, Har!" I grab my glass from the table and go to the counter to refill it. I can drink this whole pitcher. I only need to walk across the porch to get home. And I'm a cougar shifter. I metabolize alcohol quickly. At least I didn't lose that when I lost my ability to shift.

Harrison grabs my hand and leads me back to the couch. "They will be ready to cut and use for sundaes in about twenty minutes. Plenty of time to finish your story."

I grab my plate of pizza and sit back down. "My brother is a jerk. The end." I take a bite of my cooling pizza. It's better when it's hot, but it's still good enough.

"Do you want to date Burke?" Andy asks. "He's the tall one with dark hair and a beard?"

"You described half the team, hon," Harrison says.

Andy shrugs. "True. Stop rolling your eyes, Ken. It's not attractive."

I stick my tongue out at him instead. My first graders are rubbing off on me.

"If—*if* I wanted to date anyone, I'd maybe pick him. He's good looking, and he seems nice."

"You should try it, Kendall. You're too young to shut yourself off." Harrison gently squeezes my hand.

Tears fill my eyes. I'm always Ken or Kennie. They only call me Kendall when they are worried about me. Shaking my head, I try to hold back my sob, but it comes out as a hiccup.

"No. I'm not ready. It has nothing to do with Squirrel Shit." That's our private nickname for my ex. "Obviously, I don't love him or miss him or have any good feelings for him."

"Hey," Andy puts his arm around me and pulls me to his chest. The throw pillow barrier disappeared somewhere. "It's okay. Just tell us."

I take a deep, shuddering breath. Shame clogs my throat, but I know I can tell these two anything and they will love me through it.

"I can't shift anymore. I haven't shifted since before that last night when he..." I give another hiccup sob. "...when he was throwing stuff and yelling." I take a shaky breath. "I'm pretty sure he was going to hit me if you guys hadn't busted in. I couldn't shift to protect myself, and I still can't shift, and I won't put myself in a position where I'm with a man twice my size—a polar bear shifter to boot—and I have no way to protect myself."

I take a deep breath to calm down and stop babbling. Harrison rubs soothing circles on my back.

"It's obvious my judgment sucks. I can't trust he's a good guy and not faking it. I can't risk it. I'm okay alone."

Harrison snuggles in, and I'm the filling in an Andy-Harrison sandwich. "Honey, you are never alone. You will always have us."

For right now, it's enough.

5

BURKE

"Ready to hit the ice?" Coach asks as he enters the locker room. The party yesterday broke up not too long after Kendall left. It was getting ready to wind down anyway, but Kendall leaving broke the ice. We'll start moving into the barn after practice. If we can still walk.

I think Coach gave me permission to date his sister. Not that I was going to ask her out. Not that she wants to go out with me. Is that a strike against me?

"Bedard, a word in my office? Everyone else, get on the ice. Steve and Boomer are out there."

Carter shoots me a glance. Does he know something? He must read the question on my face because he gives a slight shake of his head and shrugs. I feel the eyes of most of my teammates on me as I rise and grab my stick and go to Coach's office. Dread is like a cannonball in my stomach. I hate the uncertainty eating away at me l as I approach his door.

"Come in," Coach says. "Close the door."

I do as he says, leaning the stick against the wall next to the door.

"Have a seat. You're not in trouble."

I sink into the chair across from his desk and let out the breath I had been holding.

Coach leans his forearms on his desk and clasps his hands.

"Bedard, you don't know me well yet, but I'm not the type of man who reams people out for no reason. In my experience, shifter athletes who have reached this level of achievement are harder on themselves than any coaching staff could be. If my players do their best and follow the rules, I have nothing to yell about."

I nod. I have the same coaching style. My kids are teenagers, and there will be times when they need guidance, but I've found you get the best results from building them up, not tearing them apart.

"Anyway, you're not in trouble." He grimaces. "But I am. I must apologize for yesterday. I'm sorry if I made you uncomfortable with the whole Kennie thing."

He runs his hand through his hair and leans forward.

"She's my little sister. I want her to be happy. I worry about her."

"Why?" I ask. She's a grown woman and seems to have her act together from what I've seen.

"She had a nasty breakup last year. I want her to be with a good guy. I want her to be happy."

Chuckling, I lean back in my chair. "I have a younger sister, Emily. She's twenty-two. I get it. But if Kendall is anything like Emily, the more you push or 'suggest'—" I can't believe I'm doing air quotes to my coach."—the more she's going to resist."

Coach chuckles too. "You get it."

"I do. But I'm here for hockey. I'm not looking to get involved with anyone. I want to play, save my money, and when I'm done playing, go back to Canada to teach and start a family."

"Do you have someone waiting for you at home?" Coach asks.

"No, I'm single. Hockey is my focus. But I'm looking for something to keep me busy when we aren't practicing or playing. I was wondering if the team has community service opportunities, ideally with a school. As great as things are with the team, I miss being with kids and teaching."

Coach steeples his fingers under his chin and squints his eyes. I guess this is his thinking face?

"Yeah, we can arrange something. What did you have in mind?"

"Something in the classroom. Science enrichment. I don't want to only speak at assemblies. I want to interact with the kids and teach them something."

"Let me talk to people. Daphne will let you know what we set up." Coach stands. "Enough bonding. Let's get this team in order."

"We survived. I'm not moving from this bench until we start again Monday morning." Stone Waller says from where he sprawls on the bench in front of his locker.

It's been five days since Coach and I spoke about setting up something for me to do in the community. Nothing has been set up yet and I'm okay with that because practice has been intense and we are all dragging our carcasses. We've all been through training camps before and are used to working hard. This is nothing new. But doing this as a teenager, or in college, is a different experience than doing it in your late twenties. Of course, the stakes have never been this high. If we screw up here, we are missing out on realizing a dream and a lot of money.

Coach and Jake enter the locker room and have the nerve to laugh at us. "Before you leave, we want to meet with each of you and go over the week. Get your sweaty asses in the shower and come to the meeting room when you're done. Won't take long. After we speak to everyone, we'll have a brief team meeting and then you'll be off for the weekend. Good job, team."

"You're enjoying this, aren't you?" Jake says as he and Coach leave the locker room.

Coach chuckles. "You bet your feathered ass I am." His laughter cuts off as the door closes behind him.

I manage to contain my groan as I unlace my skates. Normally

I'm all about a cool shower, but I'm longing for some warm water hitting these sore muscles. I don't stay under the spray as long as I'd like. I want to get my meeting with Coach and Jake over with. I don't know what they want to discuss. Maybe how we are adjusting. If we have a place to live. I moved into my apartment already. It's nice. Brick and Stone have obviously lived together before. They are used to each other's rhythms. I consider myself easygoing. They give me space when I need to decompress. They are up for hanging out when I feel like being social. Carter and Mac too. We've been having foosball tournaments at night and a couple of nights we did a group dinner.

Crosby leaves the office and gives me a nod as he takes a seat in the meeting room and pulls out his phone.

"Next!" Coach calls out. I look around, and it doesn't look like anyone is jumping up. I enter and close the door.

"Have a seat, Bedard." I take the seat in front of Coach's desk, next to Jake. They both seem relaxed, which is good, I guess.

Jake jiggles the foot crossed over his knee. It doesn't seem like a nervous thing, just a lot of energy looking for an outlet.

"You're living in the barn?" Jake asks.

"Yeah, moved in this week."

"Is this guy a good neighbor?" He hooks a thumb at Coach. Coach gives him the finger.

"Haven't seen him," I say truthfully.

"Be careful if you use the pool. He likes to skinny dip."

"Fuck you," Coach says.

It's cool seeing them acting like two best friends and not like the head coach and general manager of a professional hockey team.

"Anyway, how do you think the week went?" Coach asks.

I assumed they were going to ask something like this.

I sit back in my chair. "I think it went well. We're gelling. I think we need to work on conditioning. We have the skills, but most of us haven't been playing this hardcore in years. We have to build up our stamina."

Coach nods. "On the schedule for next week. Lots of ice baths in the future. You'll be in heaven."

I let out a heartfelt sigh. "I miss ice baths. I can't wait."

"We've been asking everyone a question—who do you think should be team captain? You can't say yourself."

Without a moment's hesitation, I give my list. "Carter. Absolutely. If goalies could be alternate captains, I'd say Brick. Mac is quiet, but he's solid. Crosby."

The scratch of Coach's pen on his legal pad is the only sound in the room.

"Cool. Thanks. Send the next one in."

Rising, I nod at Coach and Jake and exit the office.

Brick gets up and approaches me. "Anything I need to know about?"

"Nope. It's casual," I say.

I grab my water bottle from my bag and refill it then take a seat with Carter and Stone, who already spoke with Coach and Jake. Carter has his earbuds in and is watching cat videos. Stone is playing a match three game. I grab my iPad and kick back to read a few pages in the mystery I've been enjoying.

"Okay," Coach says. I close the case on my iPad and put it on my lap. Coach is at the front of the room with Jake. Teagan has joined them, and the rest of the coaching staff is there too.

"Thanks for hanging around. I know you're all ready to start your weekend. We had a productive week. We're pleased with how things are going. Next week we are ramping up conditioning. You know you have the skills. We need to get the stamina at the same level. Rest this weekend. Don't do anything stupid. Before you go, congratulate your new captain, Burke Bedard."

I'm in shock as the room erupts in cheers, applause, and whistles. The backslaps seem to come from everywhere. My hand raises for high fives like it's on auto pilot.

I swallow hard. I don't want to cry in front of my team. My team. "Wow, thank you."

"You earned it, Bedard," Jake says. "You were the team's unanimous choice."

Screw it. I cry. In a manly way, of course, but I'd have to be heartless not to be affected by the honor my team has given me. I vow to be worthy of it.

Conditioning week is kicking all our asses. While we spent much of it in the gym, the training staff has taken advantage of the miles of sand outside The Nest. Burly hockey players lumbering along the sand are not the same aesthetic that Baywatch had back in the day. At least we're back inside the rink today. There is a skating clinic for kids who want to join our junior hockey teams. It's not mandatory the players take part, but most of us do. A few of the players with kids are bringing them along. It will be nice, and the people who signed up to coach the kids' teams will be there.

Carter skates up to me, spraying ice over my skates to be a punk. "Ready for this?"

We can hear the excited chatter in the lobby and coming from the public dressing rooms. It's a skating day today, the kids don't have sticks yet.

"Yeah, I am. Believe it or not, I'm excited. I miss my kids back home. I miss teaching. Don't get me wrong, I love playing, and I'm grateful for the opportunity, but I miss feeling useful."

"Well, get ready to feel extra useful because here they come," Coach says. I didn't realize he had skated up to us. Even my polar bear's senses are tired from conditioning week.

For most of the kids, this is the first time they are on skates. There will be lots of tumbles and a few tears, but they'll get the hang of it. We have a fantastic turnout, but Rowena's not here. I'm surprised. I half expected her to be the first one on and the last one off the ice.

"Rowena isn't doing hockey?" I ask Coach.

"She is. Maybe she's running late?" he says.

I see a flash of red hair along the boards.

Ro is jumping alongside the ice like a little kangaroo. "Hurry, Miss Morgan! I'm late! I won't have time to skate!"

Miss Morgan. Kendall is with her.

"Ro, you need to sit down so we can get your skates on you. Come here," Kendall says.

I skate over to the gate to join them. Kendall isn't a skater, she won't be able to lace up the skates tight enough.

"Hey, guys. I was wondering where you were." I'm looking at Rowena but my statement is for both of them. "Here, let me lace up your skates for you. If you don't tie them right, your feet will hurt, and your ankles won't be supported correctly. I can do it fast. I know you want to get out on the ice now. We'll go over how to do it yourself later."

I squat down and lace up the tiny hockey skates with the pink shoelaces. They're adorable. As soon as I finish, Rowena hops up, puts on her helmet, and rushes off to the ice. I turn to watch. She's a bit wobbly, like a newborn colt for the first few strides, but soon is steady and whizzing around like she has been skating for years. I can't wait to get a stick in her hands.

Smiling, I turn back to Kendall. "Where are your skates? I'll tie you up too."

I realize what I said and feel a blush creep up my cheeks.

Kendall looks at me with an amused expression. "Not in front of the children, Burke." Does her voice sound huskier than normal?

"What size?" Damn. My voice is husky too.

She winks. "I'm betting at least nine inches."

Now my face must be scarlet. I need to think about icebergs because skating with at least nine inches is painful. And hard to hide.

"What size skates?" I have my eyes closed because I'm afraid if I see any kind of heat in her beautiful blue eyes, I'll throw her over my shoulder, take her somewhere private, and show her exactly how many inches we're dealing with.

"Size six," she says. I can hear the smile in her voice and it makes me grin. I rise and go to the skate rental desk. I buy a pair of socks too.

I hand Kendall the socks as I crouch in front of her. "Here we go, Cinderella."

"Thanks." She takes off her black Converses and pulls on the socks as I loosen the skate laces.

I help her get her foot in the skate and start lacing them up. A full body shiver runs through her, but I don't flatter myself thinking it's my touch eliciting the reaction. She's cold.

I shrug out of my zip up fleece and drape it over her shoulders.

"Here, wear this."

Kendall puts her arms through the sleeves, and when she sees they hang past her fingertips, she rolls them up. "Thanks. I wasn't planning on being here, I'm not bundled up. Teagan was going to bring her but got stuck in traffic driving from Philly and called to ask me to bring her. It's why we were late."

I help her to her feet and hold her by her upper arms to help steady her.

"Ready to go? You must have the balance and core strength. You can do this. I won't let you fall."

She nods and starts taking slow steps toward the ice, clinging to my arm. I step out onto the ice first and wrap an arm around her waist to help her get her legs under her. I know there are layers of clothing between us and the only skin to skin contact we can have is through our hands, but imagination tricks me into believing I can feel heat down the side of my body where she's pressed against me. I'm surprised there isn't steam rising from the ice, with how hot I'm feeling with Kendall in my arms.

Rowena zips over. "Good for you, Miss Morgan! You can do it!"

"Way to go, Kennie! Never thought I'd see you on the ice, sis!" Coach calls out.

Carter skates up to Kendall's other side with a huge grin. "Looking good, Ken. My turn."

She flinches away from him at first, a movement so small I almost didn't notice. Maybe I shouldn't let her go. But then she takes a breath and relaxes. Did I imagine it?

I'm slow to ease my arm from around her waist as Carter takes her hand.

"Okay?" I ask.

Kendall gives a tense nod.

"Yeah, I hate it when people touch me unexpectedly."

Carter looks offended but doesn't say anything.

When she gives me a slight smile I take as reassurance she's okay, I skate away to work with the kids. It's why I'm here. Need to remember the whole point of this event is the kids.

It's fun skating with them. By the end of the session, Kendall can skate on her own. She's still a bit wobbly, but she's upright.

I skate up to her and Rowena as everyone exits the ice.

"I'll help you get your skates off. Make sure you loosen them the right way. If you don't do it correctly, they can get damaged." I do Rowena's first since the whole point of being here is the kids. I should go help other kids, but that's why I have teammates. Instead, I do Kendall's. I take my time undoing them and revealing her trim ankles. I feel like someone from a Jane Austen novel with how turned on I am by the sight of a woman's ankle. It's ridiculous. I know it. But I don't want anyone else touching her this way, kneeling at her feet.

After I finish with Kendall's skates, Rowena takes them back to the counter to turn them in. I sit on the bench next to Kendall and unlace my skates as she puts on her sneakers. Coach sits on his sister's other side, and Carter sits on the bench across from us.

"Now that we have you on the ice, you can have your dance teams skate too." Coach says to Kendall.

Carter looks up. "There's going to be a dance team? Really?"

Kendall nods. "Teagan roped me into it. There are going to be dancers for the juvenile teams. No skating. Maybe next year, we'll have an adult team for the Devil Birds."

The talk of cheerleading stunts and plans for the weekend flow around me. I'm glad I helped tonight. I hadn't realized how much I needed it. I'm hoping helping with these junior teams fills some of the void I'm feeling from not teaching. Fill the void of loneliness I'm feeling. As much as I know I need to focus on hockey, it's hard being away from my family and friends. I don't miss my ex, Tabitha, at all, but I miss dating and physical companionship.

Surely it's why I feel this pull to Kendall. With no one else to protect and teach, I'm attaching all those feelings onto her. If that's not it, I have no other explanation. We can't be mates. A polar bear who loves the cold and a panther who loves the heat? I bet she uses an electric blanket. Mother Nature wouldn't be that cruel.

Hopefully, once the season is in full swing, I'll be too busy to be distracted by tiny blondes with luminous blue eyes who leave my jackets smelling like gardenias when they give them back. It's easy to loan out a jacket. I worry if I give my heart, I won't get it back.

6

KENDALL

"Miss Morgan!"

I turn to see my principal, Mr. Babcock, hurrying down the hall. He's a beaver shifter and a very dear man, but he's always darting around and his over-the-top energy is overwhelming.

"Good morning, Mr. Babcock. How are you today?"

His buck-toothed smile lights up his face and crinkles his brown eyes. "I'm well, Miss Morgan. I trust you are too?"

I give my best cheer smile. It's the response he's looking for.

"I have wonderful news! We have a volunteer to help with science enrichment for the younger grades. This week he will work with your class. He's going to come by during your planning period today. I'm sure you can work out something to do together."

He's so enthusiastic he's ignoring the fact I'm not thrilled beyond belief at the idea of someone random coming into my class. Whoever he is will interrupt the little planning time I get during the school day with his *enrichment,* which I will end up having to organize materials for while this dude comes in like a hero. It's not enough to oversee fifteen first graders. I'll have to babysit a grown man too. Awesome.

"Great," I say, wondering who it is. Probably a dad or a granddad. They'll show up a time or two and give up when they realize it's not all fun and games and their "lessons" need to be age appropriate. I walk toward my classroom. The kids will be here soon, and I like a few minutes alone to center myself.

"You'll be in your room for your planning period?" he asks.

I pull open my door. "Yes. Send him down. I have to walk the kids to music, but I should be back before he gets here."

The intercom crackles. "Mr. Babcock, please come to the office."

"Well, duty calls. Have a wonderful day, Miss Morgan."

I watch him scurry away. I've never seen him in beaver form, but I can picture it.

The morning passes quickly and I have playground duty today with Abby Reimer. We chat while watching the kids run and play.

Abby kicks the soccer ball back to the group of kids playing soccer. "Do you know who the enrichment guy is?"

I roll my eyes. "No clue. I'm sure it will be a thrill."

She holds up crossed fingers. "Hopefully, he'll show up a time or two and get bored."

I cross my fingers as well.

"Okay, kids, put the balls back in the bin and line up." My voice carries over the balmy air. It's still on the warmer side in September here in New Jersey, but since the humidity has given up its stranglehold, it's more pleasant.

After lunch is reading time and some spelling worksheets. I walk the kids to Mr. Garvey's music room and rush back to my room. My rubber-soled flats are quiet as I walk along the halls of the school. When I turn the corner to the hallway leading to my room, I gasp. Reading the bulletin board I have set up next to my door is a tall figure I'm coming to know too well.

"Burke? What are you doing here?" I ask as I approach. Today he is in a blue button-down shirt with rolled-up sleeves exposing muscular forearms. He must have had those navy slacks tailored to fit his muscular thighs and firm, apple-shaped ass.

"Kendall! Hi. Um...how are you?" His smile is cautious. He looks around the empty hallway.

"I'm good, thanks. Why are you here?" I ask again as I open my classroom door and walk in. He follows me and looks around the room, chuckling at some posters I have hanging up.

"I asked Liam if there was some sort of community service type thing I could do with school kids. Like science enrichment. Daphne made the arrangements, but I didn't realize it was going to be *here*. I can ask for them to find somewhere else. But I miss working with kids, and I have free time. I can't play video games all day, and hockey is my job now, not just a hobby. I figured I could make teaching my hobby." He gives a self-deprecating laugh. "Not that teaching is a hobby. You know better than anyone, but since I can't have a full-time classroom, I figured this may work. Unless you don't want me."

Oh, I want him. That's the problem. Andy always tells me I don't have a poker face. Burke's eyes flare with a sudden heat I think matches my own.

"Good, you found the classroom. Miss Morgan, you've met Mr. Bedard?"

I didn't realize Principal Babcock had entered the room while my entire focus was on Burke. My cougar senses must be on hiatus with my shifting ability.

I spin around. "Yes, Mr. Babcock. Mr. Bedard is the captain of the Devil Birds hockey team my brother coaches. We know each other."

My principal nods enthusiastically. "I thought that was the case. How lucky we are to have a professional athlete involved with our kids. And he's a certified teacher in Canada too! Quite the boon. He's passed all the background checks, of course. It was a simple matter to approve him as a volunteer."

"Yay." I wave my fist in the air like I'm waving an imaginary pom pom. When in doubt, smile and wave your poms, I always say. So do a couple mugs in my kitchen cabinet and a t-shirt in my dresser.

When you coach you tend to get some repeat gifts. Please let me sound more enthusiastic than I feel.

"Well, I'll leave you two to plan. Door open or closed, Miss Morgan?"

"Closed, please," I say.

I look up at Burke as the door clicks behind me. Did I imagine we were having a moment? Was it wishful thinking on my part or pent-up sexual frustration? It's been over a year since I've been kissed, but I'm a normal twenty-four-year-old woman. I have needs.

Burke looks back at me steadily, and his nostrils flare slightly. I can recognize signs of arousal. It wasn't solely me. That's reassuring. Maybe. I don't know. We're in school, and I have thirty minutes left before I get the kids. We need to plan something.

Grabbing a notepad, I walk over to a table in a corner and sit on a stool. Burke lowers himself to the other one, and I notice he has a leather portfolio with him. I was so focused on his physical presence it didn't register before.

I gesture with my chin toward the portfolio. "What do you have there?"

"Notes and suggestions to see if it would work. I substituted with younger grades when I was in uni, and I kept notes. It's all subject to your input and approval, of course. You know your students best." He unzips the brown leather and pulls out a worksheet and some pictures he places in front of me.

I pick them up and look through them. "Trees?"

He nods. "It's a shifter population. I assume they understand the animal world better than the average first grader. Since there are both oak and pine trees around, I thought we could cover deciduous and evergreen trees. The leaves will start turning soon. I don't know how much time you can give me, and if you want me more than once, but if this went over a few weeks, we could include a walk outside to identify some different tree species."

I grin. "Great idea! Anything that gets the kids outside more is a bonus. They have tons of energy. If they can expel some of it while learning, awesome. You're ready to do this today?"

He gives me a grin that makes me tingle in all the best places.

"I'm all yours," he says.

I wish. Wait. No, I don't. Here's here because of the kids. He's a dedicated teacher, like I am. We are two young, attractive, single people. Of course, we are going to flirt. It's natural. Doesn't mean anything. I bet he flirts with everyone and will have a girl in every town he travels to. Remember that, Kendall. But if he's good with my kids, it's going to be a struggle. While hot athletes are like catnip to me on a physical level, being good to my students is the way to my heart. The combination may prove to be irresistible.

I glance at the clock above my door.

"I need to get the kids from their music class. Will you be okay here?"

"Yeah. But why don't you tell me where the copier is, and I'll run the copies we need so we're ready to go when you get back?"

Oh...someone to make copies for me. I think this is one of the sexiest things a man has ever said to me. I hope I'm not drooling.

I blow out a breath. "Sure. That would be great. We have fifteen students."

"Okay," Burke says. "I'll make twenty copies, you always need a few spares."

If ever there is a flex to make to show you're an experienced teacher, knowing how many extra copies you'll need is it. I should not find that sexy. I leave him at the copier while I get my students. He's back in the room when we return. I introduce him and explain why he's here.

"Class, what do we say?" I prompt.

"Hello, Mr. Bedard," my class choruses.

"Hi all," Burke says. "Thanks for welcoming me to your class-room. I'm excited to be here today." I can hear the sincerity in his voice. That's sexy.

"Class, Mr. Bedard is here to help us with science today. Mr. Bedard is the captain of the Atlantic City Devil Birds hockey team."

The class oohs excitedly.

I gesture for them to settle down. When they are quiet-ish again, I continue. "Mr. Bedard is also a chemistry teacher in Canada."

"And a polar bear shifter!" Rowena calls out excitedly.

"Rowena, it's not polite to call out. You raise your hand and wait to be called upon," I say.

Right on cue, Rowena raises her hand. I try not to laugh because I knew it was coming.

Burke's shoulders shake as he swallows his laughter.

"Yes, Rowena?" I ask.

Rowena puts her hand down. "Mr. Bedard is a polar bear shifter!"

Burke nods. "I am. Wild polar bears live in the far northern part of the world. Like Canada, Alaska, Russia, around the Arctic Circle and the North Pole. Obviously, shifters live everywhere, but polar bear shifters prefer to live in places where it is cold in winter."

"Mr. Bedard is here to talk to us about trees," I say. "Yes, Casey?"

A little blonde-haired boy lowers his hand. "Do polar bears climb trees like other bears do?"

"Good question, Casey. I don't know." I turn to Burke. "Do polar bears climb trees?"

He shakes his head. "Polar bears are the only species of bears that do not climb trees. Do you know why?"

Hands shoot up around the room. He selects a little girl with dark braids and asks her name.

"My name is Ayisha. Polar bears can't climb trees because they are too big."

"Very good, Ayisha. That is one reason. Polar bears are the largest bears in the world and the largest land-based carnivores," he says. They're shifter kids. They know about carnivores. I like he's not treating them like they are clueless.

"They're huge! They're bigger than I am!" I say.

Ayisha rolls her eyes. "Miss Morgan, there are fourth graders bigger than you." She says it so matter-of-factly, I can't help it—I laugh. That starts the ball rolling, and the entire class is laughing. I glance at Burke laughing so hard he is wiping tears from his eyes.

After we calm down, Burke explains the other reason polar bears don't climb trees. "Trees don't grow where wild polar bears live. Once you get past a certain point, trees don't grow. Most of the time, it's covered with snow and ice. When it isn't, some grasses grow but not trees. Speaking of trees..."

He spends the next twenty minutes explaining the difference between deciduous and evergreen trees and the parts of a tree. We do a coloring page, and he reads a story about Franklin the turtle planting a tree.

The time goes too quickly. I could teach with Burke all day. Since his visit was the last part of the afternoon, he stays to help while the kids get their take-home folders into their backpacks and get their jackets on. The weather is still mild, but the rain rolled in this afternoon. There are lots of cute little rain slickers and zippered hoodies.

We're putting chairs on desks after the kids leave for their buses or the after-school program.

"I think it went well," he says.

I look up at him with a smile as he places the last chair on top of the table we're at and walks to the next one. "It did. The kids loved you, and you were great with them."

He is an absolute natural with my class, and I wish I was ready to date again. It would be easy—too easy—to fall for this man.

He smiles. "Thank you for letting me do this. I needed this more than I knew. I love hockey, but it doesn't fill the void teaching does."

"Did you always want to be a teacher? Are you parents teachers? With my mom and grandmother both teaching, it's almost a family tradition for me."

"No, my parents own a small market and deli back home. My sister recently graduated university with a business degree. Originally, I wanted to major in chemistry and work in Toronto for a corporation or university doing research on new medications and treatments. Save the world or cure cancer. I wanted to make a differ- ence. Then I realized I could make a more immediate difference by returning home and working with the kids. Make sure they had stuff to do and healthy role models. Even in a town as small as mine, kids can get in a lot of trouble if they aren't kept busy."

"Hey, Ken, how was it with the dead weight—oh! Hello!" Abby, my co-teacher in first grade, walks in. She stops mid-stride and her big brown eyes widen when she sees Burke is still here.

Walking forward with his hand extended, Burke says, "Hello, Burke Bedard."

I join them and my cheeks are flaming. "Burke, this is Abby Reimer, our other first-grade teacher."

Abby takes his hand and shakes it enthusiastically. "Nice to meet you, Mr. Bedard! Thank you for coming in to do something special with the kids. I was coming to see how it went. It went well?" She's babbling nervously, and I look at her with a "please shut up now" expression. Abby stops talking and keeps shaking his hand for a few seconds more and then, when she realizes what she's doing, stops and drops it like it burned her.

He smiles, and I'm not sure if it's a friendly smile or a flirtatious one. Abby is a raccoon shifter with a tall, curvy figure and lustrous dark hair. We're like polar opposites. Ugh. Not the choice of words I meant to use.

"Nice to meet you too, Abby. I think it went well. I know I enjoyed it."

"Are you coming back?" Abby asks.

"I hope to," Burke says. "I need to talk to Mr. Babcock to see if any other teachers are interested."

"Oh! I'm interested! I hope you do me next!" Abby's eyes go wide when she realizes what she said, and I let out a snort-laugh because I'm classy like that.

Abby waves her hand in front of her face like it's going to erase the last minute of her life. "I mean, I hope you visit my class next. The kids would enjoy it."

"I'd like that. Do you have an email address so we could coordinate schedules? Or should I do it through Mr. Babcock?" Burke asks.

Is he trying to ask for her email for them to arrange a hookup or is it truly to work out a time for him to work with her class? I hate that my first thought is suspicion, but I refuse to be stupid like I was with Kregg. I thought he was faithful to me, and he was sleeping with anyone he could the whole time we were married. I don't think he cheated when we were dating because Andy and Harrison were his teammates and would have told me. Plus, he didn't want to risk losing his meal ticket before he had his seat at the table.

I smile in what is hopefully a friendly and not territorial manner. "Maybe you can do the lesson we did today with your class, Abby, and then do a joint lesson with both classes. We could take a walk outside. That way they can identify some trees?"

"Good idea," Burke says.

Abby writes her email on an apple-shaped post-it note from my desk and hands it to Burke with a smile. "Let me know what works for you, and I'll talk to Mr. Babcock. Be careful, you may end up visiting all the lower grades."

"I'd love it," Burke says.

"Well, I'm grabbing my gear and heading out. Hope you both have a great weekend. See you Monday, Kennie."

I smile and wave as Burke says goodbye.

"Does everyone call you Kennie?"

I shrug. "Pretty much. Or Ken."

"Does it bother you if I call you Kendall? It's a lovely name."

I smile softly. I bet I'm blushing. "I don't mind."

We grab our belongings and head out to the parking lot. It's still raining slightly and thunder rumbles in the distance. There aren't many cars left in the parking lot.

"Which one is yours?" Burke asks.

"The Mustang. You're the Explorer?"

"Yeah, how did you know?"

"Well, the Ontario plate is a good indicator, plus I know the rest of the cars belong to my co-workers."

Burke laughs as he follows me to my car. It's bright blue with a black convertible top. And a flat front tire on the driver's side.

"Oh, no. You got a flat. Do you have a spare?" He crouches down next to her tire. "Looks like you picked up a nail."

"Damn it." I squat next to him to see the nail embedded in the tread of my tire. "I don't have a spare. It came with a can of sealant and a pump. I was supposed to get a spare, but I haven't yet." I stand up and tug on my ponytail. "Ugh! My dad and brother kept telling me to take care of it. I hate it when they're right."

"Is there a tire shop you can get it towed to where they change the tire and also get you a spare?"

My shoulders slump. "Not tonight. Shit."

The rain is coming down harder, the drizzle becoming a steady stream.

Burke grabs my hand and starts walking toward his Explorer. Opening the passenger door, he motions for me to get in.

"May as well get out of the rain while we figure out a plan," he says as I climb up. After closing my door, he jogs around the front and gets into the driver's seat. "Oh, you're shivering. Let me start the engine and get some heat going."

"Thanks." I rub my arms.

He reaches into the back seat and hands me a hoodie. "You can wear this. It's clean."

I don't put it on. Instead, I lay it over me like a blanket.

"I can drive you home and pick you up tomorrow to bring you back here to deal with the tow or whatever."

"Oh, Burke, that's sweet of you. Thank you." I can't believe he'd do that for me. Oh. Shit.

Taking a deep breath, I say what I have to in a rush. "You can say no. I have to go to my parents' for dinner. I can't get out of it because I skipped the past couple of times." I give what I hope is a persuasive grin. "Do you want to come along? Mom's a superb cook, and if we ride together, then I don't have to explain about my car."

Burke chuckles. "Sounds like we both win. I'm tired of my cooking."

"Okay, cool." I bite my lip as I think of something. "What are we going to tell my family? They will think it's a date. I can't deal with their matchmaking."

Burke looks at me with a furrowed brow. Maybe this is his thinking face?

"How about we let them think it's a date? If they think you're dating me, will they keep matchmaking? Or will they leave you alone?"

"What? Are you serious? How would it work? Why would you do it?" I know I tilted my head in confusion. I always get made fun of for doing it, but I don't care.

"We'd hang out together sometimes, which probably wouldn't be a lot because of our schedules. I'd do it because I want to focus on hockey. I'm not here to date, I'm here to skate. If I have a girlfriend, then people will leave me alone, and I'll have a defense against the puck bunnies."

"Aw, are you afraid of puck bunnies?"

"Yeah. From what I've heard, some of them are relentless. I want to focus on my career and not deal with all the other bull."

Puck bunnies and cleat chasers are supposed to be benefits of being a professional athlete. Kregg's defense to cheating was how lonely it gets on the road and how fired up he was after a game, even the away ones. He had needs, and I wasn't there to satisfy them, so he did what he had to do.

"If you're sure you're okay with fake dating, then that works for me. People need to leave me alone. I'm happy enough as I am."

I give him directions to my townhouse. I need to change out of my wet clothes before we go to my parents' house.

Sure, Burke, let's fake date! What a great idea! Could I go along with a dumber idea? Yeah, probably. I married my ex, after all.

Have dinner with my family! That won't be weird at all. Kendall, you're fricking full of brilliance tonight.

"Kendall?" Burke asks.

"I'm sorry. I was lost in thought. What?"

"What's the next turn?"

"Oh, that would be helpful. Drive until this road ends and then make a right. We'll stay on the next road for a bit."

"Do you have a house or an apartment?"

"I have a townhouse. It's in a friendly neighborhood. Quiet. There's several single shifters and young shifter families. People can be themselves."

I pull his hoodie tighter around me. With how big it is, it's really like a throw blanket. It smells of cedar and mint. Yummy. It reminds me of running in snow in the forests around here. We have cedar trees along the streams in the Pinelands where we'd run when I was younger. When I could shift. And I was young enough to think snow was fun.

"How do you like where you're living?" I ask. "Is it too much living with the people you work with?"

Burke hums low in his throat. "It's good. Brick and Stone are good roommates. We're all introverts. We stay out of each other's way. Having a rink and gym downstairs is convenient."

I nod. "I would have given anything to have a dance studio and tumbling space like they have when I was younger."

"You didn't know Trevor growing up?"

"Nope, we met in college. My roommate Randi was on the cheerleading squad and Trevor was her stunt partner. We would all hang out. It was a fluke we grew up in adjacent towns. Liam and Mallory met in Vegas and then months later realized they worked for the same company here in New Jersey. I can't believe how many intersections we have. It was fate that they found each other."

"So, you believe in fate?"

I snuggle deeper in the hoodie and reach out to adjust the vent. It's not cold out but being wet has given me a chill. I think about it.

"I believe in fate for some people. For Liam and Mallory. I don't believe in it for me. I'm in charge of my destiny, and I will decide what happens to me."

Burke nods. "Same. I'm a scientist. I believe in logic and proof. When I get married, it will be because it was a decision I made. Not a whim, not a spur-of-the-moment thing. I know there's supposed to be this whole fated mate thing in the shifter culture, but I don't believe it. People are attracted to each other, maybe they are in love, but they feel compelled to make it something mystical when really, it's just compatible personalities and raging hormones."

He glances over at me, and it's all I can do not to look guilty. Would a six-week marriage to a guy I knew less than six months and married because I thought I was pregnant count as a whim or as a spur-of-the-moment thing?

I laugh with a wee touch of bitterness. "Gee Burke, that sounds incredibly romantic. I'm sure the lucky lady will swoon at your feet. Good thing we're fake dating. I don't know if I could resist."

"You believe in fated mates?" He shoots me a quick glance.

Shrugging, I sigh. "I used to. My parents have an incredible relationship, and Dad's always talking about how it was fate he met Mom, about how she's his fated mate. It's like living in a fairy tale. But fairy tales aren't real. I think fated mates are just fuck buddies who got lucky with good sex, fell in love, and wanted to make it sound special for the kids.

Back in the day it was probably easier for an alpha to convince his daughter to marry a guy from another pack for political reasons if he tied it with a pretty bow of fated mates and not the truth—that if she didn't give up her body and her future to the enemy then her brothers and friends were probably going to be killed in a pack war."

He laughs. "Wow. Your take might be even less romantic than my own. But don't you worry about Ms. Lucky. Whoever she is will feel swept off her feet when I propose to her. Just because I'm a logical scientist doesn't mean I don't know how to treat a woman right."

I bet he can make a woman feel all sorts of things. Thinking about them is making my nipples tighten. We'll blame it on the rain.

"Your Mr. Lucky...," he says, "...poor guy has no idea the hill he has to climb to win your heart."

Huffing a laugh, I look out the passenger window, tracing a raindrop as it slides down the pane. "Mr. Lucky has no chance of getting my heart. It's locked away. He'll have to be happy enough with the rest of the package."

Burke turns on the radio and as the heavy bass of an old metal tune fills the cab, I hear him mutter, "Mr. Lucky indeed, unwrapping that package."

I can't stop the flip my tummy makes at the thought of him undressing me. No matter how high I flew in basket tosses back in my cheerleading days, it didn't flip like that. This is not good. Did I really agree to fake date a man who makes my stomach flip higher than a basket toss?

7
BURKE

I turn into her townhouse complex. It's a nice place, clean. There are mums planted in flower beds throughout the community. A pond with some geese and ducks swimming in it is across the parking lot and there are woods all around. Pleasant enough, but I couldn't live here. Too many people, too close. I'm happier out in the woods at Carter's.

She directs me to a parking spot. I pull in and turn off the engine.

"Do you want to come in? I'll be a couple of minutes."

The rain has slowed again. "Sure, thanks."

I follow her up the walkway to her front door. She has a front porch she shares with the townhouse next door. It looks like they coordinated with each other because there are matching planters of mums on both sides that the other porches don't have.

Entering her home, I'm struck by how cozy it feels. The walls are a soft gray, and the overstuffed navy sofa should look masculine because of the color, but the polka dot throw pillows on it bring whimsy. In the living room across from the seating area is a fireplace I bet she uses often in the winter since she seems to get cold easily.

If we're dating, or pretending to, we'll probably spend some time in front of the fireplace to keep up appearances. Being a polar bear shifter I'd almost always pick being cool over warm and cozy, but I'd be willing to sacrifice some creature comfort if it got me close to Kendall. If layers of clothing had to come off to cure overheating, so be it.

The kitchen is very tidy. Probably because she never uses it. I could cook for her.

"This looks like a comfy home. I envy you the fireplace," I say.

She looks around and smiles with pride. "Thanks, I love it here. Make yourself comfortable, grab a drink from the fridge. That's all that's in there. I'll be down in a couple."

She turns and jogs up the stairs, her ponytail swishing side to side. After she disappears, I'm left looking up an empty staircase like a creeper. Not cool. Turning, I go into the kitchen to check out the fridge and grab a bottle of water. She wasn't kidding. It's beverages and a pack of string cheese in there. She must eat out a lot.

Unscrewing the cap on my water, I wander through the living room looking at the pictures on the mantle. There's a picture of her at a wedding at a lighthouse. Daphne and Logan are the happy couple surrounded by family and friends. Everyone is thrilled, but Kendall's smile seems forced. I wonder why.

There are more pictures from her past—with her family, with her cheer team—and the one that catches my attention is of her dancing with a handsome black man. He's looking down at her with affection, and she's laughing up at him. They obviously have a close relationship. Is he an ex? Does she still love him and it's why his picture is on display? If he isn't an ex but a current, why would she fake date me? Can she not admit to dating this guy?

"Mom, I'm bringing a friend to dinner. Be there shortly. Need me to pick anything up?"

I turn toward the stairs and watch Kendall come down. She changed into a casual floral skirt with a white t-shirt and denim jacket. Black Converse sneakers complete the outfit. She's adorable. She catches my eye and does the puppet talking hand gesture with a grin.

"Okay, see you soon. Love you. Uh-huh. Bye."

She grabs a black purse and drapes it across her body.

"Oh good, you got a bottle of water. Don't judge me for my fridge. My cousin's boyfriend is an incredible cook, and they live next door. I let them feed me."

I laugh. "Good gig, if you can get it. I'd take advantage of it if I could. Ready to go?"

"Yep. Let's go."

I wait on the porch as Kendall locks her front door. I catch a whiff of gardenias as she brushes past me to get in the truck through the door I hold open for her.

Getting behind the wheel, I start the engine. "How far away do your parents live?"

"About ten minutes."

We drive and within minutes are parking in front of a stately home with nice landscaping on a large lot in a neighborhood full of similar homes. It's not as uniform as Kendall's development, but you can tell everything is exactly so. I'm betting it's one of those communities with a homeowners' association making rules about everything. Lovely home, but I'd hate to live here. I miss my little house with the dormer windows and blue shutters. I just miss home.

Buck up, Burke. You're here for a reason and it's to make money so you can fill your little house with a family. Homesickness is temporary.

"You grew up here?" I ask.

"Yep. Lived here my whole life until I went to college. Then I got the townhouse after I graduated."

"Where do you shift and run?"

She goes still, and I swear she pales a bit. I wonder why? I change the subject because I don't want to make her uncomfortable.

"Before we go in, should we work out the details of our arrangement? Are we touching each other? Kissing? How long are we doing this? When did we start?"

She nods. "Yeah, we need to work this out. The closer we stay to the truth, the easier it will be, so we'll say we decided today. They won't expect any major PDA tonight, holding hands maybe, or your arm around my shoulder. Making sappy moon eyes at each other. We're going to have to act like a normal couple and kiss each other sometime. Let's try it for a month and see how it's going. But we have to be exclusive. If you decide this isn't working, please tell me before you hook up with someone. I don't want people thinking you cheated and pity me."

"Fair. But you have to tell me before you hook up with anyone too."

She snorts. "No worries there, Burke. I have zero interest in hooking up with anyone. I enjoy being on my own. I'm doing this so my family stops trying to set me up. You're the shield I'm hiding behind. You probably heard the gossip from my brother or Trevor. I had a nasty breakup last year, and I have no desire to go through that again. I'm happy with how I am and want to focus on teaching and my cheer team. Maybe have Daphne teach me how to knit if I need a hobby." She opens the door and prepares to get out. "We good?"

I nod.

"Okay, let's head in before my mom comes out looking for us." She jumps out of my SUV and starts up the walkway to her parents' front door. I rush to catch up to her.

"I wish I had flowers for your mom or something. I feel like a clod showing up empty-handed.

"Don't worry about it. Mom is going to be psyched you're here at all. She's a fan."

"She hasn't seen me play yet, has she? Has she been to practice?" A few of our practices have been open to the public, but I thought she'd be at work teaching.

Kendall laughs as she opens the front door and walks in. "Oh, it has nothing to do with your playing. Hey! We're here!"

"Who's we?" Kendall's dad calls out as he comes down the hall.

"Oh, hello, Burke. Welcome." Will Morgan shoots a glance at his daughter as he holds out his hand for me to shake.

I grasp his hand, and his grip is firm. "Thanks for having me, Will. You have a lovely home."

"Is that Kennie? Oh! Burke! How wonderful!" Faith rushes forward to hug Kendall and then me. "I'm a hugger, can't help it. Come on back. Would you like some wine, beer?"

We follow her back to a family room full of people. I recognize Coach, of course, and his girlfriend, Mallory, from the barbecue. I know Logan and Daphne from their work with the team. Since Kendall was in their wedding picture, I figured they were friends, but didn't expect them at a family dinner.

Kendall takes my arm. I wasn't expecting that. I feel the eyes of everyone in the room focus on where we are touching. I don't know if it's the heat of their laser-like gazes or the fact Kendall is touching me making my arm feel warm, but I feel like I could toast some marshmallows over my skin.

"You know my cousin Logan and his wife Daphne from the team?"

I smile and nod. Now knowing of the relationship, I can see how Logan and Liam resemble each other.

"This is my Uncle Mike and Aunt Holly. They are Logan's parents. Aunt Holly is my dad's sister."

"Call us Mike and Holly, please." Mike walks over to shake my hand. Holly waves. "Hello."

I wave and return the greeting.

"This is Burke Bedard. He's one of the Devil Birds," Kendall says.

"He's the *captain* of the Devil Birds," Coach says, and I feel myself blush.

Kendall looks up at me with a huge smile and squeezes my arm. I feel it in my heart.

"You didn't tell me you were named captain! Congratulations!"

She goes on tiptoe and pulls on my arm until I bend down so she can kiss my cheek. Sparks shoot from that spot down my spine and to my dick. I know human anatomy even though I'm a chemistry teacher. Those parts don't really connect.

"Oh! We've heard about you, Burke," Holly says meaningfully. "Nice to meet you, finally."

I laugh, feeling uncomfortable. I've heard I'm a topic of conversation quite a few times, and I'm not sure it's a good thing.

Kendall leans against my arm. "All good stuff, don't worry."

Coach is looking at us with a furrowed brow until Mallory elbows him in the ribs.

"Ouch," he says. "Why did you…?"

"You're staring like a creep," Mallory says, cutting him off.

"What? I'm trying to figure out what is going on. Last thing I knew, I was getting chewed out for saying it would be okay if they dated and now they're showing up together at family dinner!"

All eyes turn to us. It's taking a lot of restraint not to run my finger along the collar of my shirt to loosen it.

"Um…" That's as far as I get.

"Burke did a science enrichment with my class today and we got to talking. I invited him to dinner as a thank you because we know I can't cook. We'll see where it goes."

She smiles up at me, and I can't help but smile back. My brain knows this is fake, but I think my heart may lose the plot.

"That's great. Hope you like beef stew, Burke. With it being dreary out, I figured it was stew weather."

"Beef stew is one of my favorites, thank you. It's one thing I miss from home. My mother is a wonderful cook." I make a mental note to call home this weekend.

We serve ourselves stew from the pot on the counter and take our seats at the dining room table. Kendall sits next to me, and I'm startled when she takes my hand, but when Daphne grabs my other hand, I realize they are saying grace prior to starting. My family does the same, another thing making New Jersey feel a bit more like home.

"Faith, this is delicious! I've been homesick, and this helps," I say after my first couple hearty spoonfuls of stew. There is thick sliced bread with butter as well, and it's the perfect meal for the type of weather we're having.

Faith smiles at me. The resemblance between her and Kendall is striking.

"Thank you, Burke," she says. "Home is Ontario?"

"Yes, I grew up in a small town north of Toronto and Ottawa. Ma mère is from Quebec."

All the women at the table sigh.

I must look confused because Logan says, "You spoke French. They are all piles of goo now."

I flush, realizing I had used the French version of "my mother." "Sorry, English is my primary language, but when I talk about home, some things are naturally always in French."

Kendall bumps her shoulder against my bicep. "Don't apologize. Speak French all you want. I won't understand it because I took Spanish, but it will sound pretty."

Everyone laughs.

Kendall's Uncle Mike raises his beer and takes a sip. As he lowers his bottle, he asks, "You were at Pine Grove today with Kennie's class? Were you showing them hockey skills?"

"No hockey," I say. "We were discussing trees."

Kendall leans forward to see her uncle down the table. "It was science enrichment, Uncle Mike. He talked about deciduous and evergreen trees and got some polar bear facts in. It was great, the kids loved it."

I smile down at her. "I loved it too. I miss being in the classroom." I look over at Coach. "Thanks for setting it up. I'm grateful for the opportunity. In the past, this time of year usually has me in the class-room. Everything is different. No students, no coaching. It's strange."

Faith nods. "I know what you mean. I'll be eligible to retire at the end of this school year, but I don't know what I'd do if I wasn't teaching. It's not like I have grandbabies to spoil!"

Kendall and Liam both focus on their bowls of stew. I guess this is a topic that comes up often?

Daphne fidgets beside me, and Logan stares at his wife intently. She nods.

"Well," Logan says, "you could always spoil your great niece or nephew."

"Oh!" Holly cries out and bursts into tears. Everyone is talking at once and congratulating the couple on their news. Kendall has grown still beside me.

I lean down to whisper in her ear. "You okay?"

She looks up, startled, and our faces are so close the slightest movement from either of us would have our lips meeting. She pulls back.

"Yeah, I'm great!" Her smile is bright and brittle. I don't know what is going on, but she's faking joy. Like in the wedding picture on her mantle.

She gets up and hugs Daphne and then Logan. "You guys! I'm thrilled for you both! How far along are you?"

"About ten weeks," Daphne says. "Turns out I was already pregnant when we started trying."

"I got one past the goalie," Logan says proudly. Mallory throws a piece of bread at him. I like this family.

"Because Brick Waller wasn't in net," Coach says. I guess I should call him Liam in these kinds of situations. That feels weird.

"Okay, that's creepy, Liam," Daphne says.

"What is *wrong* with you?" Mallory asks. "You're obsessed with hockey."

"Me?! You realize this is Daph, right? You know the nursery is going to be orange and black and the baby is coming home in a Gritty onesie," Liam says.

"Ooooh! Do they make them?" Daphne whips out her phone to Google. "They do! Oh, how precious!"

Daphne passes her phone to Logan and starts crying. All the men look on in alarm, but Faith and Holly laugh.

"Yep, you're pregnant," Holly says, wiping tears from her own eyes. "Welcome to the hormones."

Mike cuddles her. He's beaming. "We're going to be grandparents!" He doesn't bother wiping away his tears.

"Who are you texting?" Mallory asks Liam. "You can't tell their baby news! It's for them to share."

"Relax, Sparky, I'm not saying anything. I'm merely suggesting we have baby clothes as part of the Devil Birds merchandise. No way is the kid only wearing Flyers gear."

Coach's eyes widen. "Hey, can we do an on-ice gender reveal? I bet they make exploding pucks."

"William James Morgan the third. What is wrong with you? You can't do something like that!" Faith says. I don't know about this family, but in mine, if they use your middle name, you're in some deep shit.

Kendall is shaking with laughter next to me. "You got the William, the middle name, *and* thirded. You're in for it now!"

"We don't need input from you, Kendall Maureen. Thank you very much." Faith says.

"Actually," Daphne says, "it sounds like fun. But we won't know anything for months yet. Don't start planning. We weren't going to tell anyone until after the first trimester. You know. Just in case."

"You're almost there, honey," Faith says. "It's wise to wait. I'm sure all will be well, but it's hard on us human women to carry shifter babies."

"Did I tell you all Daph thought she'd lay an egg?" Logan says to lighten the mood as he hands her back her phone.

"Shut up. You were the first shifter I knew, and you're a golden eagle shifter. I don't know how all the stuff works!" She looks around the table. "It was years ago when we first started dating. It's not like they covered shifter biology in high school."

"They still don't cover shifter biology," I say. "It's expected to be taught in the home. Especially if you teach in a public school. They don't want the human kids 'confused.' It's part of the world they live in. What's confusing about it?"

"Algebra is confusing, but I still had to learn it," Mallory says. Her snarly face makes me laugh. I guess algebra wasn't an easy class for her.

"This is why schools like Pine Grove are important. It gives shifter kids an environment to learn about themselves and also *be* themselves." Kendall's eye flash with emotion. This is important to her. "We've all gone through the public schools, and we did well, but we know how many shifter kids fell through the cracks because they weren't understood. It was worse when shifting was a secret and you'd have to hope there was a shifter teacher in school who would look out for you. But kids get labeled as 'bad' or 'problematic' when really, they have extra energy. There's an animal growing inside of them, and they are doing everything they can to conform. It breaks my heart."

She looks so sad I can't resist putting my arm around her. It feels right when she snuggles in.

"You do a great job with the kids," I say. "It's not perfect, but it's better than it was,"

She sniffles and nods. Then she stiffens and looks up. I do too. Every eye in the room is trained on us with varying degrees of shock and joy. Except for Mike and Will. They are still eating their stew and talking baseball. I take my arm from around her shoulder and pick up my spoon. Kendall straightens and does the same. Eventually everyone returns to eating, and we spend the rest of the meal chatting. It's nice. But it doesn't feel fake.

We are compatible and share similar values. I could fall for Kendall without any effort, but we're doomed. She's been adamant she isn't moving away, and I'm not staying here after my time with the Devil Birds is done. My home and life are in Canada. The kids need me to guide them and protect them from making stupid mistakes that can ruin or end their lives. I lost my best friend because I wasn't there to stop him in time. I can't let it happen again. I'm going to make my money and go back home so I can keep my students safe. Give them opportunities other than drunken parties by the lake on Saturday night. Raise a family and protect them. New Jersey is a for-now thing, not a forever thing.

But Kendall feels like she could be a forever kind of woman.

8

KENDALL

"Thanks for the ride to dinner. I hope it wasn't torture for you," I say when we're back in Burke's SUV on the way back to my place. Two tubs of beef stew rest on my lap. One is for me and the other, bigger one, is for Burke.

"It was nice. Thanks for inviting me. A home-cooked meal was something I didn't realize I needed."

"My parents like you. If we were dating for real, they'd be over the moon." They were never as accepting of my ex. They were polite to him but with twenty-twenty hindsight I can see they were tolerating him for my sake and waiting for our relationship to run its course. Then I had to screw it up and marry the ass.

"Yeah, my parents would like you too if we ever got you up to Canada to meet them."

"They won't come down here for any games?" I ask.

"I'm sure they will. It's about a twelve-hour drive. They don't like to fly."

"Are both your parents polar bears?"

"No, only my dad. My mother is a witch. My sister, Emily, is both a polar bear and a witch. She'd punch me if I called her a bitch."

We laugh, remembering Rowena's exclamation at the barbecue.

We pull up in front of my townhouse, and Burke turns off his car.

He turns in his seat toward me. "What time do you want me to pick you up? Do you have a tire shop where we can get a spare to put on your car?"

"Come on in. We can look online. I know who my dad recommends, but I don't know their Saturday hours."

He nods and opens his door. He comes around to my side and takes both containers of stew so I can climb down more easily. Since his Explorer has four-wheel drive and is higher off the ground, it's a scramble to get in and out. It's trickier to do with my hands full of stew.

I let us in and turn on the lights. "Put the stew in the fridge. Did you want some wine? I have a nice red."

"Okay, thanks," he says.

I hand him the bottle and the corkscrew and grab a pair of glasses. "Do you mind pouring while I grab my laptop?"

His smile makes my tummy flip. Why does he have this effect on me?

"No problem," he says. "Meet you on the couch?"

I run upstairs to grab my computer from beside the bed. Coming back to the living room, I sit on the couch next to Burke and appreciate that he used coasters for our wine glasses. It's such a silly thing, but I like he saw I had them and respected my space enough to use them. My ex thought using coasters was stupid. If something got messed up, we could afford to replace it. That was his plan. Throw money at everything. My money.

I shake my head like it will erase thoughts of my past. Why can't my brain be like the Etch-A-Sketch my Grammy has at her house? I swallow down the tears wanting to gather at the thought of Logan's baby getting to play with it like we all did as little kids. It should be *my* baby playing with it.

I grab my glass and lean back with my laptop. We are sitting close enough I can feel Burke's body heat but not so close we are touching. It takes a minute to look up the tire place and confirm their hours for tomorrow and shoot an email I'll be by.

"Did you want to watch some Netflix?" I ask, stretching to put my laptop on the side table.

He nods. "Netflix is good. What do you want to watch? I like Lucifer."

I point the remote at the TV with a happy sigh. "Good choice! Tom Ellis is dreamy."

His low growl makes me giggle.

"I've seen them all," he says. "Wherever you want to start is fine with me."

I think about it. If we are fake dating, we'll probably have a lot of Netflix nights.

"Start from the beginning. If we hang out a lot to keep up the façade of fake dating, at least we'll have a plan."

I giggle when he bumps my shoulder with his.

"I like a woman with a plan," he says.

We start the first episode, and about halfway through I hear him sigh. I ignore him. A few minutes later, he sighs again. Growing up with Liam, I know this trick. Burke wants something. Working with first graders, I know he has words and until he uses them, he's not getting anything.

Another sigh. I bite the inside of my cheek to not laugh.

Finally, Burke leans down to whisper. "Do you have any chips or popcorn?"

"Yep. Both."

"Popcorn is my favorite if it's not too much trouble."

Dear, sweet, misguided bear.

"Mine too. The microwave popcorn is in the cabinet under the microwave. Help yourself. Please make me a mini bag of kettle corn."

He gets up and laughs. "Is this what it would be like to date you?"

"Pretty much." I rise from the couch too. "I'm going to get changed. Be right back."

"Okay."

When I come back downstairs, I move our wine glasses to the end table and remove the tabletop. I grab the plaid fleece blanket I keep in there and flip the top so the table is now a footstool. I like to get cozy when I'm watching TV on the couch. The microwave beeps as I pull the blanket over me. The popcorn smells divine.

Burke hands me my bowl of popcorn and sits next to me. It feels like he's closer than before. I don't mind it. It's weird. Any other man, I'd feel crowded and intimidated, but Burke doesn't cause any of those feelings. I only feel safe and comfortable with him. We're ignoring the fact that I'm also feeling a smidge turned on. Fake dating is not the place for feelings.

"Okay to take off my shoes?" he asks.

"Of course. I know you don't have funky feet."

He laughs. "Gee, thanks. Something to put in my dating profile when I look for Ms. Lucky."

My heart feels a little pang at the thought of him looking for Ms. Lucky. Mom must have put extra seasoning in the stew, and it's kicking in now.

Before we settle, I jump up to get us bottles of water and the wine bottle. May as well finish it.

I refill our glasses and settle on the couch with my feet up on the ottoman. Burke puts his feet up too.

He taps my foot with his. "You're tiny."

"Are you sure you aren't part Sasquatch?" I tap him back. "That's a big foot."

I can feel him looking at me out of the corner of his eye. I giggle and soon his deep laugh joins mine.

He puts his arm around me to give me a side hug. "You are such a first-grade teacher. Have you used this joke with your class yet?"

"Not yet, but I will."

I snuggle against his side with my bowl of popcorn. I pull the blanket over me.

"Do you want under here too?" I ask.

"Yeah, thanks."

He grabs the edge of the blanket and pulls it over us. His feet stick out past the end, but I'm all the way covered.

As we watch the Devil get up to mischief and solve murders in Los Angeles, we munch on our popcorn and cuddle. It's peaceful and comfortable. This is the safest I've felt with a man not related to me in over a year. I'm not sure if it's the wine, the coziness of the blanket, or the security I feel being beside this man, but I fall asleep during the second episode.

"Kendall. Wake up."

I snuggle deeper into my cozy nest. "Hmm...no."

I feel a kiss pressed to the crown of my head. This is too good of a dream to wake up from.

"Kendall, it's almost midnight. I should be leaving."

I struggle to climb out of my slumber. I'm leaning against Burke's side, his arm heavy around me with his hand resting on my hip. For a brief moment I feel a flash of panic like I'm being confined, but on the heels of that comes the feeling of certainty I'm not trapped. The arm is somehow meant to comfort and protect me. It's not going to hurt me or restrain me.

Kregg is the last man I slept with in any way that phrase could be interpreted, and in the last days of our relationship, I was afraid to fall asleep. I'd lay there, tense, awake, and alert because I didn't want to be vulnerable. What is it about Burke that keeps slipping past my defenses?

I sit up and push my hair out of my face, some of it stuck in the line of drool on my chin. Way to look alluring, Kendall. The TV has been paused at the start of episode five.

"Sorry. Didn't mean to fall asleep on your shoulder."

"No problem," he says. "I dozed off too. I should head out. I'll be back around nine tomorrow morning?"

"Don't be ridiculous. You drive a half hour home, sleep, and then come back in the morning. Stay here. I mean, in the guest room. If you want."

He gazes at me. "Are you sure? I have a bag in the car. Because of media stuff and practice, not for sleepovers."

I roll my eyes. "Yeah, this was all a master plan. You aren't fooling me. You slashed my tire to set it all in motion."

The "aw, shucks, you figured me out" snap of his fingers makes me giggle.

"Have to start calling you Nancy Drew with the way you pieced it all together," he says.

I shrug. "I'm a meddling kid. What can I say?"

"That's Scooby Doo. You're Kendall, not Daphne."

He laughs as he reaches out a finger to smooth the brow I furrowed in confusion

"You're adorable," he says.

He is too. I love the crinkling skin next to his gorgeous brown eyes as he waits for me to get his lame joke.

"Would I be Fred or Shaggy?" he asks.

"Pick one—wear an ascot or scarf down a pizza?"

"Pizza."

"Then you're Shaggy."

"I feel the overwhelming urge to go adopt a Great Dane puppy and name it Scooby Doo."

"Well, there's your Halloween costume sorted out," I say.

While he goes out to grab his bag from his SUV, I run upstairs to make sure the guest room is okay. I am setting out towels and soap in the hall bath when I hear Burke come back in.

"I'm up here!" I call.

His heavy tread comes up the stairs, and I meet him in the hallway.

"Your room is right there." I point to the open door behind him. "This is the bath. I set out towels and soap for you. Is there anything else you need?"

I step aside to show him the bathroom then follow him into the guest bedroom. It's navy and white, with pops of red to give it a nautical feel. I'm not lighthouse crazy like Logan and Daphne—their wedding was at the Cape May Lighthouse where they got engaged—with lighthouse figurines and pictures everywhere, but I live at the Jersey Shore. It's a rule to have some sort of beachy vibe somewhere.

He walks in and looks around while dropping his bag on the chair in the corner. "Very nice. Thank you. Okay if I grab a bottle of water?"

"Of course! Sorry, I didn't think of it." I turn and jog down the stairs, Burke following me. I grab our popcorn bowls and wine glasses and put them in the dishwasher to be run tomorrow. Being this tidy isn't my style, but I'm filled with all kinds of nervous energy. I'm not sure nervous is the right word.

I feel like there is electricity crackling between us. Like one of those metal ball things you touch in science class and it makes your hair stand up. It's not a painful shock, but a warm current. Is it attraction? Of course, he's an attractive man, but I can't be attracted to him. Attraction leads to feelings and feelings lead to love and love leads to being hurt. Anyway, he's here for hockey and then he's going back to Canada. He's not staying here.

"Do you want one too?" Burke asks from where he's bent into the fridge. Turns out I've been staring at his ass this whole time and been too lost in my thoughts to appreciate the view. What a shame.

"Yep, thanks." I take the bottle he's handing back toward me. My fingers brush his hand, and a tingle shoots up my arm. Great. The electrical current has glitter. Not what I need.

I check the locks and the alarm system. When I've confirmed everything is secure, I turn to go back upstairs.

In the hallway outside the bedrooms, we stand awkwardly before our doors. Should we hug? Why is this weird? I mean, other than having a man I'm fake-dating on a whim sleeping in my house. That's not the weird part. This reaction I'm feeling is what is strange. I have to get behind my bedroom door and try to figure out what is going on here.

"Well, goodnight, Burke. Sleep well. I'm in here if you need anything." I flail my hand at the door behind me. Ugh. I'm such a goober. What could he need in the middle of the night? Well...I mean, other than that.

Burke does the sexy one eyebrow quirk that makes women's wills weak, and I'm no exception.

"I'll let you know. Goodnight, Kendall. Thanks for letting me stay over."

"You're welcome. Sleep well." I walk in and close my door, leaning back against it with a sigh. Fake dating. That's all this is. Nothing more. He doesn't want anything real either. But, if—big if—I wanted something real again, he'd be at the top of my list.

I change into my sleep shorts and tank and brush my teeth in my connected bath. I hear the shower turn on as I slide between the sheets. I wish I could join him. I imagine him sleek with the water streaming over all his muscles. The soap slicking all over. His massive hands handling his private areas. More than twig and berries. A branch and oranges, more likely.

My body is thrumming with desire. I haven't felt like this in over a year. I slip my hand under the waistband of my shorts and feel the slickness between my legs. I rub my fingers on my clit, the friction against the tight bundle of nerves causing my breath to catch. It feels good. I rub faster and faster and tweak my nipple. That's all it takes for me to come apart, my legs shaking, my breath shuddering out after holding it as my orgasm hits. I've missed feeling this satisfaction.

Sated, I hear the shower turn off. I roll to my side and imagine Burke running the towel over his body. I mentally trace a water droplet running down his spine to his round, tight ass. My last thought as I fall asleep with a smile on my lips is, what a lucky water drop.

9
BURKE

I'm awakened by sunlight hitting my face. For a moment, I'm disoriented because this isn't my bed, and I close my curtains when I sleep. I blink my bleary eyes as the memories of yesterday filter through. I'm in Kendall's blue and white guest room. The bed is very comfortable, but I hate that I'm alone in it. I miss waking up next to a warm, pliant woman.

Even if we don't have sex, the intimacy of being in the same space and starting the day together is something I crave. I want to feel connected to someone. Could fake dating include cuddling and sleeping together? Sleeping for real. Not sleeping as a euphemism.

Not that I'd turn down fake dating with real benefits, but it's not a good idea if I'm going to avoid anything tying me to New Jersey long term. But if we both know it's temporary and our future plans are incompatible, we can keep deeper feelings out of it. We're adults with physical needs.

I can do casual. I can like Kendall without *liking* Kendall. Cuddling on the couch last night felt right. I'm comfortable with her in a way I never was with my ex. Yeah, it could work. What could go wrong? My bear snorts in derision, but I ignore him. He's always cynical. Now to bring it up to Kendall.

I hear Kendall moving around in her room as I pull on jeans and a t-shirt. Her bedroom door is still closed when I go into the hall bath to brush my teeth and get ready for the day. When I come out, I see her door is open and judging by the coffee scent wafting up the stairs, she must be down there. I pray she can make coffee, since it doesn't appear cooking is a skill she's cultivated.

"Good morning," I say as I enter the kitchen.

Kendall is stirring creamer into her coffee. As she clinks her spoon against the rim of her mug, she looks up and smiles. "Good morning! How did you sleep?"

"I slept great, thanks. Your bed is very comfortable." I wish it had her in it.

She gestures to her Keurig machine. "Help yourself. The pods are in the drawer and mugs are in that cabinet."

She gestures to an upper cabinet with her chin. I open it and pull out a mug with "Cheer Up!" with a megaphone graphic printed on it. I pick a dark roast pod, put it in the machine, and wait for it to brew. I am not a morning person. I fake it well enough because I have to. I prefer to sleep in until around ten in the morning when possible. However, if I had Kendall in my bed, I'd be willing to wake up early for some morning sexy times.

I startle when I realize Kendall has been talking and I've been distracted thinking about the delicious things we could do to each other under the sheets. On top of the sheets. Against the wall. In the shower.

"I'm sorry. I'm still waking up. What did you say?" The coffee machine gives its last gasping shudder. I grab my mug, put it on the counter, and grab the pod to dispose of it.

"You're not a morning person, are you?" She takes a seat in front of her laptop with her mug.

I raise mine. "Not until I've had at least two of these."

"Well then, we'll have to call off this fake dating."

My heart falls. "Why?"

"I'm a morning person! I love to get up and do some yoga to start my day. Have coffee on my deck. Get to the beach early to claim my favorite spot."

"You're one of those *perky* morning people, aren't you?"

She gestures to the mug in my hand. "I'm a cheerleader. I'm perky all the time. It's a requirement."

I sigh because her morning perkiness should be a dealbreaker, but...it's not. I'm still thinking of her in bed and showers in the wee hours of the morning. Maybe I'm not awake enough to process how perky she is right now. It's another reason our fake dating shouldn't become real, no matter how last night's sexy dreams tried to convince me it would be a great idea. Easing on to the stool next to her, I peek at her screen. It's a local tire shop.

"Did they respond to your email?" I ask. "Can they take care of you today?"

"Yep. All set. It's the tire place my family always uses, and he promised not to tell my dad or brother. They have my tires in stock. I'm going to get them all replaced. They are about due and with winter coming, I want to make sure I have good tread."

"Do you get a lot of snow down here?"

She quirks her lips to the side as she thinks. "It depends. We get less snow than you do, I'm sure. Since we're coastal, we may end up with rain when ten miles further inland gets snow. All depends on where the rain/snow line falls. We get nor'easter storms, which are like hurricanes in terms of ferocity. They can dump a ton of snow or rain. The islands can flood. There were mini-icebergs in the streets of Wildwood a few years ago."

"Is The Nest okay since it's on a pier?" I'm not sure I want to be in a building out over the ocean in a storm of that magnitude.

"Oh, yeah, it's fine. When my family did the renovation, they far exceeded code and engineering specs. It should be fine in the face of the fiercest nor'easter. We respect the power of the Atlantic."

I drain my cup of coffee. It's okay, but I could use another. Fresh brewed, not from a pod. I wonder if we can get breakfast and real coffee while we're taking care of the tire stuff.

"I'm ready to go whenever you are," Kendall says.

"Let's go. Oh, wait, let me grab my bag." I turn and jog upstairs. I had already thrown everything in when I got ready this morning. My shoes are downstairs from last night.

It's a beautiful late September day, sunny with clear skies and not too hot. I prefer winter. I am a polar bear, after all. But if I have to do late summer, this is the day I want.

We drive through the woods. Kendall warned me the tire shop isn't much to look at, but it's the best around. Her family has been using it for generations. She directs me to pull into a lot in front of a tin-roofed building sitting at the point of a fork in the road. The faded Harkord's sign swings in the slight breeze.

"Be right back!" Kendall says as she jumps down from the passenger seat.

Like hell I'm letting her in there alone.

I climb down and follow her in. The building is old, and it's been decades since the last renovation, but it's spotless.

"Hey Kennie Cat!" a guy around my age calls from the garage area where he had been under the hood of a Honda.

Suddenly, Kendall attaches herself to my side like Velcro is holding us together.

"Hey, Gage! How are you?" Kendall's arm snakes around my waist. I drop mine around her shoulders. Not sure what's going on, but I'll play along.

"Great thanks. You're looking good." He gives her a slow up and down look that makes me want to punch him.

"Aw, that's kind of you! This is my boyfriend, Burke Bedard. He's the captain of the Devil Birds hockey team."

She looks up at me adoringly. I swear she's batting her eyelashes. What the hell. I take advantage of the situation and give her a kiss. Nothing extravagant. No tongue. But it's a kiss. A proper kiss, no faking. Her lips are soft and pliant against mine. I think she's wearing a flavored lip gloss because there is a faint scent of straw-berries. I love strawberries. I'm about to pull her closer to me and wrap my other arm around her when a clearing throat breaks through the sensual haze wafting through my brain.

"Um...yeah. Well, we have your tire," Gage says.

Kendall pulls back with a giggle and a dazed look on her face. The kiss affected her too. Good.

"Sorry," I say, not meaning it. I regret nothing about the kiss except it being over. I hold out my hand to Gage. "Nice to meet you."

He holds up his hands. "Don't want to get you greasy. Hockey player, huh? I thought you hated hockey, Ken."

"Well, times change. You know how it goes. So, my spare is ready? And then I'll come back and get the others put on?"

"Yep, Luke will take care of it. Are you waiting?"

"No," I say. "I'll follow." I have my bearings now. The shop isn't far from my apartment. We can go back there for lunch or to hang out.

"Okay. Let me get your spare." He looks at me. "You're okay to get it on?"

"We're good. Thanks." I'm not insulted. He wasn't trying to be an ass. You don't want someone with no clue changing tires. Especially for a friend. I'm assuming Kendall and Gage are friends. They greeted each other like they were.

"You're paying for everything this afternoon, right?" Gage asks.

"Yeah, if you're good with it," she says.

"It's not like I can't find you, Kennie."

Kendall laughs, but I feel her stiffen alongside me. My protective instincts are kicking in again. I know he's some kind of shifter, but I can't smell him. Maybe a bird? His eyes are kind of beady. His nose is beak-like too. With his buzz cut hairstyle, he has a vulture-like appearance. Stick with your scraps, dude. I have the filet mignon right here, and I don't share.

Kendall and I walk outside, and I unlock the back of my Explorer to enable Gage to put the spare tire in. As he loads the tire, I open the passenger side door and offer Kendall a hand to get up. She doesn't need it, but she takes it for show. Gage slams the back down, and I bite back a smirk. We are getting Gage's goat, I think.

I make sure the back is latched and climb into the driver's seat. We wave to Gage as we drive away.

"We're going to the school next?" I ask right before my stomach rumbles.

Kendall laughs.

"I hear that. Let's grab breakfast at Rosie's Diner first, and then we'll take care of my car."

My stomach growls again. I think it approves of the suggestion.

"Sounds perfect. Tell me how to get there."

Rosie's is the stereotypical New Jersey diner with mirrors and chrome galore. The menu is huge, with everything from scrambled eggs to steak and shrimp. I eye the revolving display of pies and cakes. The sign outside says, "All baking done on premises." I will have to come back to see if the triple layer chocolate cake is as good as it looks.

"Anything special you recommend?" I take a sip of strong black coffee. My sigh as the caffeine hits my bloodstream is heartfelt.

"I get the cheesesteak omelet. Do you like eggs?"

I read the description. It's thinly-sliced steak with fried onions and cheese folded into eggs.

"Ooh, sounds interesting. I think I'm going to get the meat lovers."

Our server arrives and takes our order. I watch her walk away and turn back to Kendall. It's now or never.

"So, you and Gage?"

Kendall makes a "yuck" face.

"Yeah, me and Gage. He was my high school boyfriend. Quarterback and cheerleader. Prom King and Queen. We were each other's first. All the stereotypes. We knew it was a high school thing. I was going away to Wickham, and we didn't want to do long distance. We weren't in love." She exhales like she had been holding her breath. "At least he didn't cheat on me."

"He's a shifter?"

"Yeah. He's a hawk shifter."

Hawk, vulture. Close enough.

"Is he interested in getting back together with you?"

"I'm sure he wouldn't turn down a hook up if I offered, but I'm not interested. Too messy. I'm not averse to a friend-with-benefits, no-strings-attached arrangement. But it's not possible with Gage or anyone else from my past."

I run my finger along the back of her hand resting on the table. She shivers and it's not from being cold.

"How about with someone in your present?" I ask.

She swallows, and I swear I almost hear a gulp. This was a bad idea. Welcome to Awkwardville, New Jersey, population two.

Turning her hand over, she captures mine.

"Depending on who the someone is, it's a possibility."

Of course, our server chooses this moment to arrive with our breakfasts. No matter how much I'm starving, I would have been okay waiting to eat so we could finish this conversation.

Kendall smiles up at the server. "Thanks!"

I smile and nod as well and wish for her to hurry and walk away. Hell, I'll tip double if she drops the check and forgets we exist.

I take a deep breath for courage. "What if the someone is me?"

She tilts her head. I'm reminded of the old logo with the dog next to the gramophone. I'd see it when I was going through my parents' collection of vinyl albums.

The tip of her tongue slips out to moisten her lips and I'm back to craving strawberries.

"So, we'd be fake dating with real boinking, but no strings?"

I give my most charming smile. "Yeah?" I'd be a very lucky man if she goes along with it.

"Hmm...," is all she offers as she cuts into her omelet.

We take bites of our breakfasts. She offers me a sample of her cheesesteak omelet. It's tasty. I offer a bite of mine.

After taking a sip of her milk and sugar beverage she pretends is coffee, she rests her chin on her fist.

"How would it work?" she asks. *Finally.* I thought we were going to ignore that I'd ever brought it up.

"Biologically?" I croak out, choking on the last bite of my eggs. She told me she's not a virgin. There shouldn't be a question about how it works.

Her beautiful blue eyes roll. "Will you stop being a science teacher for a second, please?"

I nod.

"How will it work between us? We already agreed on exclusivity, but if we are sleeping together, it is an absolute deal breaker. No kissing someone else, no getting a blowjob from some puck bunny. I know this is casual and has no strings, but we aren't with anyone else. You want to be with someone else, fine. But be honest with me first. I'll show you the same respect. Can you do that?"

Reaching out to take her hand again, I give it a gentle squeeze. "Absolutely. I'm not a cheater."

She scrunches her nose. "It wouldn't be cheating. We aren't really dating."

"Whatever. I'm not going into semantics. It would only be me and you. I would not be involved with anyone else. Not like I could. I live with your best friend, and your brother is my coach. I couldn't bring anyone home, and I couldn't hook up with a puck bunny. If the world thinks we're dating, then I'm either sleeping with you or being celibate for the foreseeable future. I choose you."

"Wow, you are such a charmer, giving me such an irresistible proposition! Ms. Lucky is going to swoon when you ask her to marry you."

"Trust me, when I propose to Ms. Lucky, whoever she may be, she's going to be happy to be having all of this—"I gesture down my body."—freely available to her."

"All of that—" she gestures to me"—is not worth living in the frozen north."

I wink. "I will keep her warm and satisfied. She'll have no complaints."

"Good for you. Now that's settled, you need to know something."

Oh no, is this where the crazy comes out? I knew this deal was too good to be true. Men like me don't get offered no strings sex from gorgeous women like her. There's always strings.

"We need to go out a few times before jumping into bed."

I grin. "You need to be wooed?"

"Yes, I want to be wined, dined, and wooed. You know, in our free time between work, practice, friends..."

"Does breakfast and fixing your tire count as our first date?"

"Nope." She holds up a finger. "Dinner with my family was our first date. Dined."

Second finger goes up. "Lucifer. Wined."

Third finger goes up. "Changing my tire. Wooed. *This* is our third date. You know what they say about third dates..."

They say it's time to get our check and change her tire so we can finish our third date properly.

I raise my hand to get our server's attention as Kendall finishes scarfing down her omelet. "Check, please."

10

KENDALL

I GIGGLE LIKE A BABOON HIGH ON HELIUM AS WE RUSH HAND IN HAND FROM the diner back to Burke's SUV. I'm pretty sure I get airtime when he helps me in the passenger seat.

"Are you sure you need your car? Is the tire place open tomorrow?" Hope gleams in his eyes.

Shaking my head, I sigh. "I will need my car, and I don't want to Uber. Need to get the car to the shop today. But they have after-hours pickup..."

"Fine. We'll get the spare on and drop your car off at the shop, but then you're mine the rest of the afternoon." Burke says in a low, growly voice that makes all my girly parts tingle and clench.

There are some cars in the school parking lot due to team practices for the high school and enrichment activities for the younger kids. No one is parked near my car or milling about, so Burke can get the spare on quickly. If he stops playing hockey or teaching, he has a future in the pit crew for a NASCAR team.

I manage to stay within the speed limit as I race back to Harkord's but the urge to put the pedal to the metal is strong. Burke is hot on my tail. I pull into the lot and toss Gage my keys.

"I'll be picking it up after hours. Do you want me to pay now or bill me?" I ask.

Gage catches my keys with the grace of the second baseman he was on our high school's baseball team—I had a thing for guys in baseball pants for a while, cured now—and watches Burke pull in next to my car, leaving his SUV running. Knowing eyes turn toward me. "We have an app. When we're done, we'll text you a link, and you can pay online. I'll leave the keys under the seat."

"That would be great." The flush I know must creep up my neck gives me away. That's the problem with doing business with someone you've known since grade school. "Thanks, Gage! Have a great day!"

"Betting it's not as good as yours is going to be." His smirk reminds me why we didn't bother trying to extend our relationship beyond high school.

"Toodleloo!" I call over my shoulder as I walk to Burke's vehicle.

I open the door and climb up into the passenger seat. Before fastening my seat belt, I lean over and pull Burke's head down for a kiss. His lips are soft but firm, and he takes control of the kiss. His tongue sweeps out to gain entrance to my mouth, and I open to him. Our tongues tangle and dance.

A happy little beep-beep causes me to jump and pull back. Burke's glazed eyes look over my shoulder when I turn my head to see Gage sitting behind the wheel of my Mustang. He grins and waves as he puts the car in gear and drives it into the shop.

Burke's sheepish grin makes my tummy flip. No, not his grin. The grin is incidental. I'm sure it's the onions and peppers from my omelet doing the quickstep in my tummy. Yep, all it is. Because if I'm getting a flippy tummy, and I'm not being tossed in the air during a cheer routine, it means I'm at risk of developing feelings for Burke.

That can't happen. This must remain physical and casual. We're scratching itches. Neither one of us is looking for more. We have needs, but we have futures that don't include each other. I need to remember that.

Burke navigates back toward my place perfectly. He's learning his way around here with all the back roads and driving through the woods.

"Oh! Do you have condoms?" I ask. I don't think I have any at my place. It's not like I'm going to knock on Andy's door and ask for them.

Burke turns wide eyes to me. "No! I don't! Oh, shit. Is there somewhere nearby I can pick them up?"

I nod. "There's a CVS near my townhouse. We can stop there. Don't turn into my complex, keep driving. It's on the corner."

"Okay. Sorry. I don't keep condoms in my wallet or car. I'm not usually this spontaneous. I'm clean. The team tested us, and I haven't been with anyone."

His blush is adorable. I can't resist leaning over and kissing his cheek. His beard tickles my lips.

"Me neither." I clear my throat awkwardly. "It's been a while and not since I've moved in. I'm on birth control. But I'm more comfortable using condoms."

His warm hand squeezes my knee, and I swear it's connected to my heart. *It's physical, Kendall, don't forget it. You thought it was love before, and you were wrong.*

"It's on the right up here," I say, pointing to the entrance.

"Do you need anything?" He puts the SUV in park.

I want to suggest whipped cream, but I don't want to waste precious minutes for him to see if they have it. I'll have to remember to pick some up.

I can't hold back the laughter as I watch Burke run from the CVS clutching the box of condoms to his chest with the mile-long receipt flapping in the breeze behind him. Cheeks blazing, he throws himself back into the driver's seat. He tosses the box of XXL condoms onto my lap as he slams the door.

"I forgot New Jersey doesn't give bags."

"Yeah, oops."

He gives me a mock glare, then looks around before pulling out. I let loose peals of laughter when I see the end of the receipt fluttering outside his driver-side window since it got slammed in the door.

"Oh, for fuck's sake," he mutters.

"Exactly for fuck's sake," I say on gasping breaths from how hard I am laughing.

We pull into my parking spot and Burke turns off the Explorer. He undoes his seat belt and then mine.

With dark brown eyes intent on mine, he says in a low voice rumbling from his chest, "Laugh now while you can because once I have you in bed, you'll be moaning and crying out in pleasure." He leans across the console and takes my lip in a demanding kiss. The laughter dies in my throat and my panties get wet.

I note with relief that Andy and Harrison's parking spot is empty. The last thing I want to do is run into them and feel obligated to explain things. Or delay sexy times. It's been almost a year and a half since I've last been with someone, and I thought I was fine without physical intimacy. Maybe I was. But now I'm desperate to be with someone. Well, I'm desperate to be with Burke. I hope my desire isn't Burke specific, but that it's merely convenient he's here when I'm horny.

We rush into my townhouse, the box of condoms clutched in my hands and the receipt a streamer behind me. As soon as the door slams behind us, Burke has me pressed against it, his hard body bracketing mine. If it was anyone else, the size and strength he possesses would intimidate me.

But it's Burke and my gut instinct tells me I can trust him. But I thought I could trust my ex too, and I was wrong. Burke isn't Kregg though. I know he isn't. He's a good man. He *has* to be a good man. I know there are good men out there. I'm related to a bunch of them. There must be one for me. I can't keep picking duds. Burke needs to be someone I can trust. Even if we don't have a future, we can have a right now. I *need* this right now.

I stretch up on my tiptoes so I can wrap my arms around his neck and meet his lips halfway—okay, I'm short and he's a giant, it's not halfway, but I'm pretending it is—in a hungry kiss. We kiss as if we need to consume each other. I've never been this hungry for a man's kiss, a man's touch. I'm sure it's the sexual drought I've been in. I'd react like this to anyone I found attractive. Yeah, I'm feeling stuff, but I don't have any *feelings*.

Suddenly, my stomach drops with a sensation of weightlessness as Burke lifts me in the air, his hands under my ass. Now we can kiss without him having to bend in half. I wrap my legs around his waist and grind my center against the bulge in his jeans.

Gasping, Burke breaks our kiss.

"Kendall, love, where are we headed? Couch, bed, counter? Tell me where to go."

I'm pressing open mouth kisses against his neck and throat.

"Upstairs. Take me upstairs." I give Burke a tiny nip where his neck and shoulder meet, and he shivers. I love that I can give this polar bear goosebumps.

He carries me with ease through my living room and up the stairs. His feet make a rapid beat as we ascend the staircase.

"Your room?" he asks.

"Uh-huh."

I unwind one arm from around Burke's neck to reach behind me and push the door open. I lift my head to glance around and cringe, seeing the unmade bed and pile of clothes on the chair.

"Sorry, it's a mess..." I unwind my legs from around Burke's waist as he sets me on the floor.

"I don't care. Our clothes are going to end up on the floor too. It doesn't matter." He kisses me again, only breaking away to lift my shirt over my head. I didn't plan like he did, and we need to break apart again when it's time for his shirt to come off.

I saw him at the pool. I know how muscled his chest and shoulders are, but now I can touch him freely, not just put sunscreen on his back in front of friends and family. Feel his muscles flex and the warmth of his skin. Run my fingers through the hair on his chest. Kiss his nipples.

My bra disappears as if by magic, and Burke's calloused hands are on my breasts. They are huge—his hands, not my breasts—but gentle. The way he tweaks my nipples is incredible. I feel each tug low in my core. I reach for his belt buckle and in a few moments have my hands inside his jeans. His cock feels big and solid, and I can't wait to see it up close and personal. Burke's hands leave my nipples, unfortunately. Then they go to the button of my jeans. That's progress. We are both kicking off our shoes. Soon, we stand before each other, naked.

Oooh boy. I mean, Burke is *all man*. Holy crap, he's impressive. I don't know if all polar bear shifters are blessed like this, but Burke's South Pole is magnificent.

I've been with other men. Okay, Gage and my ex. Gage had perfectly adequate equipment happening below the belt for a teenage boy. Good enough for me to know what my ex-husband was lacking. But Burke has the holy grail of length and girth. But not too much of either that it's ridiculous. Please let him have rhythm and stamina. It would be such a shame to have all that and not have the skills to use it for the purpose nature intended—to give me orgasms.

"The best things really do come in small packages," Burke murmurs as he sweeps me into his arms bridal style, places one knee on the bed, and gently lowers me to the mattress. He stretches out next to me and chuckles.

"What's so funny?" I ask.

"I'm too long for your bed. My feet are hanging over the end."

I didn't think about that. I have a normal queen-sized bed, which is plenty for me. But Burke is six and a half feet tall. He needs an extra-long bed like I have in the guest room. Since shifters are often taller and bigger than humans, oversized furniture has become more of a thing.

"Do you want to move to the guest room? I know you fit there."

He gives me a devilish grin and nuzzles my neck.

"Don't worry. We'll make it work."

Our hands travel over each other's bodies as we kiss and nuzzle. I love running my hands over his muscles. I've always gone for athletic men, but Burke's body is on a whole other level. His skin is warm and smooth as it stretches and flexes. The light hair on his chest tickles my sensitive nipples, and I shiver in response.

"Are you cold?" Burke asks.

"No. Excited." I can't believe I admitted that.

He circles my nipple with his fingertip as he leans on an elbow above me. It hardens into a tight nub.

"Oh, yeah?"

Biting my lip to hold back my moan of pleasure, I nod.

He lowers his head to take my tightened nipple into his mouth. He gives it a light bite and there is no holding back the moan this time. A low rumbling chuckle from Burke causes the mattress to shake. I hope my bed frame is up to the workout it's going to get. When his tongue lathes my nipple, I whimper. I enjoy foreplay, but this is all too much. He hasn't touched me below the waist yet, and I feel like I'm ready to explode. The second he touches my clit—please let him touch my clit—I'm going to go off like a fire-cracker.

Burke must be a mind reader because his finger traces a path from my breast, down my abdomen, and between my folds. I am so wet his finger glides easily and starts rubbing my clit. That's all it takes. My back bows off the bed, and I let out a high-pitched cry as my orgasm overtakes me.

The calloused palm caressing my breast feels marvelous. If I was in my cougar form, I'd be purring. He kisses his way down my tummy. I know what's coming next, and I want it desperately, but I can't handle it now.

"No," I say.

Immediately, he stops and rolls away. What?!

"No! I mean yes! I want you inside me. Now." I'm sending all kinds of mixed signals, which isn't what I want to do.

I crawl on top of him, straddling his midsection, and frame his face with my hands. "Burke Bedard, I want you to fuck me. Now."

His gorgeous brown eyes—I don't think I've noticed the flecks of gold before—look up at me.

"Are you sure? We don't have to do anything. You can change your mind. It's your call."

This man. Why couldn't I have met him two years ago?

"I said no because if you went down on me, I'm afraid I would pass out because it would be too good, and I don't want to miss a moment of this. Now, are you going to fuck me, or do I have to fuck you?"

I stretch and grab the box of condoms that ended up on the bed with us. My hands are shaking with the aftereffects of the best orgasm of my life, but I get it open. I grab a foil packet and toss the rest of the box to the floor next to the bed. Burke plucks it from my fingers and rolls us over.

"I'll fuck you this time, my sexy kitty. You can do me next time."

He quickly sheaths himself, and I realize I haven't gotten a good look at his cock. I know it's big, but it's gotten no attention from me. I always reciprocate with the foreplay, but Burke was overwhelming in the most wonderful way. I was too busy feeling everything to do anything.

His body covers mine, his knees and forearm holding his weight off me. He strokes his cock and rubs it against my folds. It bumps my clit and even with that minor contact, I feel the fire he stokes within me again. I've never had two orgasms before. I know it can happen. I've heard Mallory and Daphne gossiping. But it's never happened to me.

I open my legs wider in a silent invitation Burke accepts. He takes his time as he enters me and oh, my. Yeah, he's big. Obviously, he fits, but I need a moment to adjust. He must be used to it because he stills and lowers his head to kiss me. This man can kiss. Let's face it, he's skilled in everything. Losing myself in the kiss, I gasp when he moves his hips in a slow, steady rhythm.

I wrap my legs around his hips and dig my heels in to get closer to him. He is filling me in a way no one else ever has. I've had good sex before. I've had bad sex too. But this is incredible. I tighten my core around Burke's cock when it's deep inside me and his growl of pleasure causes the hairs on my arms to rise.

I feel the heat and excitement building in me with each firm thrust of Burke's hips. He hits the spot inside me that makes need coil tighter. His breath comes faster and faster as he kisses my neck and the spot under my ear I didn't know I loved having kissed.

"So good, so tight, so right," Burke chants.

I tunnel my fingers in his hair and run them over his strong back, reveling in the flexing of the muscles and the warmth of his skin. As I press kisses along his jaw and on his shoulder, tears come to my eyes. I didn't know if I'd ever be this close to a man again. If I'd be able to feel what I'm feeling. It's such a relief to know I can feel this way.

A wave of ecstasy washes over me, and I cry out.

"Burke! Yes! Oh!" I may have spoken in tongues, I'm not sure. I was having an out-of-body experience.

With a few more hard thrusts, Burke follows me over the edge. Our skin is damp as we catch our breath. Burke moves to the side slightly, not wanting to crush me. The weight of his arm draped across me is heavy but comforting. There's still a connection between us, even though he's not inside me anymore. He traces lazy circles on my skin and doodles shapes with his fingers on the side of my breast. I can't get my brain cells to work in concert enough to determine if he's writing something or idly meandering.

"Wow." He kisses my shoulder. I shiver slightly. The air is cool against my skin.

"Are you cold?" Burke rises on his elbow. He runs his hand up and down my arm. The friction of his calluses causing heat but not warmth. I'm getting turned on again. Already. Wow.

"Let me get rid of the condom, and then we can get under the covers." A flash of uncertainty crosses his face. "If you want. Are you a cuddler?"

I smile at him. "Bathroom is through there."

He has a wonderful ass. It's round, like an apple on tree trunk legs. He's a huge guy, inches taller and at least fifty pounds heavier than Kregg. Unlike Kregg, he doesn't use his size to intimidate me. I feel safe with him.

I scoot over on the white cotton sheet to make room for Burke to slide in and pull the covers over us. He wraps his arm around me, and I rest my head on his chest. I press a kiss to his pec. It's there, and I can't resist it.

"We can cuddle," I say, "but if you fall asleep and snore, that's it. We're done."

"You're worried about snoring? You yodeled when you came!"

I gasp. If I was wearing pearls, I'd be clutching them. "I did *not* yodel! I cried out in ecstasy! I was enthusiastic! See if it happens again."

"I need about twenty minutes, kitty, but then I'm ready. It's a science experiment. We will have to see if it's reproducible results."

If he can deliver sex like this again, then this fake dating with benefits may be the best idea I ever have. Well, as long as I keep the satisfaction my body feels separate from any twinges my heart may feel. I can't confuse physical satisfaction with emotional attachment. This isn't forever, it's for now.

11

BURKE

"Ricola!" I cry out during the best blowjob of my life. Judging by the fact Kendall has stopped sucking my cock, it wasn't the best choice I ever made. Sitting on her heels with tears streaming down her face, she's laughing so hard she's gasping for breath. Her hand is still wrapped around my cock, kinda jerking me off as she shakes with laughter. It's good, but her wet mouth and enthusiastic tongue were better.

"What the hell was that?" Kendall asks as she catches her breath.

"Do you remember the commercial for the Ricola cough drops where someone would blow a horn and the guy would call out 'Ricola'? I thought it would go with your yodeling from before." I tilt my head. "Keep with the Swiss Alps theme?"

"Do you have some kind of fantasy with lederhosen I need to know about?" she asks. Thankfully, she's pumping my cock again. All is not lost. And by all, I mean my erection. I've never had a conversation during a blowjob before. This is different. Not bad, just different.

"Will you dress up in a dirndl?" I ask hopefully. I've never had a lederhosen fantasy before, but I'm willing to try it if that's what floats her boat.

"Do you want me to finish this blowjob or not?"

I mimic turning a key to lock my lips and toss it over my shoulder and widen my stance.

She gives my shaft a long lick and looks up at me with a smirk. "That's what I thought."

Maybe I should be embarrassed by how quickly I come, but it's more a compliment to her exceptional blowjob skills than my lack of control.

We end up in Kendall's shower. It's a tight fit for a man like me, but we make it work. I'm big enough I block the water from hitting her. It's a game of Twister maneuvering around each other to get everything washed and rinsed off. We'll have to get a suite at Devil's Den like I stayed in during training camp. Those showers are roomy enough and have the overhead shower heads. We'd be playing soapy naked Twister recreationally, not out of necessity.

It's late afternoon when we dress and get ready to go to the garage so Kendall can get her car. Then we will part ways. I need to go back to my apartment and do the laundry. I wonder if my room-mates realize I haven't been home?

When I reach the bottom of the stairs, I turn to look up at Kendall as she walks towards me. I ask what has been on my mind.

"What am I telling people about us? What are you?"

She shrugs her shoulders as she continues down the stairs into the living room. "I guess if anyone asks, I'll say we're seeing each other. I want people to leave me alone and stop trying to fix me up. If they think I'm involved they'll leave me alone. You should tell people the same thing. We want our stories to match."

She's reached the living room and turns around to look up at me as I take the last couple of steps. She's biting her lip. Doesn't she know that's my job? I take my work seriously. Bending down, I press a kiss to her lips and run my tongue over the spot she was worrying to soothe it.

"Okay." I grab my bowl of stew from the fridge. It's too good to forget.

Kendall opens her front door and stops short, almost causing me to run into her.

She bends down and picks up a package from her doormat with a post-it note on it.

Oh, no. It's a bag of Ricola cough drops. I lean over her shoulder to read the note. It's in a masculine printed style.

Here's the Ricola your "friend" asked for. Get him to give you a couple if you swallowed. A.

Kendall steps out onto her porch and spins around, shoving the bag into my chest as she looks at the bay window of the townhouse next door. I see curtains twitch but don't see anyone. However, when she shoots a double middle finger at the window, I hear deep, masculine laughter seeping through.

I chuckle but stifle it when she turns her glare on me.

"Gift from your cousin?" I ask.

"Yeah, Andy the Asshole," she shouts. Her eyes widen at the gasp coming from the parking lot.

An older woman is walking her little mop dog and gives Kendall a reproachful look over her cat-eye glasses.

"Hi, Mrs. Hudson, beautiful day, isn't it?" Kendall says with fake cheerfulness.

Mrs. Hudson harrumphs and continues on her way.

"Let's go." Kendall says, walking to my Explorer. I open the passenger door to let her in and go around the hood to the driver's side. I glance at her cousin's house and see the curtains twitch again. Kendall is close to her cousin. Is she going to tell them the truth about us? What is the truth about us? I know we are fake dating, but what happened this afternoon doesn't feel fake.

Stop it. She doesn't want a relationship. You don't want a relationship. Don't go getting feelings. This is fake dating and satisfying hormones. She's not a forever girl. She's a for-now girl.

I tell myself this, but I'm not sure if my bear is listening. He likes Kendall, even though she doesn't fit into our future. No matter what my bear thinks, I'm the one in charge here.

Climbing into the driver's seat, I shoot a grin at Kendall.

"So, Andy is quite funny," I say.

She rolls her beautiful blue eyes. "Yeah, hilarious."

I start the engine and look around to make sure it's clear to back up. I pull out of the parking spot and drive to the exit of the lot.

"Are you close in age?" I ask.

"Yeah, we're the same age. He's three weeks older than I am."

"Andy is a guy?" I thought Andy was short for something like Andrea.

"Yeah. Did you think he was a girl?"

I shrug. Admitting my assumptions is going to make me sound like an asshole.

"Because Andy is my best friend and has a boyfriend, you assumed they were female?"

I can feel the flush creep up under my beard.

Kendall reaches over and squeezes my arm. "Don't worry. It happens a lot."

Before I pull out onto the street, I reach over and cover her hand and squeeze it in return. "I'm an idiot. I'm not homophobic or anything."

She pulls her hand away and I place mine back on the wheel. "I didn't think that for a moment. Anyway, Andy and his boyfriend Harrison are my best friends and next-door neighbors. They met in college. They were teammates."

"Hockey?" I ask.

"Nope. Baseball. Andy was a pitcher and Harrison his catcher."

I don't know how I'm supposed to react.

Kendall giggles. "I know. They make jokes about it all the time. It's such a cliché. But they are perfect for each other."

"What do they do now? Do they still play baseball?" Shifters are playing professional baseball now. Since it's a non-contact sport, there is more tolerance than in hockey and football.

"Not professionally. They play on local rec teams. Andy is the Vice President of Operations for Morgan Development. When Liam left Morgan for the Devil Birds, Andy took over. It's always been the plan. He loves business, and he loves the company. The rest of us—me, Liam, and Logan—aren't interested. Mallory works in the legal department, and Daphne works in marketing at Morgan besides what she does with the team and her tour company. It's still in the family."

"Does Harrison work there too?"

"No, he's a computer guy. He develops apps and websites. I'm sure there would be a place in the Morgan IT department for him, but he likes his independence. Andy travels for work a lot and free-lancing lets them travel together when they want."

I turn on the road taking us to the garage. I'm getting better at navigating around here. Like any area, the roads have the official name you find on the map and then what it's called by the locals. I'm slowly learning the pairings.

"Sounds ideal. It's hard on a relationship where one person travels a lot or it's long distance."

I can see her nod out of the corner of my eye.

"Yeah, I will never do long distance again." She turns and looks out her window.

"You had a long-distance relationship?"

"Briefly. Last year of college. It was a disaster."

Maybe this is the bad breakup she had? It's my turn to reach out and touch her in reassurance. I rest a hand on her thigh. It's tense. I knead it gently, hoping to loosen it up.

"I'm sorry. Do you want to talk about it?"

"No. It's part of my past I want to forget."

Fair enough.

"What are your plans for the rest of the weekend?" I ask.

"Laundry, lesson plans, TV. Need to read a book for a book club. What about you?"

I sigh. "Laundry. Working out. Meal prep. Reviewing practice footage. The usual."

I glance over at her. The late afternoon sun makes her hair shine golden. Damn, she's beautiful.

"What kind of book club?" I ask.

"It's a romance book club with my mom and aunt, Mallory, Daphne, Mallory's mom, when she's in town. Sometimes Mal's sister. Abby. Most of the time we drink wine and talk about men. The book is incidental."

She nudges me with her elbow. "You're welcome to join us if you're into romance novels."

I nudge her back. "I do like to read, but I prefer mysteries or history. Canadian history. I'll have to see if I can get a library card here. Brush up on New Jersey history."

"You should be able to. If you have a problem, let me know. I know people. And talk to Teagan. Her family on her mom's side is one of the oldest families around here."

I chuckle. Who knew a benefit of having Kendall as my fake girl-friend was getting a library card? I can picture us cuddled up on her couch reading on a snowy afternoon with a fire going in her fire-place. I'd tell her a random fact, and she'd pretend to be interested. Maybe she'd want to reenact a sexy scene from one of her books. It scares me how much I want it. My ex was not a stay-home-and-read type of woman. She always wanted to go out to the club. She limited her reading to the status updates of her vapid friends through the app on her phone.

Kendall fidgets in her seat. Is she trying to get comfortable?

I reach toward the control panel. "Are you hot? Cold?"

"No, I'm fine." She fidgets som e more.

"What?" I ask.

"When did you want to get together again? I have dance team rehearsals on Tuesday and Thursday nights and Saturday afternoon. Cheer team Monday, Wednesday evening, and Saturday morning. All I have open is Friday night and Sunday. What's your schedule like?"

I hum as I flip through my schedule in my mind. "Devil Birds practice and working out during the day. I'll help with some of the junior team practices. What do you do for dinner?"

She shrugs. "I grab something from WaWa or raid Andy's fridge. Harrison is an incredible cook, and he takes pity on me. He'll leave a portion for me in the fridge. He was traveling with Andy to the outlets in the northwest this past week. It's why my fridge was empty."

"Do you not know how to cook, or do you not like to cook?" I hope I'm not insulting her.

"More not liking to cook. Not wanting to go shopping. Not wanting to do all the work and then clean up."

"We could cook something together. I could pick up the groceries and bring them over. Do something that doesn't use a bunch of pots and pans." Oh, Burke, what are you doing? That's sounding like a relationship thing to do.

When Kendall doesn't say anything, I look over at her to see if there's a horrified look on her face. She's chewing her lip again. She looks like she's thinking. I guess it's better than abject horror?

"Do you think we could make something and invite Andy and Harrison over?" She finally asks. "I hope the sooner they meet you, the sooner they stop torturing me."

I hate the hesitation in her voice.

"Sure. I'd like to meet them. What do they like to eat?"

Kendall shrugs. "They're twenty-four-year-old guys. They eat anything. Steak, potatoes, pasta, burgers, pizza, chicken. They're big guys. Not as big as you, but both over six feet. They don't want rabbit food."

"Are they both shifters?"

"Yeah, Andy is a cougar shifter. Harrison is a wolf shifter."

Okay. I can work with this. "How about salad, chili, and baked potatoes?"

Kendall makes the cutest snort. "Sure, Julia Child. Let's whip that right up."

"It's a simple meal to make. You need a bowl for the salad, a baking sheet for the potatoes and a pot for the chili. Takes about an hour and most of the time you're not doing anything but letting it cook."

"I thought chili was one of those take all day things?"

"Could be, but not the way I do it."

"Whatever you say, Jacques Cousteau."

"He was an ocean explorer, not a chef."

"Oh. He has a chef type name."

"Because it's French?"

"Yeah."

I can't help it. I laugh my ass off. I pull into the parking space next to Kendall's Mustang with brand new tires and rest my forehead on the steering wheel, my whole body shaking.

Kendall isn't laughing. She's looking at me with raised eyebrows. I stop laughing. Shit. Did I hurt her feelings?

"Hey, I'm sorry. It's a simple mistake to make, I guess. You're funny."

"I am? Really?" She sounds bewildered.

"Yeah. I think so."

"Okay."

"You don't think you're funny?"

"No one has ever said so. I'm pretty or perky or athletic. Short. Tiny."

"Well, you are those things, I guess. But you're funny and smart too. Kind. Caring." I undo my seat belt and lean toward her. "Sexy," I say, my voice low and rumbly. I can feel it in my chest.

Her pupils dilate as I close the distance between us. Our lips meet, and it's not a hungry kiss, but it's a thorough kiss. The goal isn't to turn each other on, it's to know one another. Our lips cling, our tongues dance, our breaths mingle. It is the best kiss of my life.

I feel dazed when I pull back, a feeling I think Kendall shares as she is slow to lift her lids.

Neither of us say anything. There are things I feel compelled to say, but it's crazy and if it is true, it's way too soon and nothing Kendall wants to hear, anyway.

Kendall's phone chimes, breaking the moment.

> Gage: Your car is done. You can pay using this link. Key under the seat. Please stop making out in my parking lot.

Kendall flushes a deep pink and looks toward the garage where Gage gives her a salute. She wiggles her fingers in a return wave.

"Um, we should exchange numbers, right?" I ask. Shouldn't we text and stuff? How else are we going to organize getting together?

"Yeah. What's yours? I'll put it in and text you. So you have mine."

I rattle off the number and give her my email address too.

My phone buzzes in my pocket. I pull it out and smile as I read Kendall's message.

> Kendall: I had fun. See you Friday.

I smile at the kissy face emoji she includes.

Before I can say anything, she jumps out of my Explorer and punches in the code to get in her Mustang. I have a magnificent view of her ass as she bends over to get the keys from under the seat. She catches me looking and gives a cheeky grin as she climbs in the seat. I lower the passenger window when she lowers her window once she starts her car.

"Don't you want to make sure your spare is in the trunk?" I ask.

"Nah. I trust them. I'll double check when I get home, but I know it's all good. Thanks for your help. I truly appreciate it."

I smile. The pleasure was all mine. Okay, not true. Judging by the yodeling, she had plenty of pleasure too. But it's been a great twenty-four hours. I can't believe how much has happened in such a brief span of time.

"You're welcome," I say. "Glad I could help. Reach out when you want. I'll touch base before Friday to coordinate for dinner."

"Sounds like a plan! See you!" With a jaunty wave, Kendall drives away and turns toward her home. I glance toward the garage. Gage is looking at me, and I lift my hand in a wave he returns with a nod. Good enough. I put my SUV in gear and pull out, turning the opposite way of Kendall.

Grabbing my container of stew and bag of dirty clothes out of the back, I lock up my truck and approach the barn. I climb the stairs to my apartment and hear everyone in there. Not solely my roommates, Brick and Stone Waller. Nope. There's also Carter, Mac, and Coach. Watching baseball. Great.

"Hey, Bedard. You've been gone all day. You must have gone out super early," Stone says when I open the door.

Coach's eyes have zeroed in on the stew container. He knows it's his mother's. He must realize this is the first time it's been in this apartment. Why else would I be bringing it in from outside? But the alternative is Coach knows I wasn't home last night. Damn.

"What's in the container? Did you bring us food?" Carter calls out from his spot on the couch.

I feel my face flush. I guess I will have to tell everyone about me and Kendall. Not the truth, of course, but our version of it.

"It's leftover beef stew," I say.

"Where'd you get leftovers?" Mac asks.

I look at Coach, and he lifts an eyebrow. I think he's enjoying this.

"Coach's mom made it," I say.

"Wait, why is she making you food and not me?" Trevor asks. "I've known her for years."

"I had dinner at her house last night. She sent some home with me."

"Why is it coming in now?" Brick asks. "Wait! Did you not come home last night?"

My face must look like a cherry tomato from how hard I'm blushing. Coach sits back, arms crossed, both eyebrows raised.

"Why did you have dinner at the Morgans? What's going on?" Carter asks.

Here it goes.

I open the fridge and bend to put the stew inside. "I went with Kendall. Then I stayed at her place."

If I was in a room full of humans, the fridge would have muffled most of my words. Unfortunately, I have to be surrounded by shifters with extraordinary hearing who didn't miss what I said.

Carter gasps. "Kendall? *My* Kendall?"

The proprietary tone of his voice raises my hackles. I stifle the growl, but my words still have a bite to them.

"No, *my* Kendall. We're seeing each other." I swear my bear does a fist pump and says, "Hell yes, she's ours!" I ignore him. But I agree with him. She's mine. I'm not even sharing her with my bear.

Carter stiffens. Crap. I hope this doesn't cause problems.

"When did this happen? How did this happen?" Carter turns to Coach. "Did you know about this?"

I poke my head back in the fridge. This is going to take a beer. Or twelve. I pop the top as I turn to face everyone and take a long sip.

"I worked with her class yesterday. We got to talking, decided we liked each other and to give dating a shot. She was having dinner with her family and invited me along as a thank you for working with her class. Went back to her place, watched TV, drank wine, and I slept over. In the guest room."

All of it is the truth. It's what we did today they don't need to know about.

Coach is grinning now.

"You're okay with this?" Carter asks Coach. "You're going to let him date Kennie?"

I shouldn't punch my landlord, especially since he's a friend, but it's becoming a tempting thought.

"It's not my place to approve or disapprove. Kennie's *your* best friend. You know she's going to do what she wants. I'd rather she date someone like Bedard than one of the losers from her past."

Talk about damning me with faint praise.

I shrug. "We're both single, and we understand each other. We'll see what happens."

"You like baseball, Bedard?" Coach asks.

Okay, we're coming out of left field now?

"Yeah, I played some as a kid. But as a Canadian, hockey will always come first."

"Good. The Philadelphia baseball team is having a Devil Birds night a week from Sunday. You're throwing out the first pitch." Coach takes a swig of his beer.

Way to change the subject. My teammates are excited. I'm hoping I don't embarrass myself.

Maybe my trepidation shows on my face because Coach quirks a grin. "If you want to practice, I can give you my cousin's phone number. He was a pitcher in college. He has a great arm."

"Andy?"

"Yeah, did you meet him?"

"No, not yet. But Kendall and I plan to cook dinner Friday and have him and Harrison over."

Carter makes a timeout gesture with his hands. "Whoa, hold up. You're getting Kendall Morgan to cook? Who are you and what have you done with my friend?"

Coach laughs. "Whatever he's doing, he's a miracle worker. Kennie avoids the kitchen unless it's getting ice cream or coffee. What are you cooking?"

"Chili and baked potatoes. Grab a loaf of bread and some bagged salad. Nothing fancy."

Coach rises from the couch. "This is getting too domestic. I'm going home. Invite me and Mallory over for dinner anytime if you don't kill Andy and Harrison. We'll bring wine."

We say our goodbyes, and I can sense Carter is biting his tongue.

"What?" I ask once Coach is gone.

Carter runs his hand over his face. "I'm surprised. I didn't think Kennie wanted to date anyone. She's been pretty adamant about not dating after her last relationship, and she wasn't going to date a shifter or an athlete ever again. This seems out of the blue."

I shrug. "I don't know what to tell you. We like each other. We click."

"You know she won't move to Canada, right?"

"Last time I checked, I was living in New Jersey," I say.

"For now. What if you get traded or when your career is done?"

My heart sinks. Am I being traded already? I thought I was doing well with the team.

"Carter, knock it off. Bedard, you aren't being traded. Breathe." Brick thumps my back, forcing me to exhale the breath I didn't realize I was holding.

"I don't know what to tell you. We're dating. We'll see where it goes. I don't think either of us is thinking about the future. I'm not looking to hurt her. I like her. A lot. Is this going to be a problem between us?" I wave my hand between the two of us like an idiot. We're guys. We don't talk about this shit. Not in a toxic masculinity kind of way because that's not cool, but in an "I'll knock you into the boards and settle it that way" kind of way.

"No problem," he says. "As long as you treat her right. She's like another sister to me. She's been through a lot, but it's not my place to tell."

I don't want to hear about her past. She'll tell me what she wants me to know. This isn't serious for either of us. At least, that's what we're telling ourselves. I fear it's going to be more serious for me than it is for her.

"Is there enough of the stew to share?" Mac asks.

I sigh. My plan was to get a few meals out of it. At least it's changing the topic.

"Yeah. But there's not enough to fill everyone. What else is there to go with it?"

As everyone goes to snag something to add to dinner and the stew reheats, I start my laundry. I wasn't expecting Carter's reaction. Maybe it was naïve on my part. I keep hearing about Kendall's bad previous relationships. I think by the time we reach our mid-twenties, most of us have a relationship or two in our past we'd rather forget. After the mess with Tabitha, I know I do. This isn't going to be another relationship mistake for either of us. We're going to have fun while it lasts, and when it's time to move on, we'll look back on this time together fondly. I need to remember this isn't real, even when it feels genuine.

12

KENDALL

I flop on my couch after Burke drives away and start counting down from five on my fingers. I've reached my last finger, which just so happens to be my middle one, when the knock sounds.

"Come in!"

Andy and Harrison walk through the door. Andy is giving me a big grin and wiggling his eyebrows. Harrison is a bit more sedate and carrying wine. They complement each other and it's beautiful. I want that someday.

"You da lay he whoooo?" my cousin warbles.

I look at him, blank faced. I get the joke he's trying to make, but if I act like I don't get it, then he tries to explain, and it makes him feel self-conscious. It's a way I've tortured him since we were kids.

"Because of the yodeling. We know you got laid—you da lay— but we don't know who he is—he who. Get it?" Andy looks over at Harrison for reassurance. Har pats his back consolingly.

I go to the kitchen to grab the corkscrew and wine glasses. I meet the guys at my breakfast bar and watch Harrison open the wine.

"So, what's up?" I ask as I take a sip of the yummy merlot Harrison poured.

"That's what I'm asking you about. Who was the hottie with you? Why did he yell out for cough drops? Did you cook for him?"

"Ha, ha, ha." I stick out my tongue. It's not that I *can't* cook. I'm not an idiot, I can read a recipe and follow directions. But I don't like to cook. It's boring. It's a lot of work for something gone too quickly. Maybe cooking with Burke will be more enjoyable. At least then I won't be eating alone. Hopefully, I can get Andy and Harrison to handle cleanup. That's the part I hate.

There is no stopping the slow grin spreading across my face. "That was Burke Bedard."

Andy gasps. "Burke Bedard who Liam coaches? Captain Wonderful of the Devil Birds? How did this happen?"

I shrug. "He's a nice guy, good looking, and has no plans to stick around. Perfect for a fling."

Harrison raising an eyebrow. "Since when do you do flings?"

I let out an irritated huff. "Since I picked a little piece of squirrel shifter shit whose goal was to use me for money. From now on it's physical. No emotions beyond liking the guy. Burke is great with kids, he has the respect of my brother, my family likes him, he's great in bed. He's light years ahead of squirrel shit."

Andy puts his arms around me and hugs me. Harrison joins our hug. I feel loved and safe.

After a moment, I squirm my way out from between them. They snuggle closer to each other. I want what they have. They are relationship goals.

"When you're done cuddling, I have stuff to tell you," I say.

That does the trick. Harrison turns and lifts his brows.

"Oh, yeah?" he asks in his deep, mellow voice. It's not as deep as Burke's but still rumbly. It's comforting.

"Yep. Burke and I are cooking dinner Friday night, and we wanted to invite you over."

I brace myself for the teasing and gagging that usually come along with talking about my cooking. But it doesn't come.

"That sounds nice," Andy says. "I'd like to meet him. What are we having?"

I wait a moment for the comments about stocking up on Tums or having Urgent Care on alert. When the guys wait for me to answer, my shoulders relax slightly. I didn't realize I was tense.

"Burke is going to teach me how to make a simple chili. We'll have baked potatoes, salad, and bread. I was hoping you guys could bring dessert?"

Stunned silence greets my request.

"You're learning to cook? Burke is teaching you? *And* you want us to meet him?" Andy asks.

"Yeah, I want you to meet him. He's a nice guy, and he'll be over here. It would be weird if you didn't meet. I suggested dinner. Our schedules are crazy. Friday night is one of the few times we can see each other. He had the idea of cooking. You guys know it's not that I'm incapable of cooking, right? I can make a frozen pizza or grilled cheese. I hate shopping and the prep and the dishes. It's a lot of work. I tried...before. It wasn't good enough."

I tried to be a good wife and make the little off-campus apartment a home for me and my ex when I was there. I lived there a few weeks in total since we eloped late in my semester, and I had to finish my classes. I skipped my graduation ceremony to move into the apartment and surprise him with a steak and potatoes meal. I overcooked the steak and my mashed potatoes were too milky. He dumped it in the trash, including the new dishes I had bought us. He had me order pizzas for him and his teammates instead. Using my credit card.

I blink rapidly. I am *never* crying over the jerk again.

"Oh, Ken," Andy says, wrapping me in a hug again. I squeeze him for a moment and then pull back. I grab a tissue to wipe my nose and drink some wine.

"Bring wine Friday night too, please. Whatever goes with chili. I may need to be tipsy."

Someone's phone dings. Andy's. He reads the text, raises his eyebrows, and tips it to show Harrison.

"What do you think?" Andy asks him.

"I guess we'll see." Harrison says.

"What's up?" I ask. I hate to be left out. Drove me nuts as a kid when I'd get left behind when my brother and cousins would go off to do "boy things," and it bugs me now when they have secrets and don't tell me.

"Your brother wants us to play catch with your boyfriend," Harrison says.

"What?!" I squeeze in to read the message.

> Liam: Devil Birds night in Philly next Sunday. Bedard throwing out first pitch. Make sure he doesn't suck.

> Andy: K

Andy's texting style is emojis, gifs, and abbreviations. Only place he's a man of few words.

"Are you going to help him?" I ask. I don't know if Burke is good at baseball or not. If he could use his hockey stick, I'm sure it would be fine, but throwing is risky. I don't want him to make a fool of himself.

"Yeah, if he wants it," Andy says. "Is he good with balls?"

I roll my eyes. Boys.

"He's good at using his stick, that's what I care about," I say.

Harrison gives me a high five. "Stick handling is very important. You want someone proficient with their stick. I'm happy for you."

Andy plops on my couch with his glass of wine, making sure he grabs my TV remote on the way. He turns on the baseball game and makes himself at home. Harrison sits next to him. I grab the three bags of Herr's potato chips I always keep in stock—rippled for me, sour cream and onion for Andy, and barbecue for Harrison. When we could never decide on one flavor, separate bags became a necessity. The things you do for love. With exquisite grace, I lower myself to the couch. Okay, I plopped too, but we're reframing it, like my yodel earlier.

"So, you like him?" Andy asks as he takes the bags of chips for him and Harrison.

I rest my head on his shoulder and sigh. "I do. I shouldn't, but I do."

I tell them about our plan and how there's no future for us. We want different things in life. We order pizza and watch baseball while we wait for it to arrive.

Locking up after we eat and they go back to their home next door, I think about texting Burke to see what he's up to. But I resist the temptation. I don't want to be clingy. I cringe at the thought of Burke thinking I'm the type of girl who becomes all needy once she has sex with a guy. No. I'll wait for him to contact me. The ball is in his court.

I go upstairs to my bedroom, sighing when confronted with the still-unmade bed and the scent of sexy times lingering in the air. No way do I have the energy to deal with the bed tonight. That can be a tomorrow project while I do my lesson plans. Instead, I wander into the guest room and sit on the bed Burke made when he got up this morning. Oh goodness, he's even a good house guest. Is there no end to his perfection? I pull out the pillow and hold it to my nose. I can smell the faint trace of shampoo and man. I go back to my room to change into my pjs, but I return to the guest room to sleep. On the same sheets Burke slept on last night. It's not the same as sleeping in his arms. I don't know if I'll ever get the chance. But for tonight, it will have to be enough.

Sunday morning, I wake with the sun shining in my face and an ache between my legs. I had been dreaming of waltzing with Burke across a sheet of ice. With his powerful arms holding me securely, we move together with grace. It's crazy because, first, I can't waltz and, second, I'm hopeless on the ice. But it was wonderful being in his arms. We somehow danced off the ice without me causing a catastrophe, and into my bedroom where we climbed into bed and made sweet love to one another all night long. I was about to experience an orgasm when I woke up, leaving me feeling doubly unsatisfied.

I throw back the sheets and get out of bed, and fifteen minutes later I'm munching on waffles hot from my toaster and scrolling through my phone.

Nothing much is going on in social media land. A girl I cheered with in high school has her hand held up to the camera to show off her engagement ring, her fiancé smiling at her with a loving expression. It's a pretty ring. I'm happy for them. Some friends from college posted pictures out at a club last night. Looks like it was at a local casino. Oh, it was a bachelorette party for Melanie. I didn't know she was engaged. They didn't call to see if I could join them. Whatever.

I didn't have any of those things. There was no engagement ring, just a pregnancy scare and a rush to get married. No bachelorette party, no bridal shower, not even a backyard BBQ reception. My last semester of college, I had online classes and spent a lot of my time at Kregg's school in Pennsylvania where he was finishing his senior baseball season. I'd go back to the apartment I shared with Randi the first few weeks we were married when he had away games I couldn't travel to.

The last two weeks of our brief marriage, he was home all the time in our tiny, crappy apartment I was trying to make into a home. He was missing baseball, angry about my trust fund, going out to get drunk and fuck other women. I was too ashamed to face my family, and we never came home for a party with my loved ones. There was nothing to celebrate. I had made an enormous mistake and had to figure out a way to escape. If my dad or brother knew what was going on, they would have killed Kregg. Logan and Uncle Mike would have made sure no one found his body.

Everyone knows I got married, but since it was over in a blink, I think it's one of those things people heard about but aren't sure if they should believe it. No way am I going to advertise that I was an idiot who married a cheating sociopathic squirrel shifter whose goal was to use me for money and sex. Let the world think rumors of my marriage were exaggerated.

I finish my waffles, rinse my plate, and put it in the dishwasher. I guess I'll start on my lesson plans for the week to get them out of the way. I want to spend the afternoon watching football. It's weird. My school bag isn't where I normally leave it. I search everywhere it could be—living room, bedroom, by the front door. I even check where it probably isn't—bathroom, kitchen—before jogging out to check my Mustang.

"Where the hell is it?" I say to the trees across the parking lot. They don't answer.

I walk back up my front steps into my house and look all around again in case I stashed it someplace weird, but it's nowhere to be found.

I sit on my couch and think back to Friday afternoon. Okay. It was raining. I was wet. As was my bag. Burke handed me his sweatshirt to wear. It smelled divine. I shiver in remembrance, not from any chill. That's it! I put my bag behind the driver's seat because I didn't want it dripping on my lap when I snuggled under his shirt. Damn it. I forgot all about it, and I need it for work.

I nibble on my lip. If I call Burke about my bag, is he going to think it's an excuse to talk to him? It's not, and we have plans to see each other on Friday. It's not like I need to invent a reason to talk to him. What the hell. I swipe my phone off the coffee table and open a text message to him.

> Me: Hey Burke. It's Kendall. I think I left my school bag in your car.

> Burke: Hi Kendall, I knew it was you. Let me go check, hold on.

Burke: I got it. Do you want me to run it over
to you?

> Me: No, I can't ask you to do that. Okay if I
> run by? I'll say hi to my brother and Mallory
> while I'm there. Maybe they'll feed me.

Burke: I'm doing meal prep today. I can
spare a portion of something for you. Can't
let you starve.

> Me: I can't take your food... Unless it's
> something I like. Lol.

Burke: When should I expect you?

> Me: About an hour?

Burke: See you then.

I take a quick shower and try to decide how cute I should look. Do I curl my hair and put on makeup? Ponytail and lip gloss? I don't want to look like this was a plan, but I don't want to show up in baggy sweats and a bare face looking like a schlub either.

In the end, I decide to blow dry my hair and put it in two French braid pigtails on either side of my head. Popping my lips in the mirror as I finish putting on pink lip gloss and mascara, I decide I look okay. I have on my green and white "Football is my Favorite Season" t-shirt Abby made me and a pair of jeans with the hems rolled. I slide into my black Converses, grab my keys, and I'm good to go.

The ride to Burke's place doesn't take long. I have my windows down to let in the refreshing late summer air. It would be a good day to sit with Mallory and Daphne on the balcony off the back of Mallory's house and gossip. We haven't hung out lately.

I turn into the long driveway leading to the converted barn and park next to Trevor's BMW. I tease him about having a lawyer's car. Everyone else is driving trucks or SUVs, and he has a sporty red BMW. It looks too nice to carry his stinky hockey gear. Maybe he

makes one of the other guys take it in their car as part of the arrangement for living here.

The barn doors for the rink are open, and I walk right in. Declan
and Sean are shooting pucks to Bridget, who's guarding the goal. I
know they all have cool hockey nicknames like Brick and Stone, but
I'm calling them by their first names. I watch them for a moment,
practicing some sort of set play. They're firing pucks at Bridget, and
she's stopping most of them. Crazy. Who volunteers to stand there
and have pieces of rubber shot at them in excess of ninety miles an
hour? I don't care how much padding you wear, that must hurt.
Granted, I spent years getting tossed into the air, flipping, and
hoping people caught me, all with a big smile on my face. I guess I
have a touch of sports insanity happening too.

I wave and continue walking toward the stairs. A peek into the
gym doesn't reveal Trevor. As much as I love the big goof, I hope I
don't run into him upstairs. I don't want to deal with any awkward-
ness. He's used to me having boyfriends, but it's never been his
roommate or one of his teammates. The guys were strictly my
boyfriends. They didn't have a connection to Trev other than
through me. Burke and Trev have a relationship of their own, adding
a whole other layer to this situation.

I enter the common area on my way to Burke's apartment and
am surprised it's empty. Burke must have heard me because he pokes
his head out of his open apartment door and greets me with a smile.

"Hey there." He backs up to let me enter.

"Hi," I say as I walk in and stop in the living room. My bag is on a
stool at the breakfast counter. Do I grab it and go? Should I have
hugged him as I walked in? I'm not good at this fake dating stuff.

He runs his hand down my back as he passes me to go into the
kitchen. It feels like an affectionate caress.

"Want some iced tea?" He takes a pitcher out of the fridge. It
looks like he's in the middle of cooking stuff.

I nibble on my bottom lip, unsure of what to do. I guess have a
glass of iced tea?

"Um, sure. Thanks. Is it sweetened?" I climb onto the stool next to where my bag rests.

"Yeah, it's extra sweet. Turns out Brick and Stone have a southern grandmother and it's her iced tea recipe. It's almost like drinking syrup."

He passes the glass to me. "Can you sweeten tea with maple syrup?" I ask.

Burke looks at me like I asked if he'd boink Shifty. A mix of horror, repulsion, and a smidge of curiosity. "Why would you?"

I know maple syrup is more precious than plasma to Canadians, but it's not that crazy of a question.

I shrug. "To make it sweet. People use honey in tea. Why not maple syrup? Like Canadian sweet tea."

He looks at me blankly for a moment and then runs from the kitchen to what I assume is his bedroom. In a moment, he is racing back with his laptop, a notebook, and a pen.

Taking the stool next to mine, he fires up his laptop.

"What are you doing?" I ask as he keys in his password.

"Research."

I tilt my head in confusion. "On what?"

"If you can use maple syrup to make iced tea."

"Why don't you make a pot and see?" I ask.

I thought it was a reasonable question, but again with the horrified look.

"What?" I ask, trying not to be defensive.

"I'm a scientist. I can't do things willy-nilly. There's the scientific method to be considered." He's saying this in what I imagine is his patient science teacher voice...and it's hot. I feel my panties getting damp from picturing him in a lab coat, lighting a Bunsen burner.

"Well, Mr. Bedard," I say over my shoulder as I walk into the kitchen and start opening cabinets until I find a mug. I have to stand on tiptoes to reach. "Today you're going to take a walk on the wild side."

I fill the mug with water from the tap and put it in the

microwave, hitting the buttons for it to heat for ninety seconds. I find the box of tea bags in the pantry and grab two, along with the precious jug of maple syrup.

"But... but..." Burke is practically apoplectic at my actions.

"What?"

"How will you know the temperature of the water?" he asks.

I shrug. "It will be hot. Good enough."

The microwave dings, and I take the steaming mug of water out. I unwrap the two tea bags and drop them in to steep.

"Why two tea bags?" he asks. So many questions with this guy.

"This way it's more concentrated. If we are pouring it over ice, then it will get diluted. If we have it concentrated, then when the ice melts, the tea won't be as watered down." I reach across the counter to poke him in his muscled bicep. "How's that for science?"

I decide to let the tea steep for another minute and grab two plastic tumblers from the cabinet and fill them with ice. I remove the tea bags and toss them in the trash and unscrew the top from the syrup. I pick it up to pour some in and see the label says, "Ben Bedard Maple Syrup."

"Is this your family?" I ask.

"My grandfather. He makes it."

"Is it okay if I use it?" If it's a precious family thing, I don't want to take it. I assumed it would be something from the store.

He gives me the cutest half grin. "Go ahead. I know where I can get more."

I find the silverware drawer, pull out a teaspoon, fill it with the rich amber syrup, and stir it in the mug of hot tea. Aromatic notes of the black tea and maple fill the air. I pour some of the mug into each tumbler. The ice crackles as the hot liquid streams over it. I pick mine up and swish it to mix the tea with the ice and take a sip. Burke is waiting for my reaction before trying his.

"It's good," I assure him. "Try it."

He rounds the counter to stand next to me and picks up his glass to take a cautious sip. I swear he's acting like he's at a wine tasting, letting it rest on his tongue and looking to the ceiling in contemplation before swallowing. He swirls his glass and sniffs it before taking a longer sip.

He puts his tumbler on the counter and takes mine out of my hand. He rests his firm backside against the counter and spreads his legs slightly. He grabs my hand and guides me to the vee of his legs and rests his hands on my hips.

I look up into his deep brown eyes and swoon a bit when he whispers, "You, Kendall, are beautiful chaos."

My heart skips a beat. And my stomach plummets. I pull back out of his hold. I can see his brow furrowing in confusion, but he lets me go.

I put on my cheer smile and laugh. I know it's bitter, but I hope he doesn't.

"You wouldn't believe how many times I've been told that! Well, the chaos part. Beautiful too, because, hello..." I wave my hands in front of me mockingly. "But I think you're the first person to use them together."

I cross to look out the window at the woods in the distance. If my cougar would cooperate, I'd shift and avoid this conversation, but she's still being a sourpuss. I guess I may as well get it over with.

I turn back around. Burke is still watching me. Waiting, I guess. Okay, here we go.

"No doubt Liam and Trev told you stuff about me because they are gossipy biddies. I'm impulsive. I don't take things seriously. I flit from guy to guy and my relationships never last. They're right. I have a lousy track record with guys. My last relationship was my senior year of college, and it was a disaster. I haven't dated since then. My judgment in men sucks. You seem like a good guy, and my family adores you."

Left unsaid is the *Please don't hurt me*.

Burke nods. "I have my own dating disasters too. I think it's hard to get to our ages without at least one. I haven't dated for months, not since breaking up with my ex. She cheated on me because I'm boring. She wanted to live in Toronto and hit the clubs. I love my hometown. I'm happy being home or at the rink. Once in a while, I go fishing with my dad. I wasn't enough for her."

How anyone could think Burke is anything other than wonderful is beyond me. I could imagine us cuddling on the couch talking about students. Sharing stories about coaching our teams. We won't have that because his couch and his school and his team are in Canada and mine are...here. Is it possible to mourn a future that will never happen? It must be because I am.

Standing, Burke walks over and stops in front of me. He holds out his hand, and I put mine in it. His thumb rubbing over my knuckles raises goosebumps on my arms.

"Coach and Carter have said stuff, but it's not what I see. Remember, I'm a scientist, and I need proof. I believe what I see more than what I'm told. What I see is a woman who is smart." He leans and presses a kiss on my temple.

"Kind." That kiss lands on my forehead.

"Funny." Tip of my nose gets a kiss. My breath is hitching, and tears burn behind my eyes. I blink so fast it's like being in a nightclub with strobe lights, but they don't fall.

"And sexy." My lips are the lucky recipients of a kiss that is thorough, but not demanding. My hands rise to rest on his strong shoulders as I rise on my toes to meet his lips better. He pulls his lips away and rests his forehead against mine. His quickened breaths brush my cheeks.

"You're beautiful chaos only because I'm methodical. But sometimes methodical needs chaos, Kendall, and I—"

"Oh, sorry!" Trevor's standing like a deer in headlights in the doorway to the apartment.

The oven chooses that moment to beep, and I pull out of Burke's arms. He pulls on navy blue oven mitts and pulls out a pan of what I assume is chicken and sets it on top of the stove. Efficiently, he puts foil over the chicken and somehow tents it like I've seen my Mom do at Thanksgiving.

"It needs to rest," he tells me.

I nod. I know nothing about cooking chicken other than if you do it wrong, you'll get sick. I'll take the scientist's word for it.

"Hey Trev, what's up?" I say, since he's still in the doorway.

"Nothing. I didn't know you were here, Kennie," he says.

I gesture to my school bag. "I forgot my school bag in Burke's car Friday, and I need it to do my lesson plans for the week."

"Oh, okay." Trevor looks back and forth between me and Burke, who is now standing next to me at the counter sipping his tea. "Well, I don't want to keep you..."

"No, we're good. I'm going to grab my bag and go," I say.

Burke looks at me with a furrowed brow. "I thought I was going to cook for you?"

I stretch to give him a quick kiss on his bearded jaw. The whiskers tickle my lips.

"Another time. I should get home and start laundry before the football game. I'll text you."

Scooting behind Burke, I run my hand along his back and give his firm ass a pat. I grab my bag off the stool and walk toward Trevor.

"So, what's up with you Trev? It's been forever since we've talked." I smile over my shoulder at Burke as I leave his apartment. I guess it's a good thing Trevor interrupted us because I was about five seconds from climbing Burke like a tree and retreating to his bedroom.

"Nothing much, lots of practice, working out, hanging with these guys," he says.

I'm not expecting Trevor to follow me to my car, but he does.

"Hockey is going well? You guys are gelling?" I ask.

"Yeah, it's good."

He looks up toward the apartments and steps closer to me.

"Have you told him about..." He holds up two hands in front of his chest and makes bucked teeth.

It takes a moment, but I realize he's making a squirrel gesture, and I laugh uncontrollably.

"Why are you whispering and since when do we talk in charades?" I ask.

Trev leans in. "Polar bears have incredible hearing."

"Really? I didn't know." I guess I need to read Ro's polar bear book sometime.

"They do. So...did you?"

"Kinda. Not the details like being married, just my last relationship was a disaster. This is casual."

Trevor scoffs. "What I walked into was not casual. I know you can do casual, but I'm not sure about him."

I open my car door and toss my bag in. Leaning my butt against my car, I cross my arms.

"He can do casual. It's all we want from this. Have fun. Keep the feelings in check. This is temporary. It's for hockey season, if that long."

"Kennie, he's our captain. We rely on him. Don't break his heart."

I don't believe it. He's *my* best friend, and he's worried about Burke.

"Yeah, that's me. I'm a femme fatale. Let's make sure we protect the delicate polar bear." I'm struggling to keep the hurt out of my voice.

He reaches out to rub my arm soothingly, but I jerk out of reach.

Trevor drops his hand and sighs.

"Ken, I know you wouldn't hurt him on purpose, but let's face it, you don't have a great track record. Hell, your marriage didn't last two months."

The statement hits me harder than any punch Kregg would have thrown if given the chance. I know people think I'm impulsive and flighty. I got married on a whim and got divorced just as easily. But do they think it didn't affect me? That I don't care? Of course, that's what they think because I never told them the truth. Well, screw them.

"No worries. He knows the score and I do too. Your captain and your precious hockey team will be fine."

I slide behind the wheel and hit the button to start my car.

"Glad to know where your loyalties lie, Trevor. See you later."

"Ken..." he says, but I don't hear what else he has because I punch the gas and take off down the driveway.

I wipe the tears off with the back of my hand when I turn onto the main road. I thought I knew what people thought of me, but having it confirmed hurts. Whatever. Let them think that. Better they think that than find out how weak I was. I don't want anyone to know that. I feel enough shame already.

13

BURKE

I wipe my forehead against my shoulder. It's still warm in the early days of fall, but the late afternoon sun shining down on me at the ballpark in Philadelphia isn't why I'm sweating. I hope I don't screw this up. Of course, I don't want to look like a loser, but more importantly, I don't want to do anything to embarrass the team. As captain, I'm the face of the team and have been doing a lot of interviews and other media appearances before our first preseason game in a few days.

"Throw the ball to me," Mark Ryan, catcher for the Philadelphia baseball team, offers. "You don't have to do anything fancy. Don't stress." We're in the bullpen before the game where I'm throwing the ceremonial first pitch in front of a crowd of over thirty thousand people. I've never been in front of a crowd this large. Even the championship hockey games I played in when I was younger weren't half the size.

"Yeah, that would be great, thanks," I say. I got to meet the players and do batting practice with the team. I hit some balls. Logan Morris is here taking pictures. Hopefully, I can get some shots printed. My parents would love them.

I pitch some balls and Mark catches them easily.

"You've played before?" he asks, throwing the ball back to me. I catch it in my glove and prepare to throw again.

"Yeah, as a kid. But I'm Canadian. Hockey was my focus."

"You're going to be fine. Ready to head out?"

"Ready as I'm ever gonna be," I say.

The crowd cheers when I'm announced and make my way to the pitcher's mound. I stop right before it and wave to the crowd. I'm wearing a Philadelphia baseball jersey unbuttoned over my Devil Birds t-shirt. Gotta rep both teams.

I look up to the area reserved for the team and see my team-mates and Kendall. She jumps up and down, giving me a big wave. I swear I hear her yell, "Go Burke!" over the noise of the crowd. Maybe it's her cheerleader superpower? I'm glad her smile is one of her real ones and not the fake cheerleader smile she uses when she's trying to hide how she's feeling. I understand why she does it, but I hate it. I hate that anything hurts her. I want to protect her from everything and make her life better. She deserves good things.

I'm glad she's here. I want her at all of my games. I want her at everything. We cooked dinner together on Friday, and it was wonderful. I want more of those nights. I wish it could be our future.

Andy and Harrison are good guys, and I'm glad Kendall has them next door. Especially since I can't be her next-door neighbor. Actually, no, I don't want to be her neighbor. I want to live with her. I want this weekend to be our life, and now my bear wants to let out a growl. I take a deep breath to center myself. I can't screw this up. Kendall and what can never happen can't steal my focus. I'm here to be the face of the team, the captain they need to lead them. That's what is important, and I refuse to be selfish, longing for things I can't have.

My pitch makes it to Mark without hitting the dirt. Okay, good. It looked like a strike to me. I walk to home plate and pose for pictures, then retrieve the ball. The Atlanta players are preparing to bat.

A blond guy in an Atlanta jersey calls out from the on-deck circle, "Tell Kendall that Kregg Beaumont said hi."

I don't know who he is to Kendall, but I nod in acknowledgement.

Someone from the team staff guides me back to the area where they set up the Devil Birds. I stop along the way to sign autographs and take pictures with folks. It's fun. This is my first time feeling famous. It's weird.

"Oh, my word! They make hockey players big, don't they?" A petite woman I'd guess to be in her early 50s like my mom, but trying too hard to look late 20s, clings to my arm as she hands her phone to my guide to take a picture. Her bright red nails dig into my bicep slightly. It's not painful, but it's...disconcerting. I feel like she's trying to lay claim to me.

"We don't have polar bears like you in Ohio," she says in her syrupy-sweet southern belle voice.

The staff member hands back her phone, and I pull my arm free.

"Yeah, polar bear shifters prefer more northern places. Enjoy the game." I give a polite smile and try to walk away. She follows and grabs my arm.

"Oh! I will! My son is making his major league debut. I am extremely proud!" She gestures to the black t-shirt that's tight on her ample chest, with rhinestones stretching across it, spelling out, "Nuts Abuot Beaumont #37."

I feel like a creep taking a long look, but I had to confirm the misspelling.

"Wow, congratulations. I hope he has a long and wonderful career."

"Thank you, sweetie." She gives a toss of her head, and her brassy blonde ponytail hanging out the back of her Atlanta team ball cap swings like a clump of straw. Nothing like the shining sea of golden waves streaming down Kendall's back. "I'm gonna follow you. I want to say hello to a friend in your section."

"Oh. Okay." I don't know what to say. I'm assuming her son was the guy on the other team who said to tell Kendall hi. I guess it's okay, and I don't want to be rude.

We're about twenty feet away from my section, and Kendall is like a ray of sunshine smiling at me. Suddenly, her face pales and goes slack.

My companion scampers away from me and screeches, "Kendall Beaumont! As I live and breathe! How wonderful you're here for Kregg's big day!"

I don't know how she did it, but the lady is in our section and pulling Kendall into a hug before I've taken another step. Kendall stands there like a statue, rigid and unmoving. Everyone around her appears to be in shock, but her mother recovers first and pulls Kendall away, putting her arm around her. It's weird. The three women look strangely alike—petite, blonde ponytails streaming out the back of their hats, wearing t-shirts and jeans. But where Kendall and Faith look naturally beautiful and like the mother and daughter they are, the stranger looks like she's trying to emulate their effortless beauty but missing the mark. Her hair is too brassy and dry, her clothes too tight, her makeup too harsh.

Faith stands in front of Kendall, giving off a protective vibe. "I don't think we've met. I'm Faith Morgan, Kendall's mother."

At last, I reach our seats. Will and Liam are flanking Faith and Kendall.

"Oh Faith, lovely to meet you finally! I'm Velveeta, Kendall's other mama!" She pulls Faith into a hug.

Stone is at the end of the row, near where I'm standing. "Velveeta? Like the cheese?" he asks.

Brick shushes him as she nibbles on popcorn and watches in fascination.

Velveeta's statement seems to have snapped Kendall out of her stupor. She pulls her mother back and steps in front. "You were never a mama to me."

"Well, I was your mother-in-law!" Velveeta screeches. Heads are turning our way. The people around us are snapping out their cell phones at record speed.

"Unfortunately, you were. But you aren't now." Kendall takes a deep, shaky breath. Her face is still pale, and she's trembling. What is going on? "Please go back to your seat and enjoy the game."

"Oh, but we have oodles to talk about!" Velveeta reaches out her skinny little hand with bright red nails and grabs for Kendall, knocking Faith back into her seat.

In a flash, Kendall has shifted into her cougar and is crouched, snarling. It's like the entire stadium goes silent, waiting to see what happens next. People don't shift in public.

"You're a crazy bitch! No wonder Kregg left you!" Velveeta screams. She's three rows away now, and her ponytail is puffed up and twitching up and down. Like a tail. Then she's gone.

As suddenly as she shifted, Kendall is back to herself, cowering on the cement and sobbing. I try to go to her, but Liam scoops her into his arms and climbs over seats to take her into the suite attached to our seating area.

"Married? She's married?" I hear one of my teammates say, and it hits me. Kendall was married. She's twenty-four. When the hell was she married? Why didn't she tell me? I turn and look at the field. That guy was her husband? Ex-husband, I hope. A wave of nausea sweeps over me at the thought of her still being married, making me the other man.

I follow them into the suite. Liam and Will are speaking in low voices. Kendall is sobbing in the restroom, and Faith is trying to soothe her.

"What's going on?" I ask.

Liam shrugs. "No idea. She was fine. That woman, who I guess is her former mother-in-law, says hello. She shifts, and now she's having a breakdown."

Andy and Harrison rush in.

"Where's Kennie?" Andy asks. They are both breathing hard. They must have run up however many stairs to get there.

Will inclines his head toward the bathroom. Harrison strides over and knocks on the door.

"Kendall, sweetie. Andy and I are here. Can we come in?"

The door cracks open, and they go in. I want to follow, but Faith comes out and shakes her head.

"Let them talk to her. She wants us to go back to our seats and enjoy the game."

"She's upset. How can I leave her?" I ask.

Teagan joins us. "Bedard, you are the face of the Devil Birds. We need you to step up, refocus the team, and let this fade for now. Please go back and watch the game. She'll be okay."

I slump my shoulders as I turn to go to my seat. I've spent the past two nights holding Kendall, laughing with her, watching reruns of The Office, making love, sleeping beside her, waking up with her head resting on my chest. I should be holding her now. Not walking away from her.

"No. I'm not leaving her."

"Bedard, we have this handled," Coach says. "You're team captain. You're needed out there."

I shake my head. "There are three alternate captains sitting there. Their job is to handle things when I'm not there. I think they can watch a baseball game without me."

"Burke?" I hear Kendall call from the bathroom.

I lay my hand on the door since I can't touch her. "Yeah, baby, I'm here."

Like there's anyplace else I'd be.

Andy opens the door, and I slip in. This restroom is nice, but not big enough for three big shifter males. Harrison is embracing Kendall, but she slips from his arms and into mine when I enter. She burrows into my chest and sobs. I rub her back and make shushing sounds. Not to quiet her but to calm her, like white noise or waves on the beach.

The guys slip out, and we remain in the bathroom. I can hear the

Star-Spangled Banner and the roar of the crowd as the first inning starts.

I feel it coming and step back. Kendall shifts again. Her cougar is beautiful, with tawny fur and a sleek muscled body. She looks confused and scared crouched on the floor, and it breaks my heart.

Crouching down, I lay a hand against her head. She presses her cheek into my palm. "You're okay, Kendall. Everything is okay. You're safe. Can you shift back?"

I'm worried about her. Shifting twice in a matter of minutes has to be painful and exhausting.

She nods her regal head and closes her eyes. They're gold when she's in her cat form. I miss the blue. She shifts back to her human form. I sit down and pull her onto my lap to cradle her against my chest. I'm not sure how long we sit there. The only sound is Kendall's hitching breaths as they gradually become more regular. My hand strokes up and down her spine in slow, steady strokes. I'd pick a better location and a happier reason, but I could do this for the rest of my life, given the chance.

There's a gentle rap on the door, and Faith's soft voice comes through. "Kendall?"

"You can come in, Mom," Kendall says.

Faith opens the door and looks around until she sees us on the floor. My back is against the wall and my knees are up to create a cradle for Kendall to rest in. Faith's eyes, identical to her daughter's, get watery and she puts a hand over her heart.

"Oh, honey, what happened?"

She kneels next to us and puts a hand on Kendall's knee.

Kendall lifts her head from my chest and reaches out to hug her mom. I now have two Morgan women in my lap, and if Will comes in, I think I'm going to be a dead man and maybe a polar-bear-skin rug in his den.

They're both crying now, and I'm just sitting there. I don't know where to put my hands or how to comfort them so I stay still.

"She surprised me," Kendall says. "I thought she hurt you when she pushed you, and I reacted. I'm sorry." She lets out another hiccuping sob. "Is Liam mad at me?"

Faith brushes hair out of Kendall's face. "Oh, honey, no. He's worried about you. Mallory wants to go squirrel hunting."

My chuckle jostles them like they are in a lifeboat, riding gentle waves.

Kendall sighs. "I didn't know Kregg was going to be here. If I had, I'd have stayed home."

"Kregg Beaumont is your ex-husband?" I ask.

Wary blue eyes look up at me. "Yeah. Why?"

"When I was leaving the field, he said to tell you hello."

Kendall is off my lap in a shot and is retching into the toilet. I'm dumbfounded and sit there in my cluelessness, but Faith springs into action, holding Kendall's ponytail out of the way and rubbing her back while murmuring soothing sentiments. I don't know what else to do. I rise, pull some paper towels from the dispenser, and run them under cold water. After wringing them out, I offer them to Faith, who takes them with a soft smile.

"Do you want to go home, honey?" Faith asks when Kendall sits back and wipes her face.

She nods. "Yeah."

"I'll tell your dad," Faith says as she stands.

When the door clicks behind her, I say, "I'm coming with you."

Shaking her head emphatically, Kendall says, "No! You have to stay!"

"No, I don't. This is just a baseball game. You need me."

"Your team needs you. Please stay. I want to go home and be alone. I'm exhausted."

She's standing now but weaving slightly on her feet. I wrap my arms around her, in part to help her remain upright, but mostly for my own comfort.

"I don't think you should be alone," I say.

"Andy and Harrison are next door if I need them. Please. Stay." Pleading blue eyes meet mine. "For me."

Denying Kendall is something I don't think I'll ever be able to do. I sigh. "Okay. But I'm coming by in the morning."

The sweet smile she gives me makes my heart ache. "I hope so."

When I lean down to kiss her, she puts her hand on my face.

"Dude, I was retching in the toilet five minutes ago. I am not kissable."

"You're always kissable to me, but I'll concede this time." I press a kiss to her forehead as a compromise.

Her dad hugs her when we leave the bathroom and shakes my hand.

"Thank you, Burke." The words were simple, but I could tell the wealth of emotion they carried. I know how helpless I feel, and Kendall isn't my daughter who I've protected from the day she was born.

"Let's get you home, honey. Wendy is going to take us the back way."

Nodding, Kendall gives me a quick hug and then slips out an unobtrusive door in the back of the suite with her parents.

I return to the stands and slide down in my seat as much as a six foot six polar bear shifter can. The second inning is about to start. I can't believe how much happened in such a short amount of time.

Liam is in the seat in front of me and puts his arm around Mallory, pressing a kiss to the crown of her head.

Mallory twists in her seat to face us. "Are we not going to talk about the elephant in the room?"

Jake groans. "Oh god, no elephants, we already had a cougar."

Teagan elbows him from her seat beside him.

"Her shirt!" Mallory gestures to her chest and there is no way in hell I'm following her movements. Sure, Coach is cool with me dating his sister, but if I check out his girlfriend's boobs, I'm skating never-ending laps every practice for a week.

"It was spelled wrong!"

"Yes!" Daphne cries from the seat beside her. "Rhinestone 101, triple check your spelling."

Andy leans forward. "What did you expect? He is dumb as a post. He shifted into his squirrel and went down the vent pipe to break into a sorority house to steal panties. The pipe was for the stove exhaust, and he got trapped. He shifts into his human and is in this super tight space, calling out for help. The sorority girls thought the house was haunted. They got him out, and he got suspended for a few games. He could have cost us our season."

"Who?" I ask. I'm lost.

"Her ex-husband. His name is Kregg Beaumont. He got called up to play for Atlanta. This is his debut MLB game."

As if on cue, Kendall's ex is called up to bat. The announcer says it's his debut and that he's a squirrel shifter.

Harrison stands and holds out a hand to Andy. "We need beer for this fiasco. Burke, want one?"

I nod and watch them walk off.

Turning back to Coach and Carter, I ask, "He's a shifter? Playing in the major leagues?" I know a few shifters have cracked pro team sports like baseball or cricket where there's no physical contact. And they are small shifters like raccoon or foxes, where their shifter doesn't give them advantages like strength or speed. I haven't heard of squirrel shifters playing. There aren't a lot of them around.

I'm fascinated a cougar shifter would choose to be with a squirrel shifter. I don't want to be judgmental, but in mixed shifter relationships, predator and prey matches aren't common. There's an imbalance. Is that why they broke up?

At the crack of the bat, I turn my attention to the field to see Beaumont run to first base. Good for him. I know I can't wait for my first game, my first goal, our first win.

Our seats are along the third base line with a stellar view of the field. From somewhere toward the outfield, I hear, "That's my baby!"

A mass "Aww" travels through the stadium like a wave. It's sweet. I could imagine my mom doing something similar.

"Speaking of babies," Daphne says, "even though mine is the size of a grape, it makes me have to pee all the time. Come to the ladies' room with me, Mallory?"

They head into the suite. I have no idea why they both needed to go, I assume to gossip.

"Yeah," Carter picks up our conversation where it left off. "He was a college teammate of Andy and Harrison. Andy brought him home for Thanksgiving. Him and Kennie hit it off. They were married by Easter and split up a couple of weeks after graduation. Married six weeks total." He shrugs. "That's Kennie. Fall fast, burn out faster. She's always flitting from boyfriend to boyfriend. I love her, but she doesn't take it seriously."

I look at her brother and cousin sitting in front of me, and they nod.

That's not the Kendall I know. Yeah, we said we were fake dating, but all the time we've spent together so far…it felt real. It felt like we were a couple who had friends that were couples too and weeknight routines. It felt domestic and sexy and *right*. And Kendall didn't seem bored, didn't seem like a cougar in a cage at the zoo, pacing back and forth, desperate for a way out. She didn't seem like a woman who was going to take a blow torch to my heart, set it on fire, watch it burn to ash, then walk away.

Kendall was—is—steady and loyal. To her friends, her family, even to me, and she's known me all of a hot minute. The Kendall I know watches out for her friends' feelings, loves her students, and takes her responsibilities so seriously she's willing to fake date a man to keep everyone from setting her up and distracting her from her purpose, her goals.

I swallow hard and nod, turning my attention back to the game because I don't want to talk about Kendall's short romantic attention span or what a fool I am. Now I understand why everyone was worried about us dating. They were afraid I'd get *my* heart broken, not that I'd break Kendall's.

Stone nudges me with his elbow. "Are you sure she's okay? Why did she shift? I've never seen someone do that before."

Carter laughs, and I want to punch him.

"Oh, she's fine," he says. "She was just wound up seeing her ex-mother-in-law. It was unexpected, and Kendall can be extra emotional sometimes."

Everyone keeps saying these things, but this doesn't sound like the Kendall I know. Maybe I'm naïve, and she is flaky and emotional and doesn't take things seriously. But that's not the woman I've seen. Is she putting on an act for me? Or are *they* not seeing the real her? Maybe she isn't showing them her real self? I guess I'll have to wait until she's ready to talk to me. Until then, I'm watching a baseball game and putting on a cheerful face. Kendall isn't the only one who can hide behind a fake-ass smile.

When Atlanta gets another man on base, Beaumont advances to second. The next batter hits the ball and Kendall's ex takes off toward third. It's a shallow fly ball, and the shortstop catches it. They trap Beaumont between second and third in a rundown.

Someone nearby has the radio broadcast of the game playing. "Rundowns are one of Beaumont's weaknesses," the first announcer says.

His booth partner responds. "That they are, Scott. Probably because he's a squirrel shifter."

That makes our section laugh. It's playing out on the field. Like a squirrel on the road who can't decide which way to run. Beaumont gets tagged out by the second baseman, ending the inning.

Through the rest of the game, I keep checking my phone in case Kendall has reached out. I'm anxious to see her in the morning, to talk to her, to know she's okay, and to help in any way I can. Logically, I know she doesn't owe me an explanation. I told her the basics about Tabitha, but not that I had considered asking her to marry me.

After the game, we sign autographs and pose for selfies as we head back to the bus. Some people try to ask about Kendall shifting, but everyone deflects those questions. It's no one's business. An eternity later, we get on the bus to take us back home. I climb in and take a seat at the back because I want to be alone, but Carter plops into the seat next to me.

I rest my head against the window with a sigh. Carter talks incessantly, but I don't listen. Eventually, he shuts up and starts playing a game on his phone. We get dropped off at The Nest. Since I have my car there, I give the excuse I'm getting something from the locker room to be left behind.

I change into workout gear and go to a practice rink. It's cool with a pristine sheet of ice. I'm wearing sneakers but walk out onto the ice and slide across it. I go to center ice and drop to my knees. I'm wearing navy sweatpants, and the chill and dampness of the ice seep through. It's wonderful. I bend forward and put my palms on the ice. Taking a deep breath, I close my eyes and shift to my polar bear.

This is what I need. The freedom to be my bear and enjoy the cold. New Jersey is a nice enough place, but it is still warm in early October. Too warm for my bear to be comfortable. Back home, I could go to the rink any time in the summer and get cool. I had other polar bears around. We could go out on the local lake or drive up north and shift. I'm not comfortable enough to do that here. I lay flat on my stomach and rest my cheek on the ice. I close my eyes and inhale what feels like the first deep breath I've taken in weeks.

This is the time I've needed, in my element, to think through everything going on. Not just with Kendall, but with the team, whether I can be the leader they need, how I can help back home and give them what they need. If I'm not there, will the kids still train hard enough to win? Who will boost their spirits when they lose? Will they forgive me for being selfish and abandoning them to chase my own dreams? They need hockey to keep them focused and out of trouble. I know all too well what happens when young people aren't kept occupied. I can't let another tragedy happen.

I'm not sure how much time has passed when the door to the rink opens. I may have dozed off. I didn't bother to turn on the lights when I came in. The dim security lights illuminating the ice are all I need. Maybe if I stay still, they won't notice me. A huge polar bear sized lump in the middle of a sheet of ice is easy to overlook. I'm sure I blend in.

No such luck.

Declan Mackenzie stands at the boards, looking at me. "You okay, Burke?"

I grunt.

"I don't speak polar bear. Is that a yes?"

I raise my rump in the air and use my back legs to scoot me across the ice.

"I guess it is. Okay if I join you?"

I give a big ursine huff of resignation, and he slides out. I open my eyes and see he's added a hoodie and is wearing his padded hockey shorts to be able to sit on the ice more comfortably. I knew he was smart.

"I assume you want to be alone, but I'm worried about you. I'll leave you be in a bit. Honestly, I wanted to chill out too. Pun slightly intended."

My low grumble acknowledges his statement.

"You're worried about Kendall?"

I grunt.

"Me too. Spontaneous shifting isn't normal. She wasn't expecting it, and she didn't control it. I think it scared her."

That's not something I'd considered. I've been focusing on her being okay. I didn't think about the shifting itself. Mac is right. We control our shifts. In the past, shifters who couldn't were a danger to us all and were hidden away from human society. We couldn't reveal the secret existence of shifters. Now it's not a secret, but uncontrolled shifting is dangerous. Not only for bystanders, but for the shifter too.

"I'm assuming she doesn't have a history of it, or they wouldn't let her teach. I don't think she'd hurt her students, but it could scare them."

Oh crap, something I hadn't considered. She spontaneously shifted in front of thousands of people. There's no sweeping it under the rug. Is she going to have trouble with her school? She loves teaching. She loves her students. It would break her heart if she wasn't in her classroom.

"Good job throwing out the first pitch. Glad it was you and not me. I've never played baseball. I'd throw it, and it would do some sort of weird bounce in front of the plate, and I'd look like a loser. Would have to go back home in shame." He leans back on his hands and stretches his legs out in front of him. I guess he's trying to get comfortable. He's massive, bigger than me, around six foot nine and muscular. Not as bulky. He's leaner than I am. But he's not lean. He's solid. I wouldn't want to mess with him on the ice.

"Other than hockey, I didn't play team sports. I ride horses. It's what I'll do when I'm done with hockey. Go back home, have a stud farm, breed horses. Coach riders."

I lift my head and study him. What does he ride? Clydesdales?

"I ride Friesians. Big black horses. Not a draft horse like a Clydesdale, but sturdy. Good for dressage. Once I filled out and put on all this muscle, I stopped with the cross-country. Didn't want to put a strain on the horse's joints with jumping."

Holy shit, can he read minds?

"Yes. But I rarely do."

My jaw falls open in shock and Mac cracks up.

"I'm taking the piss! I don't really read minds, but I'm intuitive. My mother is a witch, and while I can't cast spells like she and my sister can, I'm sensitive to emotions around me. I'm observant. Just because I'm quiet doesn't mean I don't pay attention."

I need to remember not to play poker with him.

He winks. "I'm not good at poker. Or I could be bluffing. Truly, people are predictable for the most part. You can direct conversations in such a way you guide them to think of something close enough to what you guess to freak them out. It's not magic, it's manipulation."

He rises from his seat on the ice. "How much later are you staying here? Are you spending the night? I can grab stuff and bring it with me in the morning if you need it."

Mac is a good guy. He's the quietest of my roommates. Hell, he's the quietest of my teammates, but there is a steadiness to him I appreciate.

With a huff, I get my paws under me and shift. Standing on my human feet again, I feel short. I should have stood on my hind legs as my bear so I could tower over Mac for once. I know for next time.

"Nah, I guess I'm good. Thanks for checking on me, man." I clap him on a shoulder more like a small boulder than a body part.

"Is your car in the garage here?" he asks.

I nod.

"How about I drive us home and you leave your car here tonight? I'm in the lot. It's closer and you don't have to deal with scanning out."

I'd have to go through the casino to get to the garage where I parked my Explorer. The surface parking lot Mac is talking about is much closer.

"Yeah, sounds good. Thanks."

As we exit the rink portion of The Nest, we make sure things are turned off and locked as they should be. There's security, of course, but it doesn't hurt to be cautious. The retail stuff on the rest of the pier housing the rink is still open, and people are milling around. We sign a couple autographs on our way out, but for the most part, we're ignored. Once we start our preseason games later this week, I think our relative anonymity will disappear. I'll miss it.

We get into his Suburban. It's a few years old, but nice.

"I'd figure you'd have a Land Rover, not a Chevy," I say.

He starts the engine and puts it in gear. "I have a Land Rover back home, but it wouldn't be practical here. This was my car in college."

I turn my head to look at him. "You went to college in the US? Where? For hockey?"

He sighs. "Cornell. I didn't play hockey there."

"How the hell did you end up there? What was your major?"

"It's a long story best told over a beer."

"Fair enough," I say. "I want to hear it someday."

"Aye."

We're silent through the rest of the drive home. I want to know his story, but I'm not ready to tell mine. I guess I'll have to wait. Apparently, that's all I do. Wait for the season to start, wait for Mac's story, wait for Kendall to tell me what the hell happened at the game and about her marriage.

I'm tired of waiting. I am ready for things to happen. Once I figure out what I'm going to do.

14

KENDALL

I'M SHIVERING AS I SIT IN THE BACK SEAT OF MY PARENTS' BUICK SUV. MOM is at my side, and her arm is comforting around me but isn't chasing away the chill. I know I'm not cold. It's shock. But my logical brain isn't helping my body. I can't believe I shifted. I had no control, no knowledge it was going to happen. It felt like puberty, when I first started to shift. With all those hormone surges, it's not uncommon for young shifters to experience surprise shifting. We quickly learn the signals of imminent shifting. Even if we can't control it right away, we know it's coming.

This took me by surprise.

Velveeta triggered me. I know it. The shock of seeing her riled my emotions. Her pushing my mom flipped my protective instinct. I guess I'll protect Mom before I'll protect myself. I'll try to shift on purpose tomorrow.

Crap. Tomorrow is Monday. I can't go to work. Do I still have a job? The game was televised, and Velveeta was creating a scene. I bet someone caught it all on their cell phone and posted it online.

A whimper escapes before I'm able to hold it back. Mom's arm tightens around me protectively, but it doesn't help. Neither does Dad's anxious glance in the rearview mirror.

I straighten from Mom's shoulder and feel around the backseat. "Where's my purse? I need my phone."

"It's up here, Ken," Dad says.

"You don't want it. Everything can wait until tomorrow," Mom says.

I lean forward to reach between the front seats and grab my bag, but I'm too short. I grunt in frustration and reach to undo my seat belt, but Mom puts her hand over mine to stop me.

"I gotta let work know I won't be in tomorrow. If I even have a job still. What if they won't let me back? Who is going to trust me with their kids?"

The tears roll down my cheeks as I take gasping breaths. If I can't be a teacher, what will I do? I have money. I could just not work and live off the money from my trust fund, but none of us do. It's there as a giant security blanket, but by unspoken agreement, we are all leaving it untouched and letting it grow for the future. But I need a purpose, and teaching gives me my purpose. What about my cheer team? The dance team for the Devil Birds. I shifted at an event show-casing the hockey team. The perception is I'm connected to them.

"Is Liam mad at me? Did I ruin his team before they ever played a single game? Oh my God." I know I'm hyperventilating, but I can't help it.

Dad takes the next exit off the Atlantic City Expressway and parks at the edge of the parking lot of some business complex. He turns off the car, gets out, comes around to my door, and opens it.

"Come on, Ken, get out and breathe some fresh air. Stretch your legs. Shift if you need to. Everything is going to be okay. You haven't ruined anything. We love you."

"You're afraid I'm going to shift and get cat hair in your car," I say between my hiccup sobs. I'm trying to stop crying, but it's hard.

"Damn right. I had it detailed yesterday."

Mom has my phone in her hand. "Tell me who you need to

contact, and I'll text them you'll need a sub for tomorrow because you aren't feeling well."

She holds the phone in front of my face to unlock it. I make a grab for it, but she quickly steps back before I can reach it.

"Mom, give me my phone. I need to take care of this." I'm about three seconds from stomping my foot like one of my students in a snit.

She holds my phone to her chest and turns her back on me. "Tell me what to text. I'll give you your phone back tomorrow. Tonight, calm down. Okay, I'm in your contacts. Who do we need? I promise I'll type verbatim what you say, and you can see it before I hit send."

I sigh. This needs to get done. "School Delancey is the contact. Say I won't be in on Monday and will need a substitute teacher. My sub materials are in the green folder in the rack on my desk. I will call in."

Mom's thumbs fly over the screen, and I hear the clicks as she inputs the message. She turns around and shows that she typed what I wanted. I nod, and she hits send. The whoosh of the message being sent causes my stomach to flip. I guess leaving my phone with Mom is the wisest idea. If I have it, I'll be stressing over Delancey's reply and checking social media to see what everyone is saying. I'll see what Burke says. Or doesn't say. He knows I was married. He must wonder about it.

Dad hands me a bottle of water, and I take a sip. I swear his car is like Mary Poppins's purse. Things keep appearing from it as if by magic.

"Feeling better?" he asks.

I nod. "Yeah, thanks." I take another sip of water and screw the cap back on.

"Ready to head home?"

I give a shaky laugh. "Not really. I want to run away."

Mom rubs my back soothingly. "You can stay at home in your old room. Maybe you shouldn't be alone."

I shake my head vehemently. "No, I want to be alone. I need to be alone. I promise to holler for Andy and Harrison if I need anything. I need my phone though. You can't keep it. Trust me, I won't do anything stupid."

I can see the uncertainty in Mom's face, but I'm standing firm on this. "I need to answer if work calls. They need to hear about what happened from me. They need to know I'm not a danger to the kids. This is my career at risk. You know Aunt Holly is going to call, and she won't stop until she talks to me. If she doesn't talk to me, she's going to be on my doorstep. And yours."

Dad's eyes glance toward Mom's in the rearview mirror. He loves his sister, but she scares him. Aunt Holly scares the crap out of me too. I love her dearly, and she thinks of me like a daughter, but she's so forthright and assertive she would have eviscerated Velveeta. That would have been lovely.

Mom elbows me, and I realize my mind had wandered.

I give her a sheepish smile. "I'm sorry, what?"

"Burke. Things are going well there? The way he swooped in there to take care of you. It was like something out of a romance novel."

Burke. Things *had* been going well. But now he knows I've been married, and Liam and Trevor are telling him all about it. Well, what *they* think they know about it. He's made his views on the seriousness of marriage clear. He'll never understand why I got married young and divorced as quickly as I did. Even if I told him everything and he understood, it wouldn't change anything. This is still temporary. There's an end date. Sure, we don't know when it is, but it exists. Home is too important to us, and home is a completely different country for each of us.

"Things are going okay, but don't get your hopes up. We're dating, not picking out a china pattern. We're having fun. Neither of us is looking for a commitment. Remember, you told me to have fun. And I am."

As expected, my parents come into my townhouse with me. I know they don't want to leave me alone, but I *need* to be by myself for a while. I have to process what happened tonight. Am I through my shifting block? Can I shift when I want and control it? I love teaching, but if I'm not confident I am in control of my shifting, I could be a risk to my kids.

"Well, this has been fun. Thank you for taking care of me. But you need to go now." I get up and walk to the door. Sometimes being blunt is the only way to be heard in my family.

Dad hugs me, and I rest my head against his chest and hug him back. It would be easy to ask them to stay. I could avoid dealing with today's clusterfuck, but avoidance won't solve anything.

"Call if you need us, Kendall. We love you." Mom presses a kiss to my cheek.

Tears flood my eyes. She called me Kendall. Unless she's scolding me, I'm always Ken or Kennie. It's a sure sign she's seriously worried about me. I blink to stop the tears from spilling down my cheeks.

"I'm good. You guys are wonderful. If I need you, I'll let you know. I need some time alone and, frankly, I don't want to cry in front of you." I walk to the front door and open it. I didn't realize until I saw my empty porch how much I was wishing Burke would be standing there, waiting for me.

"Seriously, Ken, anything you need, call out. Or bang on the wall. Or come over." Dad says as he walks outside. "I'll swing by in the morning."

I nod, knowing my voice won't be steady enough to say anything.

Locking the door after they leave, I rest my back against it and let the tears flow down my cheeks. I slide down until my ass hits the floor and pull my knees up to my chest and wrap my arms around them. I don't bother holding back the sobs.

I let it all out. I cry because I'm relieved my cougar is back. I missed her. I cry to let out the shame I've been carrying at being a shifter who couldn't shift. I cry to let out the fear I felt when I saw Velveeta and was afraid Kregg was going to pop up and hurt me. And yeah, I cry for the version of me that dreamed of the day Kregg would make his Major League debut and of being there to share it with him. Of the life I thought we'd have together. Of the baby I'd be holding.

Never in a million years did the version of me I am now expect to be at that game. I would have never gone if I thought it was a possibility. Like a hemorrhoid, Kregg pops up at the worst time to be a pain in my ass. My past, screwing up my present. Who knows what he's done to my future?

I rise from the floor and go into the powder room to wash my face. Red and splotchy is not a good look for me. I hear my phone signal a text and rush to read it. It's from Delancey at work.

> Delancey: Okay, sweetie. Don't worry, we have you covered. Talk to you tomorrow. Let me know a good time to call.

> Me: Thank you. I'll be available if the substitute has questions.

Delancey sends back a thumbs up emoji.

Okay. That's taken care of. I stare at the phone in my hand. Do I reach out to Burke? What do I say? Do I need to say anything?

I'm sore from shifting twice tonight. Not unexpected after not shifting for almost two years.

I decide to treat myself to a bubble bath. Hoping it eases both my muscles and my brain. I submerge myself in the tub, grateful it's deep enough and I'm small enough to do it. My parents' pool is already closed for the season. I wonder if the pool at Mallory and Liam's is? I sit up with a gasp when I realize dropping by their place may be awkward in the future. Especially if me and Burke are all screwed up. It's going to make things weird with my family and friends.

The pleasure I was finding in the tub disappears. I get out and do my routine of drying off and applying body lotion. As I run my hands over my body, I see the traces Burke's beard left on my skin during the previous two nights. He fit into my life, and with my friends, almost magically, as if he'd been made to be there. By my side.

I pull on my robe and walk into the bedroom where we spent the past two nights. He was going to stay here tonight too. His shaving kit is here and his duffle bag. Will he be by to get it?

A check of my phone shows no new texts. Should I text him? What would I say? *Hey, are you coming over?* Nah, sounds like a booty call. If he texted those words to me, would that be my assumption? No. I'd think he cared about me and was checking on me. But he's not texting. He's not checking on me. Does he not care? Should he care? Do I want him to? Yeah, I do.

I know what we've been doing is supposed to be fake dating with benefits. I've been adamant I don't want more than that, since he is going back to Canada when his career is over. But at least we'd have something for now. What we've done has been wonderful—in bed and with friends and family. I *like* him.

I'll explain the situation with Kregg to him. He'll understand. He's too good of a man not to. The way he held me on the bathroom floor at the ballpark. He stood up to my brother, *his coach*, in order to put me first. I know Liam and my cousins love me, but I don't know if they would risk their dreams, their futures, to care for me, protect me? Sure, they would protect me, but to hold me when I cry and just let me cry and not try to fix things? Not even Andy and Harrison would do that.

My yawn surprises me. I guess the adrenaline from my shifts is wearing off because all I feel now is bone-deep weariness. Changing into my nightshirt—Burke's t-shirt—I crawl into bed and pull his pillow into my arms to cuddle. I wish I was in his arms instead.

The knocking on my front door wakes me. Andy and Harrison both have keys. They could come in and leave my donuts on the counter. With a groan, I roll out of bed and stretch. Maybe I'll try a yoga workout today since I'm home. I'm sure there's something online. I throw on my robe and jog down the stairs.

"Coming!" I call out as I hit the last step.

I look through the peephole. It's Burke! A shot of joy runs through me, and I undo the locks and open the door. A wide smile lights my face.

"Hi!" I say.

"Hey," he says. His voice is pitched low and rumbly. No smile on his face. His brown eyes, usually warm and full of humor, are dull and bleak.

I step back and pull the door open more to allow him to enter. "Come in."

He crosses my threshold and stands in my living room, his shoulders stiff.

"What's up?" I ask. I walk into my kitchen to start some coffee and give myself something to do. "Want some coffee?"

"No." He croaks it out, then coughs to clear his throat. "No, thanks. I came to pick up my duffle and shaving kit. And see how you are." His glance bounces off me and goes back to the floor. Like he can't stand to look at me.

I'd be a hell of a lot better if he wasn't standing there stiff and awkward. If he'd touch me or at least look at me. But I wasn't a cheerleader for almost two decades without knowing how to put on my game day face and sparkle, baby.

"I'm good! Thanks for asking!" I put on my brightest smile and wish my hair was in a high pony with a bow instead of the loose braid I put it in to sleep.

His brow furrows in confusion. I guess my perkiness confused him. Good. His brooding is confusing the hell out of me.

"Don't do that," he says.

"Do what?"

"Give me the fake smile you hide behind. I hate it."

I freeze. He's the only person who has ever seen my cheer smile for what it is—a shield. "Well, I'm not a big fan of you coming into my house and not even looking at me in the

eye. If we're over, say so."

"What? No. Why would we be over?" He is finally looking at me, and now he's the one who looks confused.

"Because I was married while still in college and divorced after six weeks! You take marriage seriously, and if you judge me by my history, I don't. Let's not forget the whole 'shifted uncontrollably in front of thousands of people.' Any sane man would have second thoughts, and we know you're all about logic and sanity. And it's fake anyway. Why continue something fake when it hurts you more than it helps?" I hope I kept the bitterness out of my voice, but I don't think I'm that good of an actress.

Shaking his head, he walks over to me, takes me in his arms, and rocks me side to side. I don't think he realizes what he's doing. He presses a kiss on the crown of my head.

"I know you have your reasons, and when you're ready, you'll tell me. If you want. You don't owe me any explanations. We both have parts of our past we regret." He pulls back and rests his hands on my shoulders with his thumbs rubbing along my collar bones. His eyes are far away and bleak and his mouth is a tight, grim line. "I didn't go to a party and my best friend died."

His beautiful brown eyes are swimming in tears and my heart breaks. Taking his hand, I lead him over to the couch, take a seat, and pull him to sit next to me.

"Do you want to talk about it?"

At first he shakes his head no but then nods. He lets go of my hand and leans forward, resting his elbows on his knees and looking down at his clasped hands.

"Growing up I had a best friend, Bobby. We did everything together. We were line mates on the hockey team, hung out at each other's houses, partied, double dated. Teenage guy stuff. Our last year of high school stuff started to change. I was preparing to go to university. I couldn't wait to leave. I was going to go to a top tier school and I was working my ass off to get into a specialized program.

Bobby was staying home. He loved our town and couldn't understand why I'd want to leave. He wanted to get a job after graduation, find a nice hometown girl, get married, have kids. The whole white picket fence thing. We were bickering because we knew things were going to change and we weren't mature enough to handle it."

He takes a ragged breath and I feel my chest constricting. I know what's coming. Not the details but I know the story.

"Bonfires at the lake were the big social thing in our town because there was nothing else to do and it was the last one of the season before winter. Bobby kept bugging me to go and I told him I couldn't. I had to study for a chem exam I needed to take to get placed into the program. My future was riding on doing well on this test. I blew up at him saying just because he wanted to live in our hometown until the day he died didn't mean I did. I had plans to get out of there and I didn't have time for him right then. We'd hang out after my exam."

"Oh, no," I whisper. Dreading what he was going to say next.

"Bobby went to the party. He was pissed at me. Drinking more than usual. Everyone was drinking, that's all there was to do. Drink and hook up. We would keep each other out of trouble and not do anything too crazy. He was a polar bear shifter too so having a beer or two over the course of the night wasn't going to do anything. He had more beer than his usual two and decided to try pot for the first time and other stuff being passed around. We always avoided it, but I wasn't there to have his back and talk him out of it. He was wasted but still got in his car and tried to drive home. He hit a tree and was killed instantly."

His tears are dripping onto his clasped hands and I wrap my arms around him. He rests his head on my shoulder and sobs. My tears join his. I work with teenagers on my cheer team and this story is what I fear most for my kids. It's why I do what I do. If they are involved in something they care about then they aren't out at the beach or in the woods getting drunk and high and making poor decisions. I understand the responsibility Burke feels to the kids of his hometown. He wants to save them from Bobby's fate.

When he stops crying, I reach for the box of tissues and hand them to him. He wipes his eyes and looks down at the floor like he's embarrassed to have broken down in front of me.

I reach over and gently turn his face to me.

"My heart breaks over what you went through. You were a good friend to Bobby. You didn't do anything wrong. You couldn't have known what would happen. It wasn't your fault. You are not responsible for the choices he made. It was an accident. A horrible, horrible accident."

He's looking at me, but I know he's not listening. I can't grant him the absolution he thinks he needs. That's only going to be found back in Canada.

He takes my hands and squeezes them. "I don't talk about this with...anyone. Em once. I think my parents guess, but...no one else. I wanted to tell you though because I want you to know I trust you—with my secrets, my flaws, my fears. And I hope you can trust me too."

With a shuddering breath, Burke looks at his watch. This conversation is over.

"They called early practice this morning, and we are crazy with media before the season opener on Wednesday. I have to go. It's my job and the reason I'm here. But, for the first time, I want to say screw it and skip out on my responsibilities and stay here with you."

"Oh, Burke." I swallow the lump in my throat. Finally, someone wants to put me first, and they can't. Not if they want to achieve their goals and make their dreams come true. And now that I know how raw and personal Burke's goals are to him, I can't let him throw them away.

I press my hand to his cheek, and he closes his eyes with a heavy sigh. His beard tickles my palm, and I remember how it felt between my thighs.

"Let me go get your bag. Focus on the team and what you need to do to get ready for Wednesday night. You only get one first game as a pro, and I want you to cherish every moment. I'm not going anywhere."

I turn and run back upstairs before he says anything. I strip off his shirt and shove it in his duffle in case he needs it then pull on a sweatshirt and yoga pants of my own. I look around to make sure I gathered all his clothes and then grab his shaving kit from the bathroom.

"Here you go!" I shove the bag into his arms. "I'm pretty sure I got everything, but double check before you leave."

Since my coffee has finished brewing, I add sugar and cream. I wish I could feign nonchalance by picking it up and taking a sip, but my hands are shaking too much.

"I'm sorry," he says. "I have to go."

He looks so sad it breaks my heart.

"Go! You can't be late. Liam will kill you." I give him a gentle push toward the door. I don't want him to leave, but I can't be the reason he messes up his future. He means too much to me.

"Can we talk later?" he asks.

"Yes," I press a quick kiss to his lips and back away before he has a chance to deepen it. My morning breath is a thing. "But first you need to go be Captain Awesomesauce."

Burke runs his hand through his dark brown hair, mussing it. I remember how it feels to do that.

"Go!" I make a shooing motion and smile at him. A genuine smile, not my cheer smile.

His lips quirk in return. "I'll call you later," he says as he opens the door.

"You better!"

He stops short when he sees my dad on the porch holding a box of donuts.

"Good morning, Burke. Donut?"

Burke's face flushes, and it's adorable. "Um, no thanks, Will. Going to practice." He almost leaves a vapor trail in his rush out the door and to his car.

Dad walks in and hands me the box of donuts.

"He was getting his bag for practice," I say as I open the box and grab a chocolate frosted donut with rainbow jimmies, my favorite.

"Okay. You're a grown woman, Ken. What you do is your business. Did you sleep? Are you okay?"

"I'm good, Dad, really. I slept. I'm okay. Really."

My phone rings upstairs, and I jump up. "I gotta get that. It may be work. Thanks for the donuts. I'll talk to you later. Love you!" I press a quick kiss on Dad's cheek and run upstairs. My phone stops ringing before I can grab it, but I see the missed call notification. It's Delancey from school.

I hear my front door close. Dad must have left. Good. I hope he left the donuts.

Pressing the button to play the voicemail Delancey left, I sit on the edge of my bed.

"Hi Kendall, it's Delancey from school. Checking in. Call me when you can, please."

She sounded friendly. Not angry or cold. That's a good sign, right? I shake out my hands to get the blood flowing to my fingers. They were feeling tingly from how tightly I had been clenching my fists. I forgot I was holding my donut, now there are colorful candy sprinkles decorating my carpet. Oops. Guess I'm vacuuming today.

I hit her name on my recent calls and put her on speaker. The phone rings once...twice.

"Hey, Kendall! I just called you!" Delancey says, sounding chipper. Too chipper for a Monday morning.

"Hi Delancey. Yeah, I had left my phone upstairs, and it stopped ringing as I was going to pick it up. How are you?"

"I'm well. Are you not feeling well today? Your substitute is doing fine. Your notes were right where you said they'd be."

Does she not know about my shifting at the ball game? This is awkward.

I clear my throat. "I'm okay, Delancey. I needed to take a personal day. I wasn't sure if I should come in today or not."

"Is this about the shifting at the ball game?" Delancey asks. This is one thing I like about her. She's direct. Never unkind, but no bullshit.

"Yeah," I admit.

"What happened?"

I explain what happened and wait to hear my fate.

"Oh, honey, shift happens. It's nothing rare. You did what most shifters would do if they perceived a threat against a loved one. Wait until you have babies. You'll be wanting to shift all the time to protect them from everything."

A wave of cautious optimism washes over me, but I'm afraid to hope.

"I'm not in trouble?" I ask.

"For shifting? Nah. Shifting isn't a problem. If you were drunk and flashing your boobs on TV, then we'd have an issue. Hell, it's Philly where they grease the light poles to keep people from climbing them. A cougar shifting in the stands is the least crazy thing to happen at any given game."

We both chuckle because it's true.

"Will you be in tomorrow?" she asks.

"I'll be in tomorrow. Delancey, thank you so much. Pine Grove is lucky to have you as part of the administration."

"I keep telling them." I hear a voice in the background, and Delancey tells someone she'll be right there. "Kendall, I gotta go. Enjoy your day off. I'll see you tomorrow."

Before I have a chance to say goodbye, Delancey hangs up.

It's okay. I'm okay. I didn't lose my job. I'm still a teacher. Burke didn't break up with me. We're okay. We say we're fake dating and I know we may not be endgame, but we are very real, and while I have him, I want him. For real. Nothing fake about it, even if it is temporary.

15

BURKE

"Pass the damn puck!" I scream at Lindy. He's skating around with the puck on his stick like he's taking a Sunday stroll.

Carter skates up. "What's your problem?"

"He's not shooting the fucking puck! That's my problem! How the hell will we get goals if he la-di-da skates around with the puck on his stick?" Logically, I know I'm overreacting and being an asshole. But seriously, he needs to shoot the puck.

Coach blows his whistle. "Bedard!"

I look at him. "Yeah, Coach?"

"Hit the showers. You're done."

My stomach sinks. I've never been sent off the ice like this before. Ever.

"No, I'm good." I skate back toward the faceoff circle.

"It wasn't a suggestion. Get the hell off my ice. You're done for today."

The rink is silent. I feel heat run through me, part anger, part humiliation. I skate off the ice, and it takes every bit of my self-control to not smash my stick into smithereens. I slam into the locker room and start ripping off my gear. I get down to my compression shorts and plop on the bench in front of my stall.

I know I can't bring my emotions on the ice. I have a job to do and a team to lead. What happens in my personal life can't affect my performance. Not even two weeks. Kendall and I have been doing whatever we're doing for less than two weeks, and I'm tied in more knots than I ever was with Tabitha. Hell, I considered asking Tabitha to *marry* me, and our breakup didn't affect me like this.

I'm on the verge of everything I've dreamed of and Kendall is distracting me from it. We aren't dating for real, but I have all kinds of real feelings in my heart, and I don't know what to do. The team is depending on me, and I need to put them first. I can't be selfish. I've made promises back home I need to keep. But I *want* Kendall. I want to see her every day, hold her every night. I resent the time I have to spend at the rink when I'd rather be with her.

I scrub my hands over my face. I owe Lindy an apology. I'm right, he needs to shoot the puck, but I was reacting out of anger and frustration and that wasn't his fault. I shower, and since I'm alone, I spend extra time letting the hot water pour over me. Our first game is tomorrow night.

A lot of us have family and friends coming to town. My parents and sister will arrive tomorrow. It's a quick visit because of their schedules, and then we'll travel for two more preseason games this weekend.

I will miss not being with my family for Thanksgiving. Canadian Thanksgiving. But those are the sacrifices I knew I'd have to make to play professionally. A few years away, and then I can be home and have a wife and family of my own. I can't lose focus on why I'm doing this. I let myself get distracted by Kendall and lose sight of what I want. I'm a forever guy. I want marriage and kids.

I get out of the shower and change into workout gear. If I'm not on the ice, I can do some strength training at least. Maybe run a few miles.

I'm on mile six and cooling down when Jamie the trainer comes in. I take out my AirPods and slow down as she approaches me.

"Wasn't sure you were still here. Team meeting in ten minutes."

I nod. "Thanks. Be right there."

I walk into the locker room and head to Lindy's spot. Thankfully, he's dressed, or this would be more awkward for me than it already is.

"Lindy, I'm sorry. I shouldn't have screamed at you. You should pass the puck, but I was taking frustration out on you that you didn't deserve."

He stands up and holds out his hand. "It's okay, Cap. We all have bad days. I will work on passing the puck more."

I shake his hand, feeling grateful for his understanding.

"Bedard." I turn to see Coach standing in the doorway of his office, watching. "A word."

Aw, shit. I'm betting he won't be as easygoing as Lindy was.

Entering his office and closing the door as directed, I take the seat in front of his desk.

"I know you apologized, but you can't be pulling shit like you did today. You're the team leader, and they are counting on you to be steady. We all have bad days and there's the stress over tomorrow, but we're counting on you."

I nod. There's not much else I can do.

He sighs and leans back in his chair. "You and my sister broke up?"

My eyes widen. Why the hell would he think we broke up? Because she shifted at the ball game? Because she was married before? Those aren't reasons to throw away a relationship. At least, they aren't for me.

"I'm sorry, man," Coach says. "I was hoping she would be different this time. You're a good man and steady as a rock. You're what my flighty sister needs. I thought she had finally matured enough to stop flitting around, but I guess she hasn't. I'm sorry you got dragged into her mess."

I'm dumbfounded. I don't know what to say. Why would he think we broke up? I know what everyone is telling me about Kendall and her relationships, but I swear that's not how I see it. Is she that good of an actress? Am I that gullible?

Clearing my throat, I mumble an "Um..."

It must be sufficient because Coach nods his head. "Good talk. Get the team into the meeting room. I'll be in to go over stuff for tomorrow in a moment."

At his dismissal, I stand and walk out of his office. We fill the meeting room, and I'm seated between Mac and Carter.

Carter leans in. "You okay, man? You can't let stuff with Kennie mess with you. I tried to warn you."

Before I get the chance to say anything, or punch Carter in the face, Mac leans in as well, and now I have these two grown-ass men leaning across me, chatting like a pair of old biddies.

"This is not the time for I-told-you-so's, Carter. Leave Cap be."

Praise the Lord, Coach walks in then and calls for everyone's attention.

"Good practice. You know what you need to work on. Tomorrow is our first pre-season game. Our first home game. It's a big night. There will be a blue-carpet entrance. You are all to be in suits and ties. Brick, you can wear a skirt. You too, Mac," Coach says, looking our way.

"It's a kilt, not a skirt, damn it!" Mac calls out with a thicker brogue than usual, making everyone laugh. As he intended.

Coach holds up his hand. "I know Canadian Thanksgiving is next week while we are traveling and a lot of you will be missing time with your families. My parents would like to welcome all of you and any family or friends you may still have in town from tomorrow night's game to their house Friday night for dinner. It won't be the Thanksgiving meal you're used to, but my mom is a wonderful cook, and she'd love to have you. You don't need to bring anything. We have it all covered. Let me know if you can't attend. Their address and other details are in your emails."

Coach looks around the room and claps his hands. "Okay, that's it. Rest up tonight. No partying. We will have a walkthrough of the ceremonial stuff in the morning and a light skate. Now is the time to shut out the outside world."

His gaze flicks to me and then moves on.

"This team, this game, is your priority. This is what you are here for. What we have all been working for. Don't lose focus. Get out of here. Eat well. Rest. Don't be idiots. See you tomorrow."

We file out of the room and to our cars. Excited chatter coming from some. Others are exuding determination and concentration on what tomorrow will bring. Carter is in the former category. I'm in the latter. I hope I can have my head in the game and lead my team to victory. That's what I'm here for, what I've given up my teaching career and my home in Canada for. To be here and play professional hockey.

If I let myself be distracted by her glorious blue eyes and her even more beautiful heart, I risk losing what I'm here to get. She's not my future, and I can't risk everything on someone who is temporary. I can't have it all—I must sacrifice something. Too many people are depending on me to succeed. My heart is going to have to be pushed aside.

16

KENDALL

I love my brother. It's why I'm here. But I wish I could show my support somewhere other than the owners' box at The Nest waiting for the Devil Birds to play their first game.

"There you are!" Daphne says. "Here's a jersey for you to wear."

I accept the blue, gray, and white jersey. The colors are reminiscent of the Atlantic on a stormy day. I unfold it, excited to see "Bedard" and the number fourteen on the back. It's not. I'm wearing Trevor's jersey. I should be wearing Burke's name and number on my back, but I'm not.

"Why are you giving me a Carter jersey?"

She gives me a sympathetic smile and sad eyes. "I didn't want to make you uncomfortable since you and Burke broke up."

Before I have a chance to ask her what the hell she's talking about, there's a cheer as the teams skate out for warm ups. The Devil Birds are playing the Salem Spellbinders out of Massachusetts. My eyes stray to Burke. His helmet obscures his face, but he looks commanding on the ice. The captain's "C" on his chest belongs there. I'm happy his dream is coming true. I *want* him to be happy and have the life he wants. Even though I won't be in it.

I'm sitting with Daphne and Mallory along the front of the box. Daphne leans forward.

"When do the coaches come out?"

"I think after warm-ups," Mallory says.

All of a sudden, Liam is there, leaning between me and Mallory, to whisper in her ear.

"You know how you became my girlfriend on the day they announced the team?" he asks.

I take that as my cue to rise and get out of the way. Liam takes my place and grasps Mallory's hands to pull her to her feet.

"Yeah..." she says.

Oh crap. I know what's going to happen. I need to get out of here, but there's no way to escape now that everyone is watching. I glance out and see the scene unfolding on the Jumbotron. I'm right there on camera. Time to dust off my cheer smile again.

"I thought if I asked you another question today with it being our first game, it would be a good balance." I can hear a slight tremble in his voice. He's nervous. Bless his heart.

Liam drops to a knee, up here in the owners' suite, in a packed arena, in front of our family and friends.

"Mallory Carter, I love you. Will you make tonight the best night of my life and agree to be my wife?"

He's holding a diamond ring. It's gorgeous. Mallory doesn't look at it. She's focused on Liam's face. That's the way it should be. Tears prick my eyes.

"Yes! Of course I'll marry you! Oh my gosh! I love you!" She's babbling, and it's adorable. Her parents and older siblings are there and cheering. I look down and see Carter looking up. He doesn't have his helmet on, and a huge grin lights up his face.

Liam rises to his full height and wraps Mallory in his arms, kissing her like he has all the time in the world.

At the front of the box, Jake cups his hands around his mouth and bellows so the entire Nest can hear. "She said yes!"

The roar of the crowd is deafening, and Mallory laughs when she realizes they featured the proposal on the Jumbotron and everyone was watching with rapt attention, including the teams warming up on the ice.

They wave out to the crowd and the teams, who give them stick taps in congratulations. I see Burke, and I swear he's looking at me.

Teagan comes over and hands out flutes of champagne to everyone.

"We all want to congratulate the happy couple, and we will—after the game. But first our groom-to-be needs to get his newly-engaged self downstairs and coach our team to victory. Let's make a toast, first to Liam and Mallory. Congratulations. I speak for everyone here wishing you all the happiness life has to offer. Second, let's toast the real reason we're here." She winks. "Go Devil Birds!"

We all raise our glasses and cheer, "Go Devil Birds!"

Liam gulps his glass and presses a kiss to Mallory's lips.

"That's my cue to get down there. Hope we give you a good game!" Liam rushes from the box back down to the locker room to meet the team when they finish their warm-ups.

I ease further back into the box to make room for everyone to hug Mallory and admire her ring. My mom is crying, and Dad is hugging her.

She hugs Mallory's mother, who is smiling, and wipes a tear from her eye. Mrs. Carter returns mom's hug and says, "We can plan a wedding together!"

Mom beams with excitement. "Finally! I've been dying to plan a wedding!"

Well, that's not a dagger to the heart or anything. I know Mom didn't realize what she said, and I'm not mad. I wish life was different. That she had planned my wedding to Kregg, and we got to do all the things we dreamed of like dress shopping and talking about flowers. We were both cheated out of what we deserved.

We all stand and direct our attention to the ice as the high school choir from Pine Grove Academy sings the "Star-Spangled Banner" beautifully.

I refill my champagne when the teams do the ceremonial face-off. As captain, Burke is front and center. I watch it on the Jumbotron. He isn't wearing his helmet, and he looks so handsome. He smiles at the camera, but his eyes seem sad. I bet he's thinking about Bobby and wishing he could share this with him. My heart breaks a little for him. He shouldn't be sad. I want him to be over the moon. He's getting what he always wanted.

I settle in and watch the game. I understand the basics of ice hockey from the years Liam played. Get the puck in the other team's goal. I wasn't prepared for how physical it was. It's like bumper cars out there with players running into each other and smashing them against the boards. Even all the way up here we can hear the plexiglass rattling from the force of the impact.

Burke gets the first goal, further cementing his place in Devil Birds' history. It's cute how they all hug each other after a goal. Jake is on his phone with someone, making sure they get the puck to give to Burke after the game. I thought it was a Liam quirk to save pucks from certain games or milestones. I didn't realize it was a real hockey thing.

In the end, we win the game three to zero, and Bridget Waller is the hero of the game for having a shutout. They name three stars for the night—Bridget and Burke as one and two, and Trevor as the third for having two assists. At least, that's what Mallory tells me. I don't understand it all.

I know Burke is going to be tied up with media stuff and his family is visiting. All I want to do is escape and go home. Burke and I will text later or in the morning as I'm getting ready for work. However, I'm swept along in the wave of family leaving our box and heading downstairs to the locker room area. Since Morgan Development renovated and operates the property, we have the run of the building and can go wherever we want. Yippee.

I stop short when we enter the hallway leading to the locker rooms. Burke is hugging a beautiful young woman. A flash of jealousy runs through me before I have the chance to stop it.

"She's his sister, Emily," Daphne says from next to me. "I met her when we visited his hometown before the training camp started."

She walks forward and hugs an older couple who look to be in their early fifties. They must be Burke's parents. Burke has the dark hair and eyes of his mother but he has his father's build, tall and broad.

I catch Burke's eye as he is giving an interview. The reporter asks his mom a question before turning the microphone back to him. He gives me a sexy wink, and I blow him a kiss. I slip through the crowd and walk back down the hallway. I gotta get out of here. I don't want to be a zombie at work.

I text Andy to let him know and ask him to make my excuses. Everyone is celebrating the victory tonight at Devil's Den, but I'm looking forward to a private celebration with Burke Friday night after dinner at my parents' house. I want to give him some happy memories to take with him on their first road trip.

17
BURKE

WE WON. MY FIRST PROFESSIONAL HOCKEY GAME AND WE WON. I SCORED A goal, the first goal. I will be in the history books of the Devil Birds. We all will be.

Brick got the shutout. Lindy got the first penalty for delay of game by shooting the puck over the glass. Mac scored on our first power play.

I'm glad my family could come watch. I saw my parents wiping away tears when I scored. There was a friends and family section, and I think they kept a camera trained on it throughout the game to catch all the emotion. I hope they show us the feed.

There's a crowd in the hallway outside the locker room. The folks who have family or friends attending are getting hugs and high fives. I'm a sweaty mess and would love to get a quick shower, but I'm slated to do an interview, and my mom is insisting on pictures.

"Mrs. Bedard, how proud are you of Burke tonight? The first goal in team history, team captain, it's very impressive," the pretty red-haired reporter asks Mom as she tilts the microphone toward her.

Mom beams, and she squeezes my arm. "We are proud of him.

This has been his dream and as a parent, to see your child's dream come true..." She sniffles. "C'est magnifique. It's wonderful."

She turns the microphone on me. "Burke, you've got your first win. The team has a few days off and then you're traveling for your first road trip. Are you feeling the pressure to keep winning? Any worries about team dynamics and adjusting to traveling and playing in strange rinks?"

I take a deep breath. I hate giving interviews, but I accept that as team captain I am expected to be a face of the organization.

"There will always be pressure to win. What's the point if we aren't trying to win? Our team dynamic is strong. As for travel, at some point in our hockey careers, we have all played on travel teams and played in unfamiliar rinks. We handled it then. We can handle it now."

My answer must work because she smiles and thanks me. Coach and the other team owners are her next targets.

Mom hugs me again after the cameraman moves on. When she releases me, Emily claims a hug. I look out over the crowd. Mallory's at the back of it, watching. Daphne is with her. Daphne says something to her and comes through the crowd to join Logan, who is taking pictures of everyone. I wink at Kendall, and she blows me a kiss. Emily must have caught my wink because she pulls away and starts looking around.

"Is she here?" she asks, going on tiptoe and looking all around like she's a meerkat shifter and not a polar bear.

I watch Kendall walk away from the crowd and I assume she's leaving.

"Who?" I ask, playing dumb.

"Your girlfriend!"

That gets Mom's attention. Crap.

"Girlfriend? You have a girlfriend? Where is she? I want to meet her!" Mom is looking all around like she can magically pick her out of the crowd. Actually, I'm pretty sure she can. Not sure if it's because of her witchy powers or from being a mom, but she always seems to know.

"I don't have a girlfriend, Mom. I'm here to play hockey." The words taste like ash.

"It's not like they are mutually exclusive, Burke! Plenty of professional hockey players are in relationships."

I look to my dad for help. Like always, he's there when I need him.

"Marie, leave him be." He slips his arm around her shoulders. "I'm sure you want to shower and change. We are going to back to the hotel. You'll drop by?"

The team arranged for our guests to have rooms at Devil's Den if they wanted.

I nod. "I'll be there. They've arranged a space for us all to hang out and eat, if it's okay with you. I'm starving."

I knew saying I'm hungry would do the trick. Mom's magic is as a kitchen witch, and she can't stand for someone to be hungry. She will want to check out all the food and try to get recipes if she can.

I shower and change back into my suit. We had a blue carpet ceremony before the game where we walked in past fans and reporters. It was exciting, but it was hard to enjoy it with our first game looming ahead. It's a shame we don't have a carpet leaving. It would be fun now.

There are fans milling around the Boardwalk when we leave The Nest and cross to Devil's Den. We stop for selfies and autographs. Before we enter the steak house reserved for us, I stop Carter, Mac, and Stone.

"Don't talk about Kendall tonight. I don't want to deal with all the questions."

"Why would we?" Carter asks. "You aren't together."

I need to clear that up, I guess, but not here and not now. It's nobody's business.

Walking into the steak house, I see my luck was limited to the hockey game. My parents are chatting with Faith and Will Morgan. Crap. I join them and accept Faith's hug and Will's handshake.

"Great game," Will says. "Keep this up and the regular season is going to be incredible."

"Thanks, that's the plan." Lame. I look around for Emily but don't see her.

"Where's Em?" I ask my parents.

"Here I am," she says from behind me. "I wanted to try the slot machines."

"Aren't they fun? I love the Betty the Yeti one!" Faith says enthusiastically.

"They are! I didn't see that one. I'll have to look for it."

I introduce Emily to the Morgans and hold my breath.

"I don't know why our daughter isn't here. She was at the game. Did she say anything to you, Burke?" Faith asks.

Heat creeps up under my beard. "Um...no. I haven't spoken to her."

Mom looks interested. Oh, no. "Your daughter?"

I swear Mom is picking flavors for the wedding cake already. I wonder if faking appendicitis can stop this conversation?

Faith smiles. "Yes, our daughter Kendall is friends with Burke."

Emily's eyes widen as they look at me. "The coach's sister?" she mouths.

I glare at her.

Andy and Harrison come up to us, and I introduce them to my parents and sister and wait for everything to go off the rails.

"Is Kennie with you?" Faith asks.

Harrison shakes his head. "No, she went home. She had a headache and wanted to make sure it was gone before school tomorrow."

"Kendall teaches first grade at our local private school for shifters," Andy explains to my family.

"A teacher!" Mom is almost vibrating with excitement.

She's naming the babies now. This is bad. I don't want her to get her hopes up. There won't be babies because we can't have a future.

I paste on a smile. Now I understand why Kendall does it. It is time to end this. "Please excuse us. I'd like to introduce my family to some of my teammates."

"Oooh, yeah," Emily says.

I shoot her a look that tells her, "Don't you dare." The last thing I need is my little sister hooking up with a teammate. I'm brought up short. Coach didn't care about me dating Kendall, as long as it didn't impact the team. Something sits heavy in my stomach. If Emily were to date someone on the team, I'd be more worried about *her*. Is Coach right in protecting the team over his sister? Or is this just another example of how everyone has Kendall wrong, viewing her as some sort of beautiful tornado leaving a path of destruction in her wake?

We join Mac, Brick, and Stone at a table. Carter sits with his family across the room. There's a lot of them—three older siblings, nephews, parents. Liam is with them, and there's lots of oohing and aahing over Mallory. I wonder if Carter feels overshadowed by their engagement. This was a big night for him. He seems genuinely happy for the couple though. I guess it's a nonissue.

"Hi guys. Meet my parents, Cameron and Marie, and my sister, Emily. These are some of my teammates, Declan Mackenzie, Bridget Waller. She's our number one goalie, and her brother, Sean Waller, he's my line mate." Everyone shakes hands and says hello. Emily turns flirty eyes on Declan, who blushes and quickly pulls his hand away.

We take our seats and Emily ends up next to Stone. They do some mild flirting, but I'm not worried. Stone has a younger sister and understands hockey code. You don't mess with a teammate's sister.

"So, tell us about Kendall," Emily says conversationally. Stone looks ready to answer but Brick, bless her, jumps in.

"Coach's sister, Kendall? She's nice. She's a teacher and the Devil

Birds sponsor the school she teaches at. She's helping with a junior dance team for our junior hockey teams."

"Is she single?" Emily asks.

Brick shrugs. "No idea. She's close to Trevor Carter."

"She's not dating Burke?" Why are my parents sitting there letting Em cross examine Brick?

"Emily, knock it off," I say.

"What? I'm getting to know your friends."

"Then ask them about themselves, not random people."

"Fine." Emily turns back to Brick. "So, are you single?"

"Are you looking?" Brick gives Emily a saucy wink. Mac goes scarlet, and Stone chokes on his drink. I think it's straight soda, but maybe it's a rum and Coke.

Em's eyebrows raise, and she flushes. "Um...I like guys."

Brick does the single brow raise and gives me a feline-like smile across the table I didn't think a moose shifter could pull off. "So do I."

I know she's doing this to mess with my sister. I play along by giving her a flirty half-smile in return.

"Stop teasing your sister, Burke," my mother says over her menu.

We order and make small talk. Somehow, the conversation turns to witchcraft.

"Marie, you're a kitchen witch?" Mac asks. "Burke mentioned you were a witch. My mother is a green witch. She gets endless joy from her gardens."

"Yes, do you practice, Mac?" Mom asks.

He shakes his head. "No. I'm a wolf shifter."

"You can be both," Emily says. "I'm a polar bear shifter and an eclectic witch."

"Oh, I know. My sister is a wolf shifter and an eclectic witch too. Mam would be happy to teach me, but being a shifter is enough for me."

Sean cocks his head. "Aren't you born a witch? You can learn and gain powers for real?"

Teagan Penhall shows up behind Sean and lays a hand on his shoulder. Poor guy jumps a mile.

She gives his shoulder a gentle squeeze. "The most powerful witches are those born to lines of witches, but everyone can learn how to be more in tune with the world. Being a modern witch isn't all about spells and potions. It's about being in tune with nature, the universe, and yourself."

"Exactly!" Mom says with a big smile. "You're a hereditary witch?"

I get up to offer Teagan my seat, which she takes with a gracious smile. I pull another chair over and wedge myself between Emily and Sean, grinning at Emily's annoyed huff.

"I am," Teagan says. "On my maternal side, I'm from a three-hundred-year-old local line of witches. There's a local legend of the Jersey Devil. My family is responsible for that. The legend is my ancestor was a witch who was giving birth to her thirteenth child, fed up with her husband, and wished the baby to the devil. It was born a human child and then transformed into a winged creature and flew up the chimney to roam the Pine Barrens and Pinelands of southern New Jersey ever since."

I've heard the basics of the legend. It's part of the marketing for the Devil Birds, but to hear it from Teagan herself is powerful. We are all hanging on every word.

"In reality, the baby was a stillbirth. Even in their grief, my ancestors were practical people, and decided to use the vile rumors of their neighbors to their advantage and give purpose to the tragedy. Through the centuries, they would use misdirection and transformation spells to project the commonly perceived image of the Jersey Devil onto deer, sandhill cranes, sometimes each other, to distract from possibly less-than-legal activities back in the day. Now everyone is law abiding," she winks. "It's more to scare tourists and amuse themselves."

"So, the Jersey Devil doesn't exist?" Sean looks like he was told the truth about the Easter Bunny and Santa too.

"Sorry, Sean, as a single creature, no. But as a concept, and as a beautiful example of teamwork, he lives on."

Mom and Dad share a glance. Their silent communication is a sweet reminder of all the times they had entire conversations with a single look.

Mom smiles at everyone around the table. "It was wonderful meeting all of you. Teagan, thank you for arranging our stay and this delicious meal. Cam and I are going to turn in. Emily, we are leaving at eight in the morning. Make sure you're packed before then."

Em rolls her eyes but nods. Hey, at least they didn't give her a curfew.

When my parents stand, I do too, reaching out to pull Mom into a hug.

She kisses my cheek and whispers, "It will be okay. Have faith."

Unexpectedly, tears spring to my eyes. My mind flashes to Kendall, but I know Mom can't mean her. She must be talking about hockey.

Dad and I shake hands and share a manly hug.

"Listen to your mother," he whispers in my ear.

"About what?" I murmur.

"Everything," he says.

They bid everyone goodbye with hugs and handshakes and walk out of the restaurant hand in hand.

"What are your plans?" I ask Emily as I sit next to her.

"I'd love to gamble more and hang out in the casino. Maybe hang out with some of your teammates." She laughs at the low growl I make and bumps my shoulder with hers. "But I'm going to be a mature adult and go up to my room, pack my stuff, and get a good night's sleep. I'll save the partying for the next time I'm down when it's not an in-and-out trip."

"I'll walk you up."

Em rolls her eyes. "Burke, I am capable of getting to my room by myself."

"I know."

She tilts her head and assesses me, a slow smile spreading across her face.

"You want my advice!" She wiggles in her seat like she won bingo or something.

"No, I don't need advice."

"Yes, he does," says Mac. Brick and Stone nod. Thank goodness Teagan excused herself when our parents left.

We rise from our seats.

"See you guys at home," I say.

Of course, Em must hug everyone goodbye and get their contact details. Why did I want my family to come meet everyone? Damned if I know.

I walk her to her door. "I guess I'll leave. You have to get ready for bed and pack. I'll call for Thanksgiving."

"You don't have to go," she says. "I've only been here for two days. It will take me five minutes to pack. Including the time to change into shorts and a tee to sleep in."

"Thanks, but I'm beat. I want to get some sleep and use the massage gun on some of my muscles. Practice is nothing like playing against people who are okay with hurting you."

I hold out my arms for a hug, and she steps into them. Her arms wrap around my waist and give me a squeeze.

She turns her face up to me. "I love you, Burke. When you're ready to talk about whatever is going on, I'm here to listen."

I squeeze her in return and kiss her forehead before stepping out of the hug.

"Thanks, Em. I love you too. When I have something to talk about, I'll let you know, but don't hold your breath."

I ruffle her hair because I know it annoys her.

"Lock your doors." When I hear all the safety locks engage, I rap a knuckle on the door and say goodnight.

I'm surprised when I'm stopped for a couple of autographs and selfies as I walk through the casino to the adjacent garage. With my size and build, I don't blend into a crowd very well and as the one player most often used in the promo materials for the Devil Birds, it makes sense I'm recognized, but I still don't expect it.

Like I'm on autopilot, I drive past Kendall's condo. I tell myself it's to make sure she got home safely. When I see her blue Mustang is in its usual spot, I know she did. I see the light spilling into her side yard from her bedroom. I want to stop and knock on her door. Hold her, talk with her. But I can't.

I continue driving home. I'm here to play hockey, and I need to focus on that. Sweet, sexy blondes aren't part of the plan. Knowing Kendall was up in the box, watching me play, is what I've dreamed of. But my bear kept wanting to look at her, to be near her. I wasn't only fighting the opposing team, I was fighting with myself to stay focused on the game and win. I can't fight a war on two fronts and win.

I'm sick of fighting. What's the use? Nothing is fake anymore. My feelings for her are real.

I love her. I think she may be starting to fall for me too. That's real. What happens when an experiment's hypothesis proves false? You accept the new conclusions. No other choice. And I have new conclusions all right.

I'll do what it takes to have Kendall, to keep her. Once my bear is settled, hockey will get easier. We can focus on the game because we know we are going home to her. She'll be ours. It's going to be okay. We'll talk after Thanksgiving dinner at her parents'. Maybe we can work out a quick trip home to Canada over our short holiday break. I know she doesn't like the cold, but I'll keep her warm by sharing my body heat.

Hope blooms in my chest. This is going to work. I just had to be logical and organized. Scientific method for the win.

18

KENDALL

It's not fair. Andy and Harrison are taking a weekend trip to celebrate their engagement and are missing family dinner *again*. Now it's going to be the Liam-and-Mallory show and all about their engagement. Not that I'm not happy for them—I am—but I don't want to be stuck listening to wedding plans.

I turn onto my parents' street, cars lining both sides, and I spot Burke's SUV. They are hosting Canadian Thanksgiving for the team and any of their family still in town. I wasn't expecting such a sizable crowd. I would have gotten out of it if I could, but this is my only chance to see Burke before they leave on their road trip. With our schedules being crazy this week, it's been texts and a couple of short phone calls since he dropped by the morning after the baseball game. I've missed him.

Pulling into the driveway. Logan and Daphne pull in behind me. It won't be easy to sneak out early. Damn.

Daphne's baby bump is starting to show, and it is adorable. I ignore a twinge of grief. I have tons of children in my life—my students, the babies coming in my family. Maybe I'll have my own someday. It's okay. I force my mind away from an image of a young polar bear getting used to their size. There are no polar bears in my long-term future. No full-grown ones, no cubs. There aren't even polar bears at the Philadelphia Zoo. I will live a polar-bear-free life.

Mom is opening the front door with a big smile before we reach the porch.

"There you are! Get in here! We're ready to serve, and I want to make sure you and Daphne get some!"

Liam appears in the archway leading to the kitchen and family room. "Why are you hanging out there? Come on back. We want to eat and have been waiting for you. Mom's worked hard on this."

Reluctantly, I follow Logan and Daphne to the back of the house. Much of the team is here, and I can see Mom has outdone herself. I can't believe how much food there is. She must have been cooking for days.

"Kennie!" Aunt Holly cries and gives me a big hug. "You okay?" she whispers in my ear. I assume she's talking about shifting at the ball game.

"I'm fine," I say.

She pulls back and gives me a long look. I smile. The best I can do for a genuine smile, not my cheer smile.

"Oh, sweetie. I know breakups are hard, especially when you still have to see him. We have your back." She nods and releases me.

I look around the room and see all the gazes. Some are sympathetic, some are curious. Burke told me everyone thought we broke up, but why do they still think that? Is there something I need to know? I don't see Burke. Did he not come? I'm here because he's here.

My parents stand in the center of the dining area, their arms around each other and glasses of wine in their hands. I need to get myself one of those. Uncle Mike must have read my mind because he hands me one as he stops next to Aunt Holly. He slides his now free hand around her waist.

I love their relationship. Aunt Holly is strong and no-nonsense, and Uncle Mike loves that about her. He's not threatened by her success as a family law attorney, and he was happy to be the parent handling school drop off and pickups and sick days when Andy and Logan were little. Aunt Holly works for a firm in Philly and, as an associate working her way up to partner, it wasn't practical for her to handle those things.

Uncle Mike is the head legal counsel for Morgan Development. It was easier for him to be flexible. It's what I want my future relationship to be like. A partnership. A compromise. Not me giving up everything for a man.

Mom smiles radiantly and looks over the assembled group. She loves hostessing and taking care of people. "Thank you all for joining us tonight. I know some of you are missing out on having Thanksgiving at home with your family or at least want some home-cooked food." She smiles and everyone laughs and there are some nods of agreement.

"We are ecstatic some of your families could join us." The extra people must be some of the players' family members. I don't see Burke's family. They must have gone back to Canada already. I feel a flash of sadness for him. I finally see him off to the side, hidden behind Mac. Mac is the one guy on the team big enough to obscure Burke.

Our eyes meet, and he gives me a lazy smile. My heart flutters, and I give a soft smile in return. He's wearing a dark green button-down shirt. I love how it hugs his broad shoulders. The fabric looks soft. Maybe it's flannel? I want to rub my cheek against it. Rest my head against the brawny chest underneath. Later tonight, after dinner. I've missed him.

I focus on Mom again. She is smiling at the families. "Thank you for your help with all the cooking. We wouldn't have this without you." She claps and we all join in. Trust Mom to bring everyone together to create something special.

Burke steps from behind Mac as the clapping dies off.

"Faith, Will, and everyone who helped, I speak for myself and my teammates, thanking you for your hospitality and generosity. This makes being away from home easier. Thank you."

Everyone claps again until Dad raises his hand.

"Okay," he says. "Enough of this. Everybody grab a plate and dig in."

"Hosts and families first, then team," Burke says. "We'll be like a plague of locusts." Everyone laughs.

I follow my mom and aunt and grab a plate. Daphne and Mallory are behind me. There's a ton of food. Ham, turkey, lasagna, salad, all kinds of side dishes. It all looks delicious. I fill my plate and sit at a table on the patio. I leave a space for Burke, but Trevor takes it. Before I have the chance to say anything, Liam, Mallory, Daphne, and Logan join us.

Everyone has filled their plates and found places to sit. Some of the family members are sitting with my parents inside. Burke is at the next table with his teammates. He's facing me. Better than nothing, I guess. It's just dinner. We'll be together soon enough. I can watch his muscles flex under his shirt and it's distracting, like jiggling Jell-o but sexy. Someone at his table says what a great idea it is to do it buffet-style.

"We always do holiday meals buffet-style," Liam says over his shoulder to Burke's table behind him. "It makes it easier when you have guests." He looks at me with a crooked grin. "Kennie loves a good buffet, don't you?"

That's random. "Sure," I say.

"The last big buffet meal we had like this, you picked a husband, got your eye on anyone new? Lots to choose from here." He laughs like he's funny. Logan and Trevor join in and a few of the players chuckle, but it seems to be more out of following their coach than thinking it's funny.

I don't say anything. I'm too shocked he's bringing this up in front of our guests. That he's bringing it up at all.

Trevor explains things. "A couple of years ago, I came home with Kennie for Thanksgiving. Her cousin brought home some of his base-ball teammates. Bing bang boom, she's hooked up with the squirrel shifter from the ball game last weekend and married. Six weeks later, they're divorced. Now she's done with Cap. Time for someone new."

Liam is laughing like a fool. Logan laughs again, but when Daphne shoots him a look, he stifles it. Burke's shoulders are stiff. I want to crawl under the table and hide.

Trevor bumps me with his shoulder. "Six weeks was your record. You never stayed with anyone that long before."

"That's Kennie, love 'em and leave 'em," Liam says as he lifts his beer bottle to his lips. I want to rip it out of his hand and hit him upside the head with it.

I feel the blood drain from my face, but there is fire in my blood. I'm fucking sick and tired of this. I stand, my chair scraping on the slate tile of the patio. My parents look over. The French doors are open. They'll hear what I have to say too.

"Since it's been brought up and I'm sure everyone is curious, how about we clear the air about what really happened? That way you can stop gossiping about it."

Daphne reaches for my hand, probably to get me to sit back down, but I shake her off and step away from the table. I walk over to the patio doors to make sure those inside can hear me too. I'm going to embarrass my parents with what I'm about to share, but I'm done with this.

"Two years ago, my cousin Andy brought home some teammates for Thanksgiving. One of his teammates was Kregg Beaumont. He was charming and good-looking, with sweet midwestern manners. I fell for him."

I take a deep breath. I don't want to say this in front of my parents. In front of anyone. But in for a penny, in for a pound.

"We had a pregnancy scare."

Mom gasps, but I can't look at her. I'm not looking at anyone, I'm looking over their heads out to the trees. I wish I could shift and run away, but I need to get this out. When I realize my hands are shaking, I ball my fists and tuck them behind my back.

"He convinced me we were in love and should get married right away. Especially if there was a baby on the way. I thought I loved him. I thought it was romantic. Of course, I would want to be married if we were having a baby. So, I agreed. On the day I was supposed to try out to become an NFL cheerleader with my best friend, I was in a boring courtroom in rural Pennsylvania standing before a justice of the peace. Getting married without my family and friends there."

I take a shuddering breath. I can feel my eyes prick with tears, but I'm determined to finish. I put on my cheer smile.

"We were living in a crappy student apartment I was trying hard to make into a home." I shake out my hands because I gripped them too tightly and restricted the blood supply to them. "Kregg wanted me to get early access to my trust fund. I didn't care about the money. We could support ourselves. We didn't need the trust fund. I asked Dad because Kregg insisted, but it wasn't a big deal to me. He said no. But it infuriated Kregg." I give a bitter laugh. "He married me for my money. He thought if he could get me pregnant, we would be his meal ticket."

Dad gasps, and Aunt Holly calls Kregg a motherfucker under her breath. I grin. It's such an Aunt Holly reaction.

"Anyway," I continue. "It turns out I wasn't pregnant, but at least he still had me as his wife. My parents wouldn't want me living in poverty and doing without. When I told him I wanted to make it on our own, to support ourselves, he went crazy. He'd yelled at me before, but I chalked it up to him being stressed with finals and the upcoming draft. He always apologized. It was okay. It *had* to be okay."

A tear slips down my cheek, and I blink to hold back any of its compatriots that may want to follow. "But...but this time, he started throwing things. Our glasses, dishes. He almost clipped me with a lamp. Thank goodness he played shortstop and wasn't a pitcher."

No one joins me in my bitter laugh. Maybe they had to be there.

"He had me pinned up against a wall, his fist cocked back like he was going to punch me." I hear gasps around the room, but I can't look at anyone. I need to get this out and be done with it. "That's when Andy and Harrison busted in. Andy took me out of there. They were our downstairs neighbors and were supposed to be gone. Pretty sure it's the reason Kregg felt brave enough to do what he did, because he was always charming and doting when we were with people. I don't know what Harrison said or did after we left. I know his knuckles were bloody. Until that day at the ballpark, I had never seen Kregg again. I could tell he had a broken nose sometime since the last time I saw him. I don't know if it was from Harrison or someone else. Andy and Harrison are the only ones who know any of this."

I gesture to Liam. "As you know, my family thinks I just got tired of being married. I realized Kregg was a loser, like they knew all along. They don't know I thought I was pregnant and was excited to be a mother. That I was dreaming of a future with a husband who loved me and children. They thought I was being flighty again. Silly Kendall. She's too impulsive. Takes nothing seriously. Flits from guy to guy."

Mom is sobbing, and Dad is trying to comfort her. I know I have ruined what was supposed to be a special time for the team, but I'm sick of being the butt of snide comments. I know Liam is being a pain-in-the-ass older brother, and if he knew any of this, he would have beaten the hell out of Kregg. That's why I said nothing. Kregg wasn't worth throwing away his future over.

May as well tell the rest of it. "I hadn't been able to shift since we got married. The time at the ball game was the first time I've shifted in almost two years, and I wasn't expecting it. His mother confronting me and pushing Mom triggered it. I'm relieved to know I can shift again."

I give a mirthless laugh and shake my head. "I was terrified, pinned against the wall and unable to shift to protect myself. I'm a cougar shifter, and I was afraid of a fucking squirrel shifter. In our animal forms, I could kill him with one swipe of a paw and have him for a snack. But as a man, he's bigger than me and stronger. He used his size to intimidate me. I'm ashamed I couldn't protect myself. If we ever had children, would I be able to protect them? I couldn't risk it. So, I left him."

Okay, almost done. I can do this. "I missed my college graduation ceremony because I was at one of his games being a loving, supporting wife. I didn't apply for any teaching positions here because we were waiting to see what was going to happen with the draft. I gave up so much and ended up back home two weeks after graduation with the divorce pending and no job lined up. The true reason I have the job at Pine Grove is because I'm a Morgan and my family supports the school. They didn't hire me when I applied. Then the team pledged support to the school and poof," I make an exploding fingers gesture, "there's a position for me as a long-term sub for a pregnant teacher. I got my class now because she decided not to come back. It's all that ever matters—I'm a Morgan. Does it matter that I'm Kendall?" I shake my head. "What really matters is I'm a Morgan."

I put on my cheer smile. "Thanks for coming to my TED Talk. Please enjoy your meal and download your application to be my next fling at KendallMorganisatramp.com."

"Mom, I'll talk to you later. I have to go now. I love you." I rush off the patio. I don't know how I'm getting home. I guess I'm walking.

"You are both such assholes!" I hear Mallory shout.

"We didn't know!" Trevor cries.

"It shouldn't matter! What is wrong with you?" That's Daphne. It's nice knowing they have my back.

"Ken, I have the car keys," Daphne calls out.

"Take two bottles, Mal," Aunt Holly calls. "Love you, Kendall."

That seems to have opened the floodgates and there's chatter. I can't make out any of it other than Liam insisting he didn't know. If he had known, a professional baseball career wouldn't have been a possibility for "the squirrel-shaped shit stain."

Shit. I forgot Logan's Jeep is blocking my car. How am I going to get out of here? Like magic, I hear a vehicle unlock as I reach the front of the house and the lights on Logan's jeep flash, and I head toward it. At least something is turning out right.

"Kendall, wait!" Burke's ragged voice cuts through the early evening, and my hand hovers above the door handle.

He pulls me into his arms, and his flannel shirt is as soft as I imagined it to be. We are rocking back and forth, and I think I feel tears fall to my temple. Is he crying? Over me?

"You are the bravest woman I know, Kendall Morgan. I am proud of you." He leans back and there are tears on his face. This dear, sweet man is crying. Over me. When he presses his lips to mine, I can taste the salt of our mingled tears. I'd rather the salt was on the rim of a margarita glass, but I wouldn't trade this kiss for anything.

"I love you, Kendall."

And that's when my heart breaks. We can't do this.

"I love you too, Burke." The smile he gives me is glorious, and I tuck it away in my heart forever. "But we can't do this. It's not going to work."

The smile is gone, replaced by confusion. Mallory and Daphne come around the corner of the house. Mal has a couple of bottles of wine in her arms. Good, I'm going to need them.

I lead Burke away from the Jeep, into the shadows of the side yard. His hold on my hand is tight. Not to be hurtful, but in shock.

"Wha...what are you saying? We love each other. Of course it's going to work." He's holding both of my hands now, and I can feel the tremble in his.

Daphne and Mallory are in the Jeep. I'm sure they have the window down to hear what we are saying. Fine. It will save me from having to explain it later.

"We love each other, but our dreams are taking us different places. I am never giving up everything to follow a man again. My home and my life are here. You will go back to Canada. It's where your dreams are. Yeah, we could be together while you're here, and it would be wonderful. But you're never going to stay, and I'm never going to leave. It will hurt more months or years down the road. It's better to end it now before we really start. Maybe we will eventually find the Ms. Lucky and Mr. Perfect who fit our dreams."

I don't believe I'm going to find anyone, but I pray he does. I'd have to give up too much to be his Ms. Lucky. This time I'm going to love myself as much as I think I love a man. Telling my story out loud like I did tonight made me realize I've been running, reacting, hiding. I'm done. I'm going to chase my dreams out in the open without any hesitation. I'm going to be Kendall first, not a Morgan, and prove to everyone Kendall is good enough. Because she is. The love I have for Burke is a million times more than the infatuation I mistook for love with Kregg. That's why I know I need to let him go.

His beautiful brown eyes show sorrow when he recognizes the truth of what I'm saying. He swallows hard and nods.

"Kendall, I'm a scientist. I need proof, and now I have it. You are my mate. It's written in my heart, and there's no changing it, but it means your happiness matters most to me. I'd never hold you back."

I can't do this. But I do. Somehow, I walk away from him and get into Logan's Jeep. They left the passenger seat for me.

"Your house or mine?" Daphne asks after I close the door and she starts the engine. I see Declan walk up to Burke and clap him on the shoulder. Good. I don't want Burke to be alone.

"Mine, please. I'm sorry to have ruined dinner." I start crying. I've cried more in this past week than I have in the past two years. It's like all the tears I've held back have been unleashed.

I told Burke I didn't believe in fated mates anymore, but now, because of him, I do again. But just because you find your other half doesn't mean you don't still have to make hard choices. Finding your mate doesn't mean happily ever after.

Mal reaches between the seats to rub my arm. "Let it all out. I'm sorry we both have assholes for brothers."

"Yay for being an only child," Daphne mutters.

I laugh. This is all ridiculous. I can't believe I told all my business to total strangers. What must they think? I realize I don't care. Numbness sets in, and I welcome it.

19
BURKE

To say I'm stunned is the understatement of the year. Kendall rushes outside after sharing her story. She was magnificent. And brave. She's gotta be cringing in embarrassment, having said all that in front of strangers, but good for her for standing up for herself. Coach, Logan, and Carter are at their table, looking shell-shocked. Mallory hit her brother upside the back of his head as she got up to leave.

From across the table, Lindy sweeps the scene with wide eyes. "I like this Thanksgiving! Everyone says something...uh..."

"Embarrassing," Sean supplies.

"Ja. That." Lindy says, pointing at Sean. "I go next."

He goes to stand, but Bridget and Mac each grab an arm and yank him back into his chair.

"It's not a Thanksgiving thing, Linds," Brick says. "You're thinking of Festivus and the airing of grievances. That's in December."

Their chatter breaks me out of my stupor, and I get up to race after Kendall. I cut around the house and jump over the fence to reach Kendall before Mallory and Daphne do.

We talk.

It's over. I'm numb.

Mac joins me in the side yard as I watch Kendall drive away with Daphne and Mallory. She's crying. I head toward my SUV to follow her, but Mac grabs my arm. I could break away, and if I shifted, my bear could kick his wolf's ass, but I'd never do that. Mac is being a friend.

"I love her," I whisper. "She loves me too."

"Aye, I know," is his equally quiet reply.

"How am I supposed to let her go?"

Mac's sigh is heavy. "You let her go because you love her. What she needs is more important than what you want. And you pray every day the universe brings you back together."

Now I'm letting Mac lead me back. I have no clue how he thinks I'm going to be able to face all those people and make it through without sobbing or punching someone.

Reluctantly, I take my seat. Everyone attempts to act like nothing happened, but it's impossible. Dinner continues, but it's awkward. The food is delicious, and Coach's parents are superb hosts, but what Kendall revealed devastated her family. I heard Coach's aunt telling Faith she had everything covered if she wanted to go to Kendall. Faith said she knew Mallory and Daphne were taking care of her, and she and Holly would go over after dinner.

I have the feeling there is going to be a family meeting with Coach, Logan, and Carter first. Whatever. I don't care. I had it. Everything I wanted—my career, someone to love, *a mate*, a glimpse into the future I dreamed of. That I've always wanted to share.

And it's gone.

***

"Do you have ice on your ribs to ease pain or because it's cold?" Mac asks as he walks into the hotel room we are sharing in Vegas. We play the Las Vegas-based Area 51 Aliens tomorrow night for our final preseason road game. We played the Omaha Ogres last night, and it was a bruising physical game. I got out a lot of aggression and frustration over the situation with Kendall, but I took some hard hits. Nothing I can't handle, but I'm feeling it. Our practices have contact, but we aren't trying to obliterate each other.

"Both," I say. "It feels good. The Ogres hit harder than you guys do in practice."

Mac puts the pizzas we ordered on the table. "You're welcome."

"Thanks." I sit up from where I was reclining on my bed. I'm not thanking him just for the pizza. I'm grateful he hasn't gone full tilt at me. He's not aggressive or mean on the ice, and he doesn't take cheap shots or hit someone for the hell of it. But Heaven help you if you're between him and the puck or between him and the goal. He goes right through you and you're left flattened on the ice, hoping someone got the license plate of the truck that hit you. The sports reporters have nicknamed him the Mac Truck.

There's a knock on the door and Mac opens it to let in half the team. He leaves the door propped open. We are on a private floor since we're staying at one of the Penhall casino properties Teagan's family owns. We don't have to worry about random puck bunnies coming by. Since we are all rookies, we share rooms while traveling. Brick shares with Gina, one of our equipment managers, or Annie, our assistant trainer. This time, they share a suite, giving them each a room. We should hang out there since they have more space, but Annie and Gina insist they don't want our "boy cooties" in their space since they know how gross we are.

Carter brought his game console along and hooked it up to our TV. People are taking turns playing games. Some folks are sitting in the hall, chatting and hanging out while eating their pizza. The guys who didn't want pizza are downstairs getting burgers or pasta.

"Hey, Carter, since you and Stone are in here, okay if I go to your room to make a phone call?" I ask.

Carter looks up from his slice. "Are you calling Kennie?"

"No, my sister. Have you spoken to Kendall?" I wonder if she's forgiven him. I'm hungry for information about her, but I can't reach out.

"No, I'll call her when we get back and get her cupcakes from the Half-Cocked Bake Shop. She can't resist them."

I know. She told me she worked there in high school, and we stopped there once. She loves the peanut butter chocolate ones.

He jerks his head toward the door. "Go ahead. Tell Emily I said hello."

"Yeah...thanks."

I grab a bottle of water and head to the room Carter and Stone are sharing a couple doors down. They left the door propped open, but I close it behind me. No one needs to hear me pouring out my soul to my little sister.

I settle on the sofa and text Em to make sure she's free to talk. She calls and her smiling face fills my screen.

"Happy Thanksgiving!" I say. "How was dinner?"

"Delicious, as always," Emily says. "You had yours on Friday, right? I know Faith Morgan had asked for recipes."

"Um...food was good."

"But...?"

"There was an incident."

"So, what's up? Is this about Kendall?"

I give her a wary glance. "What have people told you?"

She shrugs. "She's the coach's younger sister. You guys have been dating. Trouble in paradise?"

"Yeah...no. I don't know. If I tell you something, you can't tell anyone else," I say.

"Oh, no. Did you get her pregnant?"

My heart jumps at the thought of a baby. But since we were always safe, the chances of a pregnancy happening are slim.

"No."

She settles onto her couch like she's getting ready for story time.

"Okay. Our plan was to let everyone think we were dating, and they'd stop trying to fix us up with other people. But really, we are...

were…fake dating. Fake dating with benefits. We have different goals in life and views on things making us incompatible long term. But we like each other, and we have…needs." I feel a blush creep up from underneath my beard. I never thought I'd be talking about sex with my sister. Wait. That came out all wrong. Brain bleach in aisle two, please.

Em's eyes widen, and she shakes her head. "I don't want to know what you were thinking about."

"You're right, you don't."

She waves her hand to motion for me to continue. "Okay, you're not compatible, but you like to hook up. What's the problem? Is she getting clingy?" She gasps. "Are you?"

"No one is clingy. I'm in love with her. And she loves me."

A huge smile spreads across her face. "Yay!" Her brown eyes, lighter than mine, narrow. "Why aren't you happier?"

I sigh. "It won't work. We broke up."

She holds up her hand like a stop signal. "Wait, what? You fake date with benefits, you fall in love, and you break up? You suck at this."

My huff of laughter holds no humor. "I do."

"What's the problem?"

I tell her everything—well, almost everything. She doesn't need to know about the Ricola. I have them stashed everywhere, little talismans from a wonderful time in my life. I can't believe we were only together for a few weeks. I always scoffed at people who talked about fated mates and insta-love, chalking it up to lust and hormones, but it's real. It happens. I'm living proof.

"Have you spoken with her since dinner?"

"No. What's the point?"

"The point is you love her, you idiot!"

"We want different things! We aren't compatible. There's no point starting something that doesn't have a future."

"What do you want?"

"To play hockey, save money, come home, get married, have a family, teach, and coach." "Okay, what does she want?"

"Teach, get married, have a family, stay in New Jersey."

"Okay, you want the same things. The problem is geography. One of you moves. Problem solved."

"I can't ask her to move. She did it for her ex, and she won't do it again."

Em's sigh is long and pitying. "Burke, for such a smart man, you are an idiot. Of course you're not going to ask her to move. After everything the poor woman went through, I don't blame her for not giving up the security she has. You stay there."

It's my turn to sigh. "How can I stay? I promised I'd come back! I can't break my promise!"

"Dude, do you think everything has stopped up here and is frozen in time, waiting for you to come back? There's a new chemistry teacher, there's a new head coach. Life is moving on. Of course, we'd welcome you back, but it's not like you will just step back into your old life if you come back after five or ten years. As for helping the kids and being a role model, you aren't the only player from town in the PHL. There are other guys who can be role models and do stuff too. It's not all on you. I know you have your hero complex—"

"I do not!"

"Yes, you do. You have to take care of everyone and fix everything, and people let you so they don't have to deal with it, but it's not your responsibility. Bobby's accident wasn't your fault. He decided to go to the party, drink too much, and try to drive."

"I was his best friend, if I was there, he wouldn't have..."

She cuts me off. "Yes, he would have. Just because Bobby is dead doesn't mean he's a saint. If you went instead of staying home to study for your exams what would have happened was you both would have been wrapped around the tree and you'd be dead too. I'd be without my big brother. You're allowed to put yourself first. It's not being selfish. It's being human."

When did my little sister become wise? I'm usually the one giving advice. Maybe she is right about my need to be the hero.

"So, what do I do?" I ask.

"Figure out what you truly want. If you need to be in Canada, it's okay. It's a great place. We had a wonderful childhood living here. I know you love the school and the team. Living here was Bobby's dream, not yours. Remember how excited you were to be going away to school? You wanted to go to new places. You don't have to live the life Bobby wanted as some sort of penance. He would want you to be happy and live the life you dreamed of. They have schools and teams in New Jersey. There are kids there who need mentors and role models. Canada will still let you in for vacations and holidays."

"Yeah..."

Emily is making sense. That's annoying.

"But if you aren't without a doubt certain you are willing to commit to not coming back here, then don't string Kendall along. She's been through too much and doesn't deserve to be jerked around. Don't go into this thinking you are going to change her mind. You go into it with *your* mind changed."

"How do I convince her I've changed my mind?"

"Burke, you're not a stupid man. Figure it out. You know her. I don't. Because you didn't introduce us, you ass. But whatever. You're the scientist. You're always talking about logic and proof. Apply that scientist's brain of yours to the situation and figure out a solution. I know you can do it."

My scientist's brain is churning with things I can do to fix the mess we're in.

"Thanks, Em. I love you."

"I know. Love you too. Work this out and then introduce us! You owe me someone wonderful after having to put up with Tabitha all those years."

This time my laughter holds humor. My blue-jay-shifter-ex was crazy. I can't judge Kendall for what she went through with Kregg. I could have easily ended up in a similar position. We should fix our exes up with each other. They would be perfect for each other. Keep the crazy contained. Then I think about their children and shudder. No teacher deserves to be subjected to the spawn of those two.

We say goodnight and hang up. Em has given me a lot to think about. For the first time in days, I feel a tiny bit of hope.

"How do you play professional hockey and still find time to volunteer here?" Delancey Kasper-Ridge, wombat shifter and Vice Principal of the elementary school portion of Pine Grove Academy, asks.

I shrug. "I make time for things that are important to me. I'm grateful the Academy has been so welcoming to me and willing to accommodate my crazy schedule."

"Are you kidding?" Delancey asks. "If we could have you here more, we'd snap you up in a heartbeat. It's always a challenge to find STEM teachers, especially those with a shifter background. Many of our high school teachers in the math and science departments aren't shifters. They are excellent teachers, of course, but middle and high school are where it's most helpful for students to have shifter mentors in education. Male mentors in particular."

"How do you get away with wearing a Wilcox Wombats t-shirt?" She's wearing a black t-shirt with a wombat dressed in teal and pink hockey gear. The Wombats are a team in another league, not the PHL.

She laughs, "I have to represent the Wombats and this way I'm not playing favorites between the teachers and the students."

We're walking down the school hallway toward the gym. The Devil Birds have donated floor hockey equipment for the gym classes, and the teachers are playing a fundraising exhibition match against the academy's high school kids the Friday before American Thanksgiving. I'm coaching the high schoolers. Carter is coaching the teachers. The community will start arriving in about an hour. We're using the time before to get our teams ready.

Brick is Carter's assistant coach, and Stone is mine. Of course, there is trash talking between the siblings. Between the teachers and students too. It's all good-natured, but it will change once the heat of competition kicks in.

Carter walks up to me with a shit-eating grin on his face. "Ready to lose, Cap?"

"No, I'm ready to beat you, Carter."

Brick joins us, laughing. "We have a secret weapon. You're going down."

I look over at their team, and I catch my breath when I see Kendall. She's wearing the teachers' team shirt and watching Coach Morgan intently as he explains something and points to the goal.

"If you think you're going to distract me by having Kendall here," I say, "you're wrong. I'm a professional."

In the end, it turns out Kendall wasn't the secret weapon. Her friend, Abby, was a star field hockey player in high school and a ninja at floor hockey. The teachers beat the students ten to two.

"You didn't even take mercy on us!" Robbie, one of Kendall's cheerleaders, says.

"When have I ever taken mercy on you, Robbie?" Kendall asks. "You shouldn't have bet me fifty burpees you guys would beat us."

"Mr. Bedard, how could you let this happen to us?" Robbie says with a mock pout.

Kendall turns around and takes a deep breath as she looks up at me. At least she's still breathing. I feel like someone has stolen the breath from my lungs every time I see her. Considering I'm at the school every chance I get, it's amazing I don't pass out from lack of oxygen.

We're cordial with each other. I've worked with her class, but it's hard not being able to touch her, to hold her. I think Kendall is suffering as much as I am. I've caught her pulling her hand back when she's reached out for me out of instinct. We see each other a lot between school and our work with the junior teams. Her dance team is a fun addition to the Devil Birds family.

I hold up my hands in defense. "Not my fault. I warned you guys to take them seriously."

"Well, we know Ms. Morgan sucks at anything with balls!" Robbie cries out in a room that, unfortunately, was at the moment silent.

You can tell the moment he realizes what he said and is torn between laughing like the fifteen-year-old boy he is and wanting to sink through the floor in embarrassment.

Kendall starts the snickering and soon uproarious laughter fills the gym. Thankfully, since most of the audience has left to go to the cafeteria for snacks, it's only the players on both teams, the coaches, and some of the Devil Birds players and staff here to sell raffle tickets and give autographs.

"Miss Morgan, I am really sorry. I didn't mean it that way." Robbie is earnest in his apology. He's a good kid.

Kendall is laughing so hard she's crying, and she wipes her tears from her eyes. She lays a hand on his forearm.

"Robbie, I know. It's fine. It was hilarious. I'm the one who is going to get in trouble for laughing about it."

She is beautiful when she laughs. She's always gorgeous, but laughing and happy brings a flush to her skin and a radiance to her eyes that makes my heart ache. I want her looking at me with that joy and happiness. I had it for a moment and let it slip away. I am the biggest idiot in the world.

I hope she lets me fix it.

20

KENDALL

Grabbing the gift bag holding a bottle of whisky and scratch-off lottery tickets from the passenger seat, I get out of my car and approach Liam and Mallory's house. The Carter family has a tradition of having a holiday open house for family and friends.

One of Mallory's uncles owns the Christmas tree farm next door and delivers a tree for the family to decorate. This year they brought a second tree and Mallory asked everyone to make an ornament to add to it. I love the idea. I always think creating mementos at events is special. If I ever get married again, I'd love to have people sign scraps of fabric I could have sewn together into a quilt or a wall hanging.

I let myself in and see everyone in the great room at the back of the house, looking out into the backyard. I hang up my coat and put my gift bag on the table. We're doing a Secret Santa type gift exchange where each gift gets a number and whoever draws that number out of the bowl gets the assigned gift.

"What's up?" I ask. Being shorter than everyone sucks at times like this because I can't see what they are looking at.

"The boys are playing in the snow," Aunt Holly says, moving aside to let me slide in.

Oh. My. Ovaries. The backyard is full of shifters playing in the eight inches of snow we got yesterday. Wolves, cougars, and a moose are all running around. Mallory's nephews are building a snow fort with Logan and Uncle Mike. I guess they didn't feel like shifting into their golden eagles and flying, so they are playing with the boys.

What has my attention, though, is the giant polar bear making snow angels. Suddenly, he flips to his tummy and, with his butt in the air, buries his muzzle in the snow and flings his head upward to create a snow shower. Burke is gleeful, and it makes me happy to see him like this. It also breaks my heart because it's more proof we have no future. This snow is a fluke. I mean, we get snow in New Jersey, but it's nothing like he gets at home in Canada. A few inches in a couple of storms isn't enough to satisfy him.

I step out on the patio because the outdoor heaters are on.

"Hey, Ken! You going to shift and play?" Logan calls out.

I shake my head. "No. I hate having snow between the pads of my paws. Too cold."

Burke's head swivels to face me. He has snow on his black nose and it's adorable. He lifts a massive paw in a wave, and I wave back. He lumbers over to where I'm standing at the edge of the patio and stands before me. I feel sad. I'll never know what it's like to watch him play outside in the snow with our children.

Tears prick my eyes as I give him my cheer smile. "You got your snow! It's rare we have a white Christmas. You got lucky!" I back away and gesture to the yard. "You better get back out there and soak it up while you can. See you inside." He grunts, but I turn and walk away before he shifts and says anything. I can't talk to him now. Everyone in the house is watching me, and I'm tempted to walk around the corner of the house, get in my car, and go home. But because I don't want any more gossip following me, I straighten my shoulders and reenter the house.

"There's a hot cocoa bar if you need something to warm you up," Mallory says with a kind smile.

I take her advice and use the excuse of getting a mug of cocoa as a chance to compose myself. They set it up in the butler's pantry. I love these big old houses with genuine old-fashioned touches. Mallory's family built the original home in the 1700s, before the United States was a country, and added onto it throughout the generations to make it the spacious, casual-but-elegant farmhouse it is today. What is now the butler's pantry was the original main floor room of the original cabin. The years have seen counters and cabinets added, but the original pine floor remains.

I fill my mug with cocoa and add caramel sauce, white chocolate chips, whipped cream, and a sprinkle of rainbow jimmies because jimmies make everything better. I see they have Bailey's. I may need some spiked cocoa later depending on how today goes.

Daphne joins me. "Birdie loves hot cocoa," she says, patting her baby bump.

They call the baby Birdie since they don't know the gender yet. I watch as she loads her mug with peanut butter cups, M&M's, marshmallows, and whipped cream. On the whipped cream, she adds coconut and a chocolate drizzle. Grabbing a spoon, she turns to leave.

"You didn't put any cocoa in," I tell her.

Daphne shrugs. "There's no room in the mug. Oh, well!"

Male voices echo down the hall. The guys must have finished playing in the snow. I turn to leave when Burke enters the space.

"Hello, Kendall," he says.

"Hi, Burke," I reply. Wow, this isn't awkward. "Did you have fun?"

He nods. "I haven't played in the snow like this in years."

I tilt my head. "You haven't? I figured it's something you'd be doing all the time back home."

"No. I'm always busy teaching or coaching. We do a polar bear plunge in early December before the lake freezes. It's not like we're out walking around as our bears all the time. I maybe shift a couple times a winter." He shrugs. "It's not a big deal."

"You're not hanging out on an iceberg watching the northern lights?"

He laughs. "No. Do you want to see the northern lights?"

"Yeah, but you have to go north, and it's cold and snowy. I don't like cold and snowy." I hand Burke a mug and move to give him room to get some cocoa. No one knows about the websites I have book-marked full of cold weather gear like subzero coats and water repellent gloves. The ugly boots to keep my feet warm and dry. I know they have heat in Canada and real houses. I'd only have to bundle up while outside. Inside I could be toasty warm, especially if I was in a certain someone's arms.

I know this won't work, but I keep trying to figure out a way we can both have what we want and need. I've been drinking my morning coffee on my deck trying to get my blood to thicken up so I can stand the cold better. Maybe my family wants to open outlets in Canada? I bet I could convince Andy and Harrison to move north of the border with me. They like snow. They had fun outside. Andy could head that division of Morgan Development.

We live near an international airport. It's not like my parents couldn't afford to charter a plane and visit. Maybe they'd like a second home. I want this to work, but I don't know how. Would Burke want to figure out a compromise?

He fills his mug and adds a couple of marshmallows.

"That's it?" I ask. "All the wonderful stuff you could go with, and you choose marshmallows?"

There's a commotion in the kitchen.

"I want cocoa! Why can't I go in?" Liam grumbles.

"Burke and Kendall are in there. Here's a packet of Swiss Miss," Mallory whisper-shouts. We don't need shifter hearing to know what they are saying or to hear the rustle of the cocoa envelope.

"We're done!" I call out, easing past Burke and entering the kitchen. Mallory looks disappointed. I feel disappointed. We should form a club.

We spend the afternoon chatting, snacking, and making our ornaments. I filled a glass ornament with red and gold tinsel and used a white paint pen to write "Making Merry Memories" with the year and my initials. It turned out cute.

As the sun sets, we gather for the gift exchange. I'm in the family room on the sofa next to Mom. Burke is on a stool at the island in the kitchen with Trevor and Sean. Teagan walks around with the bowl full of numbered slips. I draw my slip and see I am number thirteen, my lucky number.

I look over at the table of gifts to see if I can figure out which one is mine. But the table is empty.

Mallory stands before the table. "I figured we'd make the gift exchange more fun this year and make you hunt for your present. We scattered the presents around the first floor. They could be behind a pillow or under a table, but they aren't in a cabinet or closet. When you find your present, come back, and we can open them together. Okay?"

We all nod and murmur agreement.

"Then go find your presents! If you need a clue, ask me or Teagan."

Everyone scatters and, one by one, they return with wrapped boxes, gift bags, and envelopes. I see Aunt Holly ended up with my gift. It's Sassenach Whisky, she loves to watch the cutie pie Scottish guy on *Outlander Otter*. I know she'll get a kick out of the name since it's what he calls his lady love.

"You didn't find your present, Ken?" Andy asks from his spot on a loveseat he's sharing with Harrison.

"No. I've looked everywhere."

"What number are you?" Mom asks.

"Thirteen. It's my lucky number, but maybe not this year."

Mallory looks at Teagan, who shrugs.

"We have a back-up plan in case a present got lost," Mallory says. "Go refill your cocoa, and we'll hide a substitute present."

I want my damn present. I'm tired of playing hide and go seek, but I don't want to be a dud. Holding back my grumble, I head to the hot cocoa bar. I enter and see an envelope with "13" written on it propped up against the cocoa pot. Grabbing it, I turn to return to the others and run into Burke's chest. How does he keep sneaking up on me? Someone so big shouldn't be able to be quiet like he is.

He tilts his head toward the red envelope I'm holding. "Found your present?"

"It appears I did," I say.

"Open it."

I cock my head. "Shouldn't we join the others?"

"After you open your gift."

"Do you know what it is?" I ask.

A shrug is my answer.

Being a cougar shifter, the phrase "curiosity killed the cat" applies in spades. I'm dying to know what's in it.

I slip my nail under the sealed flap and open the envelope. There are a few folded sheets of paper inside. I pull them out and unfold them. The first is a letter written in a strong, masculine script.

Dear Kendall,

I hope this is a gift you don't want to return.

XO Burke

I look up at Burke. "My present is from you? What is it?"

"Keep reading."

I flip to the next page. It's a letter on Pine Grove Academy letterhead. I scan it and see it is approval to be a substitute teacher at the academy and the position of science enrichment consultant.

"What's this mean? You'll be working at the school? What about hockey?" I'm confused.

Burke nods and smiles. "I'm still playing hockey, but I'll be working at the school as my schedule allows during the season and full time in the off season. I love teaching, I don't want to give it up. One of the things I don't want to give up."

I look at the next sheet of paper. It's a deed. To a house in Canada. Burke's house. He's selling his house.

"You're selling your house? What? Why?"

"Keep reading."

I flip past the pages of the deed and get to the last page of the bundle.

SW Polar Bear ISO SW Cougar to be my Ms. Lucky

Moody, boring polar bear shifter who sometimes is an idiot, seeks a beautiful, brave, smart cougar shifter to date with an eye toward a long-lasting future relationship. Must love kids. Snow not required. Must be willing to visit rural Canada in the summer and reside in New Jersey the rest of the year.

If interested, please respond to...

I snort-laugh. "Seriously? Your email address is SexyPuckingPolarBear? You rather think a lot of yourself, don't you?"

"I mean, I made you yodel. I think that's rather impressive."

"Yodel, what does he mean?" Mom asks.

My eyes widen and blood rushes to my cheeks. Shit. Everyone was listening. Burke casually reaches back and closes the pantry door. And locks it.

"Let's open our presents," Harrison suggests from behind the door. "I have number one." Paper rustles as he opens the package and enthuses over whatever is in the package.

"I see why he's your favorite," Burke murmurs in my ear.

"One of my favorites." I wave the bundle of papers. "What does this mean, Burke?"

"It means I'm in love with you, Kendall, and I will do whatever it takes for us to be together. I understand you're cautious, and I respect that. I am willing to commit to making a life here, we can date and see if we can have a future together that makes us both happy."

Tears spring to my eyes. "But what about Canada? You want to raise your family there. It's hot here. I love you too, but I don't want you to give up everything important to you."

He raises a calloused palm and rests it against my cheek.

"Kendall, *you're* important to me. I want to raise a family *with you*. Whether it's in Canada, New Jersey, or Timbuktu, it doesn't matter. What matters is it's you by my side. The rest is pesky details."

I do a combination laugh/sob thing. I can't believe this is happening.

"Do I have to apply online, or can I apply in person?" I ask.

"I guess I can accept an in-person application, if the person is you."

I tilt my head back for a kiss and giggle. "Look." I point to the sprig of mistletoe above our heads.

Burke lowers his head to mine, and we indulge ourselves in the mistletoe's missive, only breaking away when there's a knock on the pantry door.

"Kennie, it's number thirteen's turn. Did you find your present?" It's Liam, sounding like a smug jerk.

"Was everyone in on this?" I ask.

"Most of us," Liam says from the other side of the door. "Come on out, guys. You're hogging all the cocoa."

Clasping my hand, Burke unlocks the door, opens it to Liam's smirking face, and leads me past him.

Mallory giggles from her spot in front of the fireplace. "Found your present, Kennie?"

Blushing, I nod. "I did."

"Who has number fourteen?" Teagan asks.

Burke raises his hand, "I do."

I look around. "Where's your present?"

"Turn around."

I turn around, and the room erupts in laughter. I glance over my shoulder at Burke's smiling face with narrowed eyes.

"What did you do?" I ask with mock severity.

He reaches out and removes a sticky note from my back with the number fourteen written on it.

"You agreeing to give us a chance is my present." He leans down. I'm expecting him to kiss me, but instead he whispers in my ear, "And my future." And *then* he kisses me.

***

Did you enjoy Burke and Kendall's story? Want a peek into their future? Get a bonus scene by subscribing to my mailing list here - https://BookHip.com/PKQATGL or scan the QR code

If you want to leave a review for Sexy Pucking Polar Bear, I'd really appreciate it! Visit https://books2read.com/SexyPuckingPolar-Bear to choose the vendor of your choice.

ALSO BY JENNY FENSHAW

KEEP IN TOUCH!

Follow Jenny now for her romantic stories, stay for her ridiculous personality.

Warning: Snort laughing possible.

If you'd like to keep in touch with Jenny Fenshaw check out Jenny's website for all the ways to connect

https://jennyfenshaw.com/
Or just scan the QR code!

ACKNOWLEDGMENTS

There is no way to acknowledge everyone who has helped me achieve a dream I was too afraid to admit having—being an author. If you know me, consider yourself acknowledged and thanked.

There are a few people who I have to especially acknowledge:

My family, especially my husband, who has supported me every step of the way and listened to my random mutterings about seagulls and polar bears.

Andie Wood and the TNRC Writers Incubator - I would have never started writing if it wasn't for Andie and the TNRC anthologies. The knowledge and support from the Incubator is incredible.

All the independent authors who inspired and mentored me (whether they know it not) to be brave and reach for my author dreams. I'm honored to walk the trial you've blazed.

ABOUT THE AUTHOR

Jenny Fenshaw is a funny, goofy, and creative author of contemporary paranormal romantic comedies who loves daydreaming about ordinary events, making them ridiculous, and including them in her stories. A native of southern New Jersey, Jenny loves to set her stories in the area she knows so well. From the Atlantic City Boardwalk to the Pine Barrens, her stories are a love letter to her hometown just as much as they are the love story of her characters.

When she's not writing, Jenny enjoys watching ice hockey (for research!) and reruns of *Murder, She Wrote*. She has been married to her cinnamon roll of a husband for over thirty years and has a grown son who has the best adventures.

facebook.com/JennyFenshawAuthor

instagram.com/jennyfenshawauthor

bookbub.com/authors/jenny-fenshaw

www.ingramcontent.com/pod-product-compliance
Lightning Source LLC
Chambersburg PA
CBHW031955240626
47153CB00003B/995